SADDLEBAG DISPATCHES MAGAZINE PRESENTS

BETWEEN HELL AND TOMBSTONE

WHERE LEGENDS ARE FORGED IN SILVER AND LEAD

Saddlebag Dispatches, LCC
A Subsidiary of Oghma Communications
Bentonville, Arkansas
www.saddlebagdispatches.com

Between Hell and Tombstone: Where Legends are Forged in Silver and Lead
Description: First Edition | Bentonville: Saddlebag Dispatches, 2023
Identifiers: ISBN: 978-1-63373-908-6 (trade paperback)| ISBN: 978-1-63373-909-3 (eBook)
FICTION/Westerns | FICTION/Action & Adventure |
FICTION/Thrillers/Historical

Trade Paperback edition December, 2023

Cover Design and Interior Design by Casey W. Cowan
Editing by Dennis Doty, Anthony Wood & Amy Cowan

SADDLEBAG DISPATCHES MAGAZINE PRESENTS

BETWEEN HELL AND TOMBSTONE

WHERE LEGENDS ARE FORGED IN SILVER AND LEAD

Last of the Buffalo by Albert Bierstadt

TABLE OF CONTENTS

Law of a Broken Land by Alex Slusar 3

Prelude to a Gunfight by Paul Colt 23

The First Shot by J.R. Wolff 31

Wait There, Cochise by Keith "Doc" Raymond 43

The Wild Ones by Dan Walker 61

Players and Prayers by David Bowmore 77

So Far From God by Steven McFann 97

The Ballad of Cochise's Granddaughter by P.A. O'Neil 111

Beast of Burden by Julianne Metzger Taylor 131

Unwanted by Anthony Wood 139

The Hunt for Augustine Chacon by Rickey Pittman 151

Johnny Reb and the Gunfight at the O.K. Corral by James A. Tweedie 163

Tales of Padre Rojo by Barbara L. Clouse 175

Until Then by Megan McCain 193

Desert Fish by Michael Woods 201

No Tomorrow by Leigh Alver 219

The Package by Dennis Doty 229

Action at Skeleton Canyon by Andrew Salmon 225

A Light in the Night by Frank Tenney Johnson

LIST of ILLUSTRATIONS

Last of the Buffalo by Albert Bierstadt vi

A Light in the Night by Frank Tenney Johnson xi

The Challenge by Henry F. Farny xiii

Indian Telegraph by John Mix Stanley 2

The Wolf River, Kansas by Albert Bierstadt 60

A Cree Indian by Charles Marion Russell 76

Assiniboin Indian Medicine Sign by Karl Bodmer 96

Fight for Water by Charles Schreyvogel 130

Cowboy by Frank Tenney Johnson 150

Pointing Out the Trail by Charles Marion Russell 162

Indian Maid at Stockade by Frederic Remington 174

The Horse Thief by Frank Tenney Johnson 228

Mexikanischer Cowboy by William Herbert Dunton 244

The Challenge by Henry F. Farny

PREFACE

IN THE VAST, untamed landscapes of the American frontier, where dust and destiny swirl together in the golden haze of opportunity and danger, the tales of the West come alive. Welcome to *Between Hell and Tombstone*, a collection of short stories that beckons you into a world of grit, guns, and gallantry—where the horizon stretches as far as one's dreams, and every heartbeat echoes the rhythm of a thousand stories. Within these pages, you will ride shotgun with eighteen riveting tales that traverse the rugged terrain of the Wild West, each one a distinct testament to the indomitable spirit of those who dared to chase their destinies beneath the ever-watchful gaze of the setting sun.

Our headliners this time around include Will Rogers Medallion Award-winning authors Paul Colt, Anthony Wood, and P.A. O'Neil. They're joined by an all-star cast of talented wordsmiths, some of whom you've heard of, and some of whom are completely new to the Western genre.

In this collection, "Law of a Broken Land" is a cautionary yarn about incompetent bounty hunters whose recklessness teaches them a lesson in the high cost of prejudice. Meanwhile, "Action at Skeleton Canyon" unfolds a relentless dance between survival and revenge, where the shadows of the mountains conceal both danger and redemption, and the tables can turn on a dime.

In "Unwanted," a youthful bridegroom finds himself thrust into a world of betrayal and murder, navigating the treacherous paths of loyalty and deceit in a town that brooks no forgiveness and where only his bride can save him. "The Package" follows the harrowing journey of a cavalry scout assigned to return a captive torn from her family and reunite her with those she holds dear. But the real question is, who does *she* hold dear?

"Tales of Padre Rojo" reveals a poignant narrative as a young adult orphan discovers an extraordinary gift in the hands of his parish priest. Meanwhile, a young cowboy's aspirations take center stage in "The Wild Ones," where he hatches a daring plan to capture a magnificent horse of his own.

As the sun dips below the horizon, casting long shadows over dusty streets, "Beast of Burden" introduces peculiar sights in town, and a strange creature lurks at the fringes of the community.

The Punny Express by George "Clay" Mitchell & Victoria Marble

You'll find that every tale weaves a tapestry of the Wild West's multifaceted soul, blending the echoes of gunshots, the whispers of wind through canyon walls, and the heartbeat of a land teeming with untold stories. So, saddle up and join us on a journey through the sunsets and showdowns of the untamed frontier—where the dust settles and legends are born.

—Dennis Doty
Publisher, *Saddlebag Dispatches*
December 19, 2023

SADDLEBAG DISPATCHES MAGAZINE PRESENTS

BETWEEN HELL AND TOMBSTONE

WHERE LEGENDS ARE FORGED IN SILVER AND LEAD

Indian Telegraph by John Mix Stanley

LAW ❀ A BROKEN LAND

ALEX SLUSAR

THREE MEN RODE to Contention on two horses. One mounted a dappled appaloosa. Two rode a dusky roan—one in the saddle, the other wrapped in white canvas and lashed down over the rump with hemp rope. The canvas was marked by rusty patches of blood and wet from crossing the San Pedro River, which was swollen with autumn rain and churned past the silent abandoned mills along the banks.

Paul Keller saw the riders coming. He'd stabled his chestnut gelding for the day and stood under the awning outside Davis's, the only general store left in town, watching the empty street from the early afternoon shade. He smoked a cigarette and contemplated asking Sadie Davis if she'd ride with him tomorrow. Keller was heading to Bisbee next, and it would be weeks before he returned to Contention—if there'd be a Contention left by then. An evening ride with the tall, tawny blonde, emerald-eyed beauty who clerked her father's store would give him a chance to make his feelings plain, he reckoned, yet the very thought of asking her put a cannonball of ice in his gut like nothing else did.

He felt the cannonball now. The cigarette wisped to a nub. He pitched it into the street and saw the riders enter town from the north road. They were middle-aged and sun darkened. The appaloosa rider was squat and hairy in a battered leather hat slouched low and a sweat-stained duster, with a fleshy ridged scar running down the right side of his face. The thin man on the roan looked like a scarecrow in his straw hat and ragged work clothes and hauled something like a large bedroll. They tracked dark gouges in the street, raising clods of red earth wet from the recent desert rains as they passed the Western Hotel. Keller found them odd. As he considered them, the hemp lashing separated.

The package slid off the roan and unfurled. The corpse hit the street with a sound like a sack of wet feed and splayed on its back. It was a young Mexican man naked but for ragged green trousers cinched with a grass belt, pockmarked with bloody holes, his bushy head blown in half, lolling over with the jaw loose. He faced the sky with a brain-shot gaping mockery of a smile.

"Creek!" the appaloosa rider said. "Look what you done, you dumb son-of-a-bitch."

"Hellfire," the scarecrow yelped. He swung the roan around, slid out of the saddle, snatched up the canvas, and threw it over the corpse. The hands and feet stuck out.

"I said we needed a wagon, Harl," he said, coiling the rope.

"Didn't say nothin', you horse's ass."

"Did so!"

Keller went into the street. With his limp, his spurs jingled.

The scarecrow tucked canvas under the body. He looked over and saw Keller—a lanky, dark-haired, clean-shaven youngster of maybe twenty in jeans and work clothes, walking with a noticeable hitch in his step.

"Hey, kid!" he said. "Give a hand."

Keller stopped. The scarecrow saw Keller's hand resting near his holstered Colt Single Action Army revolver and the sun flash on the tin star pinned to his denim jacket.

"Sheriff?"

"Deputy," Keller said.

The appaloosa rider came over, trailing the roan. "Deputy?" he said. "Just who we're looking for. I'm Harlan Dobbs, 'n this is Wallace Creek."

"Paul Keller. Why you riding with a dead man?"

"Well, that's Gustavo Suarez."

"I should know who that is?"

"Sure, Deputy." Dobbs's scar bent and twisted along his gap-toothed smile. "You're gonna pay us for him."

———◆———

IN THE SHERIFF'S office, Keller unfolded a poster Dobbs gave him. It was curled and stained and proclaimed a reward of five hundred dollars for the apprehension of Gustavo Suarez, laborer for the Southern Pacific Railroad and thief of a pay box from San Simon Station. Centered in the type was a line drawing of a slender Mexican with dark eyes and a thick beard.

"Don't know why you ain't heard," Dobbs said. "You new to this?"

"Questions are mine to ask, Mister Dobbs," Keller said.

Dobbs snorted. "Mister," he said to Creek.

Keller set the poster on his desk. The office was spacious, with four cells and a room above for whoever was on duty. The cells were empty but for the bullet-riddled corpse, which was laid out on a rack. Keller had Dobbs and Creek bring it in, Creek asking not to be locked up with the body. Keller dissuaded him, had them sit at his desk where set out their confiscated pistols—a rust-flecked Army Remington from Creek, an oily Smith & Wesson .44 Russian from Dobbs, and a pitted Navy Colt from Dobbs's saddlebag with four empty chambers.

Keller studied the sketch of Suarez. He nodded to the body and swallowed. "Ain't enough of his face left to compare," he said.

"His fault," Dobbs said. "Should've come quiet."

"Why are you so sure it's Suarez?"

"Someone in Benson said he passed through from Tres Alamos. We wagered he was makin' for Sonora off the roads. This morning, we found a camp at a spring west of here."

"Iron Springs? I know it."

"He was there, dryin' his shirt over a fire, singin' to himself. We snuck up, close enough to tell he looked like that picture. I told him to come out quiet. He said he didn't speak English. I know a little, told him we were takin' him to San Simon. He said he wasn't Suarez, didn't know anyone named Suarez. You could tell he was lyin'. He got twitchy and went for that Navy Colt. We put him down, wrapped him in his lean-to, and brought him here."

"Where's his horse?" Keller said.

"Weren't one."

"What about the money?"

"What about it?"

"He stole a pay box. Where is it?"

Dobbs and Creek looked at each other. "Weren't one," Creek said.

"You're certain?"

"Damn sure," Dobbs said.

"You didn't hide it somewhere, figure to keep it, and collect the reward, too?"

"You callin' me a liar?"

"I'm just askin' questions."

"It's as we said it was. We'd like our payment now."

"All I have is your word against a dead man who can't be identified."

"It's Suarez."

"That's for the judge to determine."

Dobbs's eyes widened. "The hell you say?"

"You killed a man and brought him to Contention. This'll go before a judge."

"That ain't necessary."

"It's the law."

"But that's Suarez!"

"Then where's the money?"

"Probably spent on liquor and whores!"

"That body could be someone you mistook. The law's got to have a say."

"Law says we're owed a reward."

"That ain't the law. The rail company put that poster out, and it ain't a county warrant."

"So?"

"So, the county don't pay. If it's Suarez, you'll have to collect at San Simon."

"That's three days' ride," Creek said.

"At least."

"This ain't fair," Dobbs said. "We done a service."

"Can't just kill a man and demand money for it," Keller said. "Maybe you're new to this."

Dobbs scoffed. "I'm done talkin' to you. Get the real sheriff."

"He ain't here."

"Send for him."

"Even if I could bring John Slaughter over, you'd wish you were talking to me."

Dobbs and Creek sat still a moment.

"Listen, fairness is the aim here," Keller said. "You ain't under arrest. You're free in Contention, long as you stay out of trouble. I'll send for Judge Easton. With luck, he'll come quick, review the facts, and decide. And I'll get word to San Simon for you."

"And our guns?" Dobbs said. "You can't take them."

"You're right," Keller said. "But leave that Colt."

Dobbs and Creek got up and collected their weapons.

"Don't use them in town," Keller said. "Folks like things quiet."

"Hardly nobody here."

"The ones here like it peaceful."

Dobbs's scar twisted against a confused smile. "Ain't you somethin'," he said.

Keller pocketed the poster. "Just doin' my job, Mister Dobbs," he said. "I'll find you when you're needed."

Dobbs stomped out. Creek followed. Keller watched them leave. When they were gone, he locked the Navy Colt in a drawer. He glanced at the shrouded body in the cell and thought it made no sense to incarcerate a dead man. He took up a pencil and a bit of paper and started writing a note.

───────◆◆◆◆───────

MCDERMOTT'S SALOON WAS empty. Dobbs and Creek drank quietly until Dobbs said, "Goddamned whelp."

"What'd you say?" John McDermott asked from the other side of the bar.

"Not you. That gimpy kid deputy."

"Who, Keller?" McDermott said. "He's a good egg."

"Took him for a ranch hand," Creek said into his beer.

"He was. Worked nearby. Couple months back, with the Jack Taylor Gang hiding in the mountains, Sheriff Slaughter called for a posse. Keller put his hand up. The gunfight that followed, they killed two of the gang, and he got shot in the leg. Must have done well though, considerin' Slaughter gave him the job after." McDermott shrugged. "Cattle's less trouble."

"I don't care," Dobbs said. He put a coin down. "I want another drink and my money."

"Our money," Creek said.

McDermott refilled Dobbs's glass. The whiskey sloshed. McDermott took the coin.

"Harl, that's four already," Creek said. "We ain't got much left."

"Don't I know."

"We could get a game going," Creek said.

"Good luck," McDermott said. "Town's clearing out. Gillis at the telegraph and post is near blind as a bat. Sam Davis, owns the dry goods, won't play. Hector Gonzales plays if he's around. And there's Keller."

Dobbs scoffed. He downed the whiskey and belched.

"We'll play you," Creek said.

McDermott shook his head and wiped the counter. "There were lots of players, until Tombstone struck water. No need for the San Pedro mills, so they shut down. The earthquake this spring down in Sonora flooded the mines here and broke open the ground. Water and muck spewin' out of the sand like lancin' boils."

"We worked the Callahan claim, Pima County," Creek said. "Hit enough water the pumps wouldn't clear. They closed it. Threw us out."

McDermott nodded. "You ask me, Providence is killin' things off in these parts."

"I didn't ask you," Dobbs said, placing another coin, "but I'll drink your whiskey."

McDermott frowned and poured. Creek bit his lip. Dobbs swallowed whiskey and spat on the floor.

"Not in my place," McDermott said.

"Nobody around to mind."

McDermott corked the bottle. "I do. You don't, go to Tombstone."

"I'm stayin' long as I like," Dobbs said, pointing at the empty glass.

"You've had enough."

"Town barman don't serve drinks. No wonder it's dryin' up." Dobbs got up from his stool. "Fine by me. 'Bout time I found a poke for the night anyway."

"None here," McDermott said. "They're all in Tombstone."

"Bound to be a filly somewhere."

"None'll let you near 'em. Unless you meant horses."

Dobbs went for the Russian in the holster. Creek clamped down on his hand and kept the gun leathered. "Come on, Harl," he said.

"Take my money 'n insult me," Dobbs said.

"Insult?" McDermott said. "You've drunk enough, and I've heard enough. Clear on out or I'll call the law."

"I'd like that," Dobbs said as Creek hustled him out the saloon door.

"Don't know why you're so angry," Creek said when they were in the street.

"Don't know why you ain't!" Dobbs said. "Nothin' for months till Suarez ends up in our lap, and we've lost it."

"Judge might see us right."

Dobbs spat. "You blind, Creek? The moment that kid deputy saw the reward, he says maybe it ain't Suarez, needs a judge. Locked up our bounty where only he can get at it."

"What're you sayin'?"

"I'm sayin' he'd like us out of the way to collect on Suarez."

Creek stiffened. "How you figure?"

"Think about it. We ought've been paid straightaway. Now he's holding our answer to an easy five hundred. No reason for that, less he figures it for himself."

"Jesus," Creek said.

"Bet the judge charges us with murder. They'll hang us, have the company pay 'em out."

Creek's eyes widened and darted. "What do we do, Harl?" he said.

"All we can do is get Gustavo to San Simon and collect the money ourselves."

"How?"

"Like we did with the Callahan claim office. Poke around town, get the right tools. Store's probably got some. Then wait till dark, get in where it's locked up, take what we need."

Creek considered it. He nodded. He winced. "I never robbed a sheriff," he said.

"Christ's sake, Creek," Dobbs said. "It ain't robbin' if you're takin' back what's yours."

AT THE POST office beside the tracks, Keller dictated a message for George Gillis to telegraph San Simon Station. He relayed what he'd learned about the possible death of Gustavo Suarez. The key rattled under Gillis's gnarled finger. His rheumy eyes went wide as gold pans.

"Be some time before a response," Gillis said.

"I'll keep things in line in the meantime," Keller said.

He found Hector Gonzales splitting wood behind the old laundry. They went to the sheriff's office, bundled the corpse, and carried it from the cell to a shed behind the building, laying it out over empty barrels. Keller snapped a heavy padlock over the door.

"A burial soon, God willing," Gonzalez said.

"You ride to Tombstone for me?" Keller said.

"Depends. Am I deputized?"

Keller handed him his note and a bill. "Just paid. It's for Slaughter. He's likely at a game. That should buy you in."

The *vaquero* touched his hat. "Done. I plant this at a table, you'll see it grow," he said, crossing the street to find his horse.

The street was empty and quiet as Keller limped along the boardwalk. He considered the day's events, and figured if he could handle Dobbs and Creek, he could talk to Sadie Davis. He thought it over. *Sadie, would you do me the honor of....*

Too formal, he thought. *Sadie, before I leave for Bisbee, would you come for a ride with me?* She'd understand. He'd known her since he'd worked the Thorne Ranch northeast of Contention. He'd come in for supplies, they'd share words, and he'd be struck by her beauty and how bright she was, how fundamentally decent to talk to. She made his day every time. And when he'd ridden off with Slaughter, returning with a tin star and a bullet in his leg, most folks regarded him as the brave—if a little pitiable—"Deputy." Sadie still called him "Paul" and smiled whenever he entered the store. You had to ask a girl like that. And if she refused? Maybe that was what stoked the fear, he thought.

The ice in his stomach built up as Keller reached the store. He went in and felt it drop hard.

Sadie was behind the counter in a white blouse and work slacks, golden rivulets of hair spilling around her freckled face and bright green eyes as she turned to him. Standing at the counter was Dobbs, hand nudging the grip of the .44 Russian while he leered over Sadie. Behind him, Creek leaned against a barrel of nails, a stick of striped hard candy in his smiling mouth.

"Well, howdy, Deputy," Dobbs said.

"Everything all right, Miss Davis?" Keller said.

Dobbs scoffed. "You reckon we're bothering the lady?"

"Don't assume my meaning. I'm...." Keller looked at Sadie. "I'm making my rounds."

"One lucky town," Dobbs said. "Don't have nothin' but a single watchful protector."

"Everything's fine, Paul," Sadie said. "These fellows are just buying."

"Hardly anything here to buy, anyway," Dobbs said.

"Mister Dobbs said they caught an outlaw this morning," Sadie said.

"Only someone ain't so sure," Dobbs said.

"You done buying, Mister Dobbs?" Keller said.

"I'll buy lots more, when I have my reward."

"*Our*," Creek said.

"Yeah, yours too, jackass."

"Better leg it," Keller said. "Miss Davis is closing up."

"When?"

"Right now."

"Shame. I hoped she'd be open. Nice and open, for a good, long while, if you take my meanin'."

Sadie's eyes went wide. Creek chuckled. Keller grit his teeth.

"Pay up and get out," Keller said.

Dobbs smiled. He picked an apple from a nearby basket and rapped two nickels on the counter. "Bartender said you was a cowhand. What makes a dude trade rope for a star? I figure you lucked into it and found you like bossin' people around." He bit into the apple. Frothy flecks ran down his chin into his beard.

"You like runnin' your mouth," Keller said.

"Try and stop me."

"I'll hear you apologize to Miss Davis."

Dobbs bit the apple again and dropped it. It landed on the floorboard with a wet thud.

"Let's go, Creek," he said.

Creek went out the door first. Dobbs stopped at it, beside Keller, and leaned in. Keller caught the scent of whisky.

"I know what you're after," Dobbs said.

"Keep walking."

"You reckon wearing the tin makes you better. But I don't know you are. Don't know you're fast enough."

"You'd pay to find out."

"Better be." Dobbs glanced down at Keller's feet. "Man ought to be fast somehow."

Keller watched Dobbs and Creek saunter down the street. The blood pumped in his ears. "I'm sorry," he said to Sadie.

Sadie's face was low, her mouth turned down. "Some people are awful," she said. "That's a fact of life."

"You should close for the day and go home. Keep away from those two."

"I shall," she said.

"Your father might keep his shotgun close tonight."

"I'll have it. He's in Tucson. He's… looking to move the store there. Maybe join one."

Keller blinked. "You're leaving Contention?"

"I meant to tell you."

"When?"

"Pretty soon."

At a loss, Keller ran his tongue along his teeth. The ice hardened inside. "Well."

DARKNESS SETTLED OVER Contention. The faint glow of lamps in the windows of the few residences winked out like embers as Dobbs and Creek crept along the street toward the sheriff's office. They skirted the building, passed the shed at the rear, and found the back entrance. Dobbs took out a heavy rasp he'd found from a box of farrier's tools in an abandoned stable. He wedged it into the doorjamb and leaned on it until the door quietly snapped open. He waited in the dark, listening for any response from within, then slipped inside with Creek in tow.

The office was empty, silent, and dark. Dobbs found the oil-lamp on Keller's desk and lit it. The amber light showed them that all the cells were empty.

"Suarez ain't here," Creek whispered. "He's gone."

"See? What'd I tell you? That crooked gimp."

"What do we do now?"

Dobbs pointed above. "We go up there quiet. We make him tell us where Suarez is."

They started toward the stairs. Something made them stop. They felt it before they heard it—a deep rumble underneath the building. The floor thrummed and vibrated. The walls shook.

"The ever-lovin' hell?" Dobbs said.

KELLER WAS PICNICKING with Sadie by the San Pedro when the water rose and carried her away. He snapped awake in his quarters above the sheriff's office. Instinctively, he reached for his gun belt hung on the bedpost. Something was moving in the darkness. No, he thought, that wasn't right—the dark itself was moving. The room oscillated, the joists creaking and groaning as they trembled and strained.

He swung out of bed, yanked on his jeans, gun belt, and boots. He ran for the door, snatching his hat off the wall peg, and clambered down the stairs as the walls pulsated around him. He reached the office, saw the oil-lamp on his desk with the low flame flickering—he'd extinguished that, he thought—and saw Dobbs and Creek by the cell.

"What in hell?" he said.

Dobbs raised the Russian. Keller went for his Colt as the Russian jerked and spat flame. Something heavy hit Keller in the left shoulder. He spun and fell. The floor rushed up to meet him. In the tremor, he heard heavy footsteps, the door unlatching, and the shatter of glass as the oil-lamp fell off his desk. There was a roar and a flash of light as the oil ignited and flared.

Keller came up on his elbow. He touched his shoulder on the meaty outside where it burned. His hand came away wet and slightly sticky, and though it felt as though a hot lance had creased the flesh, it still worked. He found the Colt on the floor and took it in hand. He saw tongues of flame licking up the legs of his desk, his chair, the interior beams.

He scrambled, launched himself out the open door, tumbled, and caught himself on a pole supporting the awning. He scanned the dark street which rolled and shook under him. Shapes and sounds emerged—people coming out of the saloon and homes farther down, frightened muttering, distant whinnies. A woman in a blanket near McDermott's shouted, "God, not again!"

Two shadows moved outside the Western Hotel. They stumbled over the shifting, quaking ground.

"Dobbs!" Keller said.

A shot answered. The ground spat at Keller's feet. He cocked the hammer back and aimed. The Colt thundered twice in his hand. He heard a yelp. He scuttled along the boardwalk, got behind a water trough, fired twice more over his head as rounds snapped in the air. Behind him, a rising orange glow flickered as gunfire cracked above him. A window shattered, spilling glass onto the boardwalk.

Keller peered around the trough. Dobbs and Creek were braced up against the Western, near the entrance. They shifted and disappeared inside. He gauged there was a shy fifty feet between him and the hotel—a hard run in the dark could close the gap, he wagered, if they didn't fire out the windows and if he was fast enough.

Sure, you're fast, he thought.

Suddenly the tremors stopped. The ground underneath Contention shivered and went still.

Keller got up, lunged past the trough, and made for the hotel, expecting gunfire. He heard only blood pulsing in his ears, his own shallow breath, and the uneven thudding of his boots in the dust. He crossed the street, nearly slamming into the hotel. He pressed his back to the wall, slid over to the entrance, and peered around the doorframe.

A shot pealed. Wood splintered just inches from his face. He jumped back.

"Stay back," Dobbs said from inside the hotel.

"Dobbs, Creek," Keller said. "Hear me out. Ain't too late to throw down your guns."

"You'd like it that easy, cripple," Dobbs shouted.

"Don't want anyone hurt."

"Then you let us ride out with Suarez."

"I can't do that."

Dobbs laughed. "'Cause you want that reward. That's why you hid the body."

"I put him somewhere safe," Keller said. He crouched and peeked gingerly around the doorframe. He caught movement behind the railing at the top of the stairs and the top of a straw hat behind the front desk. "You figured on stealing him and running?"

"Stealing back what's ours."

Keller fingered rounds out of his gunbelt and reloaded the Colt. "You've just lost any chance you had at any reward," he said. "I got you for attempted robbery, disturbin' the peace, attempted murder of a peace officer. Drop your guns, and maybe the judge'll chalk it up to bein' plain stupid."

"You got us for nothin' if you're shot to pieces."

"I'm hit, Harl," Creek said. He sounded tense and reedy. "Kid shot my rear."

"So, shoot him back, you ass!"

"Creek," Keller said, "this is one time you should listen to someone other than him."

There was a pained grunt from behind the front desk. Creek said, "I don't want no more trouble."

"Don't you dare," Dobbs said.

"Don't shoot, Keller, I'm comin' out."

Keller heard footsteps lumber toward the doorway. They crossed the threshold. The slender outline of Wallace Creek appeared before him as a shot rang out from inside the hotel. Creek jolted as the round took him in the back, and he crumpled, pitched forward, and fell through the doorway. He landed stone dead at Keller's feet. The Remington clattered beside him.

Keller swallowed and gritted his teeth. "Dobbs."

"Had enough of him, anyway. Now you got a choice here, Deputy. You drop your gun and take me to Suarez, I'll leave quiet. You come in, and after I've shot you to hell, I'll burn this one-horse town to the ground."

Keller picked up Creek's Remington in his free hand. He checked the load. There were four rounds left in the cylinder. He cocked it. He thought of Sadie.

He went through the doorway.

Volcanic exclamations shattered the air in the hotel. Keller kept moving, sighting the top of the staircase and a shadow there as he fired the Remington and the Colt in tandem. His shots peppered the railing and the wall where the low shape moved among the splinters, and he heard a cry, saw Dobbs there darting down the short hallway toward the upstairs rooms.

The Remington clicked empty. Keller dropped it and bounded up the staircase. He reached the top, saw Dobbs at the end of the hallway, leveled the Colt, and fired as Dobbs disappeared into the farthest room. Keller ran to it. He got to the doorway and bolted inside.

Dobbs was making for a window and the street below. He reached it and scrabbled at the pane, trying to force it up and get through. The glow of a wall lamp threw Keller's shadow across the floor and Dobbs turned, swinging the Russian around.

Keller fanned the Colt, emptying it as he slapped the hammer back. The rounds blew Dobbs through the window, and he fell to the dark street below, accompanied by the concussive report from the Colt, the sound of shattering glass, and his own strangled howl—then silence.

Keller approached the broken window and looked down. Dobbs lay motionless, splayed out in the street. Across the way, the sheriff's office was ablaze—small figures moved around it carrying water pails. The dancing firelight caught the shards of glass surrounding Dobbs's body. They glinted like coins.

Keller made his way shakily back through the hotel and down the stairs. At the front desk, he tore a strip of paper from the ledger, thinking that when the fire was out, there'd be a hell of another note to send to Tombstone.

DAYS LATER, KELLER stood outside Davis's store, where the door
and windows were boarded up. He lit a cigarette and saw two men on
horseback coming up the drag. He recognized them—Hector Gonzalez and Deputy Burt Alvord. It *would* be Alvord, Keller thought as he
smoked. They'd met in the posse, and though he respected Alvord,
there was an uneasy intensity there which made Keller wary, though
he knew Slaughter appreciated it.

"Look who I done found in Tombstone," Gonzalez said as they
approached.

"Found, hell," Alvord said. "Hector cleaned out a table. Some idiot
nearly ran him through with a knife. I got ordered to find you and
bring him home."

"These things happen," Gonzalez said.

"Slaughter figures with people leavin' Contention, it'll do with a
town constable."

"As I say, these things," Gonzalez said, pointing to the badge pinned
to his chest.

"Slaughter got your notes," Alvord said to Keller. "I see you got
shot again."

"Just a scratch."

"He asked if you're gonna catch lead every time it gets interesting."

"I seem to deal more'n I get."

"Fair enough. The men you killed buried?"

"I only killed the one. They're buried. The dead man they brought
burned up in the fire."

"Suarez burned?"

Keller shook his head. "I heard from San Simon. Suarez was hiding
out near Wilcox. A friend of his turned him in to the company the

same day these men rode in. He tried to escape, and a rail detective shot him. They found the pay box, even recovered some of the money."

"Who'd they kill, then?"

"Some poor drifter."

Alvord spat. "They burned down the office over a drifter?"

"The quake did that, actually," Keller said. "Tombstone get hit, too?"

Alvord nodded. "Small quakes, left over from the big one. Nearly every day this last week there's been a rumbling. God knows why."

"I know why," Gonzalez said.

"All you know is cards and mescal."

"I know those, too, very well. You're both young, I can forgive this. But remember, this is where Cochise fought people like us, who stripped and pillaged his land. Since the Chiricahua buried him in the Dragoons, the land has trembled and broken, the mines have flooded, the towns burn and dry up."

"There's a thought," Keller said.

"Mescal talkin'," Alvord said. "Hey, is that blonde beauty still workin' her dad's store?"

Keller shook his head. "It's shuttered. The Davises left for Tucson."

Alvord whistled. "She'll have every man there wrapped around her finger."

"I suppose."

"Just as well. I'm on to Benson. And you're for Bisbee."

"Yeah. Doubt we'll ever come back here."

"What's there to come back to?"

Alvord and Gonzalez rode away. Keller watched them, then turned and limped south down the main drag of Contention. He passed along its silent remnants, the markings of something like a town—the burned-out shell of the sheriff's office, the broken window of the empty Western Hotel, the shuttered buildings, the sparse cemetery with its new graves. He looked to the road south. It wound into the rolling horizon and disappeared amid the furrowed scars in the earth.

—————•◦◦◦◦•—————

—Alex Slusar writes crime and Western fiction. His work has previously appeared in Saddlebag Dispatches *and* Grain. *Alex is a member of the Saskatchewan Writers Guild and in 2022 was selected for the SWG Mentorship Program. When he's not writing, Alex works as a political attaché and serves as a reservist with the Royal Canadian Navy and can occasionally be found exploring the northern wilderness, kayaking the St. Lawrence River, summiting peaks in the Adirondacks, or hiking in the Sonoran Desert. He divides his time between the Canadian prairies and Eastern Canada.*

PRELUDE TO A GUNFIGHT

PAUL COLT

POLITICS IS THE same everywhere, only different. I should have known from my Dodge City days. Respectable folks and the reformers who follow want one thing. Those with their eye on profit or ill-gotten gains want another. The law we brought to Dodge walked a line between keeping peace and prosperity. Buffalo the rowdy with a gun butt to the head and let 'em sleep it off in jail. No need for the business end of the gun. Those cowboys was customers. We kept the peace with law and order. The customers lived to talk about and come back for more. Business folks liked it that way. I figured my reputation would travel to Tombstone and a fresh start.

Earp's the name, Wyatt Earp. My brothers and I, along with our wives and live-in ladies, chased a silver strike to Tombstone in '80. Got there too late for silver but in plenty of time for me to take interest in the Pima County sheriff's election that November—not as a candidate. Too new in town for that. My interest lay farther down the road. Word was, the territorial legislature planned to divide Pima County. According to reports coming out of the territorial capital in

Prescott, the legislative plan would hive off a stretch east of the Huachuca Mountains to New Mexico Territory and south to the border to form what folks in Tombstone were calling Cochise County. The new county would need a sheriff, an office that offered steady pay with extra pay for tax collection. The office promised a prominent position in the community and a comfortable living. All I needed to do was get my reputation in front of the voters, or so I thought.

Take interest in running for office and next thing you know you're face to face with local politics. Pima County and Tombstone had its own brand. Politics, Pima County style, divided along lines that felt familiar from my Dodge days. Shouldn't have. The county suffered depredations from an outlaw element known as cowboys. Not rowdy Texas trail hand, Dodge City cowboys. These cowboys were rustlers, posed as small ranchers when they weren't stealing cattle in Mexico or robbing stages this side of the border. Tombstone business and civic leaders valued civil society, favoring law and order. My cup of tea if I was to drink tea.

Pima County Sheriff Charlie Shibell, a Democrat, courted cowboy and small rancher support with "look-away-law." Shibell's cowboy bargain, "You scratch my back, I won't arrest yours," looked like opportunity to show a tougher brand of law and order. Tougher and beneficial to a run for sheriff once Cochise County came to be. I signed on as Shibell's deputy to put my brand of law side by side his. Shibell faced reelection that November. His Republican opponent, Bob Paul, a former lawman and Wells Fargo shotgun messenger, brought a tough law and order reputation like mine to the campaign. A win for Bob would set me up come time to elect a sheriff for the new county. Cowboys took a different view of the race.

Cowboys came and went in a loose confederacy of roughnecks, cutthroats, villains, and ne'er-do-well ranchers. "Old Man" Newman

Clanton, sons Ike and Billy, along with McLaury brothers, Frank and Tom, led cowboy outlaws the likes of John Ringo, Curly Bill Brocius, Pony Deal, and others. With Shibell's blind eye turned the other way, cowboys had the run of the territory inside and outside the law. Outside the law, we knew plain enough. Inside, we didn't understand right away. We had plenty of reason to believe the cowboys could not abide the prospect of Bob Paul being elected Pima County sheriff. We didn't know how far they'd go to keep him out of office.

In the run-up to the November election, John Ringo and Ike Clanton got themselves appointed precinct captains in San Simon, a precinct populated by small ranchers and those who rode with the cowboys. When election day rolled around, Bob Paul lost the county by some fifty votes. He lost San Simon by one hundred, with Ringo and Clanton doing the counting for all fifty eligible voters. Bob contested the stuffed ballot box. I resigned as Shibell's deputy, in support of Bob, fully expecting the election to be overturned in Paul's favor. By showing Republican loyalty, I figured to sign-on as Bob's law and order deputy, strengthening my claim on the party's nomination for the new sheriff's office.

Shibell replaced me with Democrat Johnny Behan. A political opportunist and gladhander, Behan likely saw prospect of a Cochise County sheriff's office much as I did. He figured to get the cowboy backing, keeping Shibell in office. At the first sign of trouble, he proved himself no more lawman than his boss and a perfect partner for cowboy favored look-away-law.

Trouble showed when cowboy crony and gambler, Johnny O'Rourke, shot and killed a well-liked blacksmith in the small town of Charleston, southwest of Tombstone. Town Constable, Heck Thomas, arrested O'Rourke right enough. Lacking a proper jail and fearing a lynching by the blacksmith's many friends, Thomas figured to transfer his prisoner to safer jurisdiction. Knowing Shibell couldn't be counted on where cowboy cronies were concerned, Thomas delivered O'Rourke into the protective custody of Tombstone City Marshal, Ben Sippy, who welcomed the prisoner like a case of cholera.

Thomas's hangin' bee fears turned up the following day when the blacksmith's brother, a man named Bannister, and a passel of his friends arrived in Tombstone. They wasted no time bellying up to a bar stocked with liquid courage at Hafford's Saloon on Fourth Street. Sippy got word of trouble brewing and put out a call for help. Brother Virgil, who served as part-time deputy for Sippy, answered the call along with Behan. The situation made a perfect law and order pose for Johnny. With no cowboy on the wrong side of the law this time and no personal risk if he played his cards the way he did, he could look like a lawman without performing any meaningful duty. Brother Morgan and I didn't see things that way. Where one Earp goes in the face of trouble, you can count on finding the rest of us there. Doc Holliday came along, too, out of personal loyalty and a taste for trouble.

The City Marshal's Office, with its two cell jail, was housed in the courthouse on Fremont Street. In his last term of office before retirement, Sippy went through the motions on everything except his monthly pay envelope. He and Behan took up positions in the jail to "guard" the prisoner, leaving the street and the mob to Virgil, Morg, Doc, and me. Virg, armed with a sawed off eight gauge borrowed from Sippy's unused gun rack, set us up on the boardwalk, blocking the courthouse door. We didn't have long to wait.

By sundown, the mob roused itself to righteous demand for vigilant justice fortified by all the john barleycorn bravery needed for the blacksmith's brother to lead them up Fourth Street like a slow rolling storm cloud cloaked in blue evening shadow. As they turned the corner on Fremont, Virg mused to no one in particular.

"Who you s'pose is leadin' that bunch?"

"That matter?" Morg said.

"He's the one needs convincin'."

"Blacksmith had a brother," I said. "Bannister's the name."

"That'll do."

Virg let 'em close to hailing distance. He stepped off the board-walk, into the street. Tall dark duster silhouetted with a pancake hat and a scattergun cradled in the crook of his left arm, made no mistake for the man in command.

"Stop right there."

A burly figure separated from the crowd.

"We come for my brother's killer."

"The only one comin' for our prisoner is the circuit judge."

"We got all the judge O'Rourke deserves right here. Jury too. C'mon boys, they ain't gonna stop us." The mob murmured forward.

A shotgun blast on a dark confined street even fired in the air makes a statement hard to misunderstand. Bannister's backers stopped dead in their tracks.

"I said far enough, Bannister. The next barrel's got your name on it."

The big man paused. Morg, Doc, and I drew and cocked our guns to press the point. Somethin' soberin' 'bout the discharge of a heavy-gauge shotgun. The mob began to dissolve from the rear, shadows slinking back toward Fourth Street. As mob courage drained away, even Bannister thought better of his bluster.

"I'll see the sum-bitch hang."

"Sure, you will, should a court 'a law say so."

We stood shoulder to shoulder resolute, backing Virg. The threat slowly cleared, having caused little more than minor disturbance of the peace to make a statement 'bout the brand of law and order the Earps stood for.

With the matter no longer in doubt, Behan and Sippy emerged from guard duty in time to be seen as Tombstone breathed a sigh of relief. Behan ran his mouth for his part in settling the matter peacefully for the benefit of John Clum's *Tombstone Telegraph* newspaper. Behan's look-away-law depended on looking like law. Clum published underserved flattery for him in an editorial that also gave Virg well-deserved credit, balancing the scales with word around town from those who knew the truth. All things considered, I felt good where I stood for the time Cochise County needed a law and order sheriff.

As expected, the Territorial Legislature made Cochise County enactment official, leaving appointment of an interim sheriff to Republican Governor John C. Fremont, pending formal election the following November. That was an appointment I fully expected to get based on my reputation and Republican loyalty supporting Bob Paul's Pima County election challenge.

No sooner had the legislature taken action, then Doc caught up with me, tending my gambling concession at the Oriental Saloon. Ravaged by consumption, the Georgian looked the part of a well-dressed cadaver, lacking only a pine coffin to lay out in. Still, I valued him as a friend for life, after the night he saved mine back in Dodge. We'd had each other's backs ever since.

"Evenin', Wyatt."

"Doc. You come to play?"

He coughed into an ever-present linen handkerchief. "Later. A moment first, if Ah may?"

I nodded. Always time for Doc. He signaled the bartender. Always time for Doc to drink. We took a table."

"What's on your mind?"

He swirled whiskey in his glass, took a swallow. Poured another. "Territorial Legislature finished their county work."

"They did. Won't be long now, I s'pect."

"The interim sheriff appointment."

"Yup."

"You expect it, then."

"I do."

"Have you been to see the governor?"

"What for?"

"To tell him of your interest in the office."

"My interest? Law and order is everybody's interest. My reputation speaks for itself."

"You know that, and Ah know that. Does Fremont know that?"

"Fremont's a Republican. My support for Bob Paul and party loyalty are well known."

"You sure?"

"Hell, if he don't know, he ain't payin' attention. Besides, who else is he gonna appoint?"

"Behan."

"Behan? He's a Democrat and no lawman, to boot. Fremont would never do that."

"He might."

"Why would he do such a thing?"

"He's got a Democrat legislature to deal with. Horses get traded, you know."

"What's appointment of a sheriff got to do with horse trading?"

"Deals, Wyatt. Politicians make deals. One scratches one back, while another the other."

"You mean to tell me I need to go up to Prescott and kiss Fremont's ass so's he does the right thing?"

"No. I'm telling you that you need to go to Prescott and convince Fremont you're the man for the job."

He coughed again, likely to let that sink in. "I got nothin' to prove on account 'a my reputation and besides, I ain't much for kissin' politician ass, even if he is governor."

"You can bet Behan has been pressin' flesh in Prescott along with a sympathetic Democrat legislator or two."

"Politics shouldn't enter into matters of law and order."

"Maybe so, but appointments aren't law or order, Wyatt. They're political favors."

"Shouldn't be."

"Easy for you to say. Ah seen what comes out'ah cahpetbags."

POLITICS. IT'S THE same all over, only different. Should have listened to Doc. Fremont appointed Behan interim sheriff. The cowboys would have look-away-law in Cochise County. With the stroke of a pen, Fremont drew battlelines for a gunfight politics couldn't see comin'.

Events of this story are based in historical fact. As is true of all Paul Colt historical dramatizations, the story is intended to entertain and inform. "Prelude to a Gunfight" is retold here from Paul's new biographical novel, Lunger: The Doc Holliday Story, *only from Hat Creek.*

—Paul Colt's critically-acclaimed historical fiction crackles with authenticity. His analytical insight, investigative research, and genuine horse sense bring history to life in dramatizations that entertain and inform. Readers say, "Pick up a Paul Colt book, you can't put it down." Paul lives in Wisconsin with his wife and high school sweetheart, Trish.

THE
FIRST SHOT

J.R. WOLFF

IT WAS EARLY, and he'd been in the chicken coop. From an open window, he could hear the house radio reporting that Truman had beaten Dewey. His pregnant wife called out from the porch. "Your grandma's on the phone, Cal."

Cal sighed and took a swig from the bottle that was stashed behind some wooden planks and nestled it back. "All right, all right. Hold your damn horses," he called out, striding up the porch in his wranglers and denim pearl snap. The kitchen smelled of coffee. His wife extended him the receiver, covering the bottom with her hand.

"You be nice now."

He grabbed the receiver and tugged it away. "Howdy, Gran," he said listening. "Well, I don't understand the big deal. He's always been like that."

His expression dropped. "Oh, I see. Well, in that case, I'll be there."

He hung up the receiver and looked at his wife nervously. "I have to drive to Tombstone."

"Today? What about church?"

"He's put on his uniform from the Indian Wars. He's patrolling the neighborhood with a loaded pistol, won't put it down. Shot the neighbor's cat."

"Lord Almighty, is he gonna hurt your grandma?"

"Not unless she's a Comanche. Anyway, she says I'm the only one who can get him to reason."

"Well, if we leave now, we can go to church first, beforehand," she said, hopefully.

"Told you, I don't like going to church anymore," he snapped. "You go if you want."

"All right," she said coldly, leaving the room.

He shook his head. She was *always* leaving rooms. No winning with her, he thought. Since the day was spoiled, he figured he might as well go to Tombstone and sleep there too.

He put on his tan hunting coat and beaver Stetson, palmed cigarettes from the counter on his way out, and patted his jacket to make sure he had not forgotten his flask.

He didn't really want to make the drive to Tombstone. He wanted to stay home and drink. He had been feeling anxious lately, and the road cleared his mind, but soon, even the thought of his granddaddy brought him down. Old Sam was nearly a hundred years old and still as feisty as could be. He'd fought in the Indian Wars under General Custer and was always telling grandiose, tall-tales about his past in Tombstone. To hear him tell it, he was a lawman, a rustler, and a wealthy prospector. He'd ridden with both the Earps and the Clantons. He'd taught Doc Holliday how to improve his draw. He'd cornered the silver market for a month in 1877. Cal had heard so many of these stories that he'd lost count. But Cal's own daddy had taken a bullet in the head at the Somme before he was born, so he couldn't exactly chime in with his knowledge.

After the Second World War, Cal joined his mother's family's cattle ranch where he grew up. It was on the other side of the Dragoon Mountains, a rough patch of land with Sycamore trees and just enough water for their small herd. His mama had died in forty-seven and was buried on the land with a simple cross. His wife, the daughter of a neighboring ranch, was pregnant with their first.

He thought more and more about the war these days. Not in a good way. Sure, he'd been there and done his job. Killed quite a few Japanese along the way, but he didn't have a lot to show for it. Far from a model soldier, he'd been jailed numerous times for drinking on duty and had been dragged out of a Hawaiian brothel by military police after going AWOL. He left the Army with the same rank he had gone in with.

He also wasn't sure about his daddy. There were no medals, nothing. He simply went to France and got his head blown off in a trench. He hadn't even been facing the right direction, something that had not sat well with Cal.

The last person he wanted to see was Old Sam, who had gone off the deep end sometime during Ulysses S. Grant's administration. What a family, he thought. "If someone needs me around for stability, that's a big problem."

He took a sip of road brandy, lit another cigarette, and before long, the desolate, rugged mountain roads began to calm his mind. He had loved going to Tombstone as a kid. He would run around the O.K. Corral with his toy gun, drawing his pistol here and there, re-enacting where Wyatt Earp, lawman of lawmen, and Doc Holliday had killed the outlaws Billy Clanton and the McLaury brothers.

In Cal's boyhood, it was all very clear. There were firm lines that separated good guys from bad guys. It was readily apparent what a man should do and what a man should not do. He heard it from his mother. He heard it at church every Sunday—it was important for a man to draw a line, to know where he stood and what he was about. In the West, when push came to shove, as it always did, you'd better have been ready to back up those beliefs.

Lately, Cal wasn't sure what kind of guy he was. That plagued his mind a lot. Deep down, he supposed he was a good guy, but more often than not, he was the kind of guy who always wanted to be somewhere he wasn't. The kind of guy that hated coming home. The kind of guy who had killed people. The kind of guy who lost a lot of money playing cards with his minister, which is why he always had excuses not to go to church. The kind of guy who came home late. "What kinda guy is that?" he wondered.

He passed through the Dragoons and thought about his great grandfather who had been killed there in an Apache raid—scalped, left for dead, and found half-eaten by coyotes.

Cal entered Tombstone and found his grandfather's small, one story home in a sparsely populated neighborhood. He stopped the truck, took another sip to warm his chest, and walked up to the front door. It was cold and howling with wind.

He knocked hard a few times. Nobody answered.

"I'll be damned. All the way here for nothing. Maybe they're both dead." He flipped up his jacket collar and attempted to light a cigarette.

The *click* of a pistol hammer made him freeze—the flame from his Zippo flickered in the wind.

"You move one goddamn inch, and I'll take yer head off."

The raspy voice was unmistakable.

"Grandpa? It's Cal! Your grandson. Don't shoot me for chrissakes."

Cal slowly turned to see a gigantic gun barrel between his eyes, held by a shriveled, old man wearing an oversized Army Cavalry uniform. To be fair, it was Old Sam's uniform from nearly eighty years earlier. Except now, Old Sam was a shrunken version of his former self. Everything about him had gotten smaller—except the wild blue eyes and the gigantic, walrus mustache.

The old man squinted and moved closer to his face. "Ah, shit, Cal. Why didn't you say something?" The old man tucked the huge pistol into his waistband and entered the house, holding the door open for Cal. "I swore you was sent by Geronimo."

Inside, a fracas was in full swing. The grandmother—actually Old Sam's fourth wife and of no real relation to Cal—was having a hysterical fit. Her makeup was smeared, and by the looks of the bottles and the smells on their breath, it was clear they'd both been drinking since the night before. She was angry that he had gambled away their money on a poker hand. Cal wondered who Old Sam could possibly be playing poker with, since all his friends had been dead for decades, and for his part, Sam was happy that he had lost the money because he claimed that she was a "nasty woman" and out to steal his "riches." Cal had to keep from laughing, though it was curious that her last three husbands had indeed died mysterious deaths.

On top of this, Old Sam did not know what year it was. He truly believed it was still 1882. Cal sunk into a dusty sofa and watched as the couple yelled at each other. They paid him no mind and offered no airs. She began breaking plates one by one, and finally when a plate flew across the room and shattered on the wall over Cal's head, Old Sam had had enough. He raised his huge pistol in the air and fired a shot into the ceiling to shut her up—it worked.

This got Cal's attention, and he managed to pry the ancient pistol out of the irate old man's shaking hands and put it into his own jacket pocket. "I'll watch this."

"I expect it back when I go on patrol," Sam snarled.

"Yeah, I'll talk to Custer about that."

Cal shook his head in anger. He had been duped. Roped into a domestic dispute between two drunk, geriatric lunatics. He had his own damn problems, dammit. He sat on their couch, lit up another smoke, and noticed a range of bullet holes in the ceiling.

Old Sam was impatiently pacing the room, muttering something about his favorite Indian Scout. "Bloody Knife, now he was something. If it weren't for him, I reckon I would've been kilt by the Sioux ten times over! He was a Ree. A fine man he was."

Cal couldn't take it. "For God's sakes, you're makin' me nervous. Don't you wanna talk for a few minutes?" Old Sam was briefly offended, but after a moment, he seemed to forget why and walked slowly toward Cal. Like a sack of potatoes, he dropped onto the sofa, landing next to Cal in a cloud of dust.

"Say, got anything to drink?" asked Sam with a twinkle in his eyes.

Cal hesitated, then handed him his flask. They each took a sip. He never really knew what to say to his grandfather. "Well, Grandpa. No bull, I'm asking you for real this time. What really happened at the O.K. Corral? Were you really there?"

Old Sam eyed his wife across the room to make sure she wasn't listening. He slid closer to Cal and lowered his voice.

"No, I was not."

Cal's eyes dropped.

"But," continued Old Sam, "there *is* something that I haven't told anyone. Because it's a state secret."

A "state secret" was the exact type of grandiose tale that Old Sam would tell, yet something about the tone of his voice was different, deeper, and less affected.

"Go on," said Cal.

"You have to swear you won't say nothing because it's still being worked through by the Cochise County court. Only when I'm dead."

"Okay."

"Okay ain't gonna cut it. You shake my hand, look me dead in the eye, and swear you won't say nothing."

Cal offered his hand, which his grandfather gripped surprisingly tight. He looked him in the eye. "I swear that I won't say anything."

Old Sam pulled Cal close to him and whispered into his ear.

"The outlaw Frank Stilwell was not killed by Wyatt Earp."

"He absolutely was," replied Cal, confused.

"Wrong."

"It's a fact, Grandpa. I read all the—"

Old Sam let go of his arm. He looked at him incredulously.

"You read the books? And who do you think *writes* the books in Tombstone, scholars? *Think,* boy! The history was written by those of us who lived."

"But you weren't even there," whispered Cal, trying to remain calm. "It was Wyatt Earp, Warren Earp, Doc Holliday, Sherman Mc-Master, and 'Turkey Creek' Johnson."

"Listen, I'd known Frank Stilwell from my days in Prescott City," said Old Sam. "Anyways, I looked him up when I came to Tombstone, and we played cards every now and then. One night, not long before he killed Morgan Earp, I was on a hot streak, and I cleaned Stilwell up real good. He was licked fair and square. Well, I tell you, I never saw a man's face turn so ice-cold as he handed me those dollars....

"Anyway, that evening, I decided to celebrate and see a woman," he said, with a mischievous grin. "Well, she and I were just becoming acquainted when the door to my hotel room bursts open. Guess who I see standing there? It's Stilwell, drunk as hell with his gun drawn and fire in his eyes. He buffaloed me over the head with his pistol, took all my money, and tossed my clothes out the window. And then...." Sam looked away, indignant.

"Then what, Grandpa?"

"A demonic look comes over his face. At gunpoint, he orders me and the lady to slow dance. We was buck naked! He then begun shooting at our feet. 'Pick up the pace!' he yelled, howling with laughter. Then he lit my hat on fire."

This story had gotten so bizarre, Cal acually began to believe that it might be true.

"Just as I reckoned we was about to be kilt, we heard shouts from downstairs that Morgan Earp, rest his soul, was riding up. That's when Stilwell jumped out of the window."

Old Sam looked away, his blue eyes burning with rage as he relived the experience.

"I had to go down to the street, holding my burnt hat over my *cojones* to fetch my clothes. I swore I'd never forgive that sonuvabitch, and that if I had the chance, I'd kill him."

"So, what happened next?" asked Cal.

"Sometime later, I'd headed to Tucson for a couple days for business. It was the evening of March twentieth, and I was due to return. I'd had a bit to drink, and I realized I was going to miss my train. I ran as fast as I could to the station when someone crashed into me so hard that it nearly knocked me down.

"I couldn't believe my eyes, but it was Stilwell! I tell you, I didn't have a second to think before I see Earp and a few others chasing him down from the other direction. They was armed to the teeth. I reckon I never saw so many guns.

"Well, this was my chance. So, I started running, and I was fast. It was so dark that nobody even noticed that I had caught up and ran alongside Wyatt Earp. It was pandemonium. We stood on the tracks, trains coming and going, and people in Tucson were firing their guns to celebrate something or the other.

"At this point, I'm sprintin' so quickly that my hat flies off, and I can't hardly breathe. I draw my pistol and extend my arm, and as I'm running, in a shaft of light from an approaching train, I take dead aim on Stilwell and pulled the trigger. I reckon it was the luckiest shot of my life, but I hit him right under the armpit as he ran. He fell hard and rolled, dropping his gun. Like a wounded beast, he got back to his feet. I lost him for a moment, and just as I could make him out in the dark, Earp walked right up to Frank and planted a double barrel shotgun right into his chest. Stilwell's eyes were wide open. He grabbed the barrels just as Earp fired and damn-near cut him in half. Well, goddamn if it isn't true, but the bastard was still alive. That is until Warren Earp, Doc Holliday, Sherman McMaster, and Turkey Creek caught up and had a few parting words with Mister Stilwell. Seconds later, he was shot up like swiss cheese."

"Grandpa, what year was it again?"

"1882. Something wrong with you?"

"Nobody saw you?"

"They did. They all knew me from Tombstone and knew how much I hated Stilwell. Unlike the cowboys, I never had a problem with the Earps. I didn't even know until the next day that Morgan Earp had been kilt by Stilwell. Anyway, as they dragged Stilwell's body down the tracks, Earp handed me his big pistol, which I forgot to give back."

"Wait a minute. Why didn't you take credit?" asked Cal.

"Well, something about the way they were hiding the body... I ain't never seen deputy marshals do that. I wasn't sure if they even knew I had fired my gun, and I wasn't much in the mood for jail. So eventually when Wyatt told me to git—I listened and kept my mouth shut."

"Wait, jail? You were the outlaws?"

"Well, not really in my opinion. But yes."

"Wyatt Earp was a deputy marshal. How could he be an outlaw?"

"Hell if I know. This is America, son. Days later, they was all brought up on charges, and every newspaper in America wrote about the 'Vendetta Ride,' as it came to be known. And *I* fired the first shot."

"For chrissakes, Grandpa. That's quite a tale."

"Keep it low," whispered Old Sam.

The story was a bit much. Cal decided to take a leak and found himself chuckling at the old man's tall tale. He had actually been pulled into the delusional rantings of a man who believed Chester A. Arthur was still president.

When he emerged, the couple were back at it and yelling again. It had been an unexpectedly entertaining few hours, and Cal decided that this was the time to leave. There was no way he could sleep here.

Old Sam walked him to his truck, and as Cal started the engine, his grandfather leaned into the window. "Please don't tell anyone that story. Promise me that."

"Sure thing, Grandpa," he said with a wink.

Cal had almost backed out when Old Sam motioned for Cal to stop. "Hold on."

A moment later, Old Sam came out of the house holding a box.

"What's that?" asked Cal.

Old Sam passed it through the window. "My wife says this stuff is for you. She wants it out of here."

"What's in it?"

"I dunno, she handles all the mail."

Cal rolled his eyes and put the box next to him on the truck's bench seat, "All right, then."

"See you, and watch for Apache in the pass," cautioned Old Sam. He went back to the house, slamming the door behind him.

As Cal drove, he warily eyed the box. It was just like Old Sam to burden him with clerical things like unread mail and old bills. He turned up the radio and continued to drive. As he made his way through the Dragoon Mountains, he could no longer take it and pulled his truck to a sudden stop. He turned down the radio, reached into the box, and quickly withdrew his hand in pain—something had pricked his finger. He looked inside.

There was a needle sticking out of an old envelope. Inside was something hard.

He emptied the contents of the envelope. Speechless, Cal brushed a tear from his cheek.

When he came home, it was quiet. He gingerly climbed the stairs and found his wife napping in their bedroom. Not wanting to wake her, he carefully opened his dresser, and with a smile, he placed an official letter and a bronze medal, issued posthumously to his daddy, Calvin Richardson, Sr. He'd gone back to save a comrade, and that's when he lost his life. He closed the drawer.

"How was your grandad?" asked his sleepy wife.

"He's all right. Got some interesting stories for you," he said, rubbing her big belly. "And eventually, some great stories for Cal the third, too."

She smiled with her eyes closed, "I thought you didn't want to continue that name?"

"Just an idea."

She grinned and went back to sleep.

Cal rose, and as he took off his coat, he felt something in his pocket. It was his grandfather's pistol. He'd forgotten to give it back. He took it out and marveled at the design. It was a highly unusual antique revolver with a beautiful wooden stock and a very long barrel. The metal was finely engraved with Western patterns. As he quietly placed it alongside his daddy's war medal, something caught his eye. There was something carved into the gun's metal—*W. Earp.*

"Sunnuva bitch," he exclaimed aloud, startling his wife.

"What's that?"

"Nothing, honey," he said, closing the drawer. "Know what?

"What?"

He sat down beside her and kissed her forehead. "Think I'll go to church with you."

———————————

—A California native, Jon "J.R." Wolff comes from a family of writers, storytellers, and horsemen. Growing up, Jon spent a few summers on a ranch where he developed a lifelong passion for all things Western. Jon attended the University of Texas at Austin, and it was during these years, and on roadtrips into Mexico, that he began to pen short stories and plays of his own. After graduation, Jon had stints as a ditch-digger, traveling salesman, and as a fisherman on the Sea of Galilee. He now manages his own business, acts in films, and writes teleplays, short stories, and novels.

WAIT THERE, COCHISE

KEITH "DOC" RAYMOND

THEY THREW TAISHAN Xinhui into the horse trough. Xinhui disappeared beneath the murky water and came up sputtering. He stared at the angry faces of white men employed by what we would later know as the Southern Pacific Railroad. Just before, he was busy banging on the boiler of a locomotive in the San Francisco railyard.

One of them grabbed Xinhui by the shirt, pulling him from the water, while the others made fists. He was about to get a tarnishing, when a young Peter Donahue leaned out of the engineer's cab and called them to order.

"He found the leak," Donahue yelled. "That Chinaman found the steam break, causing the pressure to drop. You leave him be!"

The muscular railroad bull was about to flatten Xinhui's nose when his fist paused in mid-air. He turned to the kid on the locomotive covered in grease, holding a big wrench. The bull answered, "I don't work for ya. I work for the P&A (Pacific and Atlantic Railroad company). If this chink is damaging company property, he earned himself a pasting!"

Two Tong thugs raced over from the other side of the tracks, drawn by the hubbub. They started yelling at Xinhui in Mandarin. Their armed presence, men dressed in black despite the heat, made the rail workers and even the bull pause and take a step back. Xinhui fell back in the trough, dunking his head, only to sit up sputtering and tell them what he was up to. The Tong dragged him out and stood him on his feet.

"Is that right?" the thug said to Peter.

"Sure is."

"Okay boy, you work for him now," the Tong with the slashed face said, pointing at Donahue.

"Yes, Boss," Xinhui nodded, and ran out of the circle of men back to the locomotive.

The year was 1853. Xinhui and hundreds of other coolies worked for two years cutting trees and clearing brush on the rail bed route between San Francisco and San Jose. The Tong made a deal with the P&A to provide cheap labor to the railroad for the price of feeding them. Xinhui was in the rail yard preparing the rails and making spikes when he heard the leak.

Peter Donahue looked down from his perch below the firebox at the dripping Chinaman, soaked to the skin. "You been around boilers, coolie?"

"The name's Xinhui, and yes, I know a little."

His fluency and even his talking style impressed Donahue. "How, Shin-wee?"

"Worked over at Pioneer Steam Coffee and Spice Mills for a while. I was even a partner before they took me," Xinhui said, nodding over at the Tong. "The principles are the same. Coffee roasters and loco-motive boilers aren't much different when it comes down to it."

Peter could hardly believe this Chinaman was a business partner, but he saw the man understood boilers, at least a little. "In fact, Shin-wee, they are a great deal different. It takes a lot more steam pressure to drive them steel wheels. Look, I'm not an expert. I'm just a kid, but I'm going to put you with Lou Hanshaw. He knows steam engines inside and out. You'll be his apprentice."

"How can someone so young own a railroad?" Xinhui asked.

Peter laughed. "I don't own it. My father's a major investor. I just like to hang around the rail yard and pick up a trick or two. Maybe someday be an engineer. Hey Lou—"

"What do you want? Can't you see I'm busy?"

"I can't see you, but I can hear you working around the steam stator. Got someone for you to meet."

"Don't have time to meet anyone. Have to get this locomotive fixed up."

"Well, this Chinaman can lend a hand. Get into places you can't. You'll need him. If not now, then later."

"Okay, young master Donahue, send him down here. And Peter quit messing with the boiler. I heard you making a racket."

"Not me, him. He found the problem."

"We'll see about that," answered Hanshaw.

So began Xinhui's apprenticeship, after which he'd be a boiler-maker. He worked hard, learning the trade as best he could. Watched his mentor closely, taking in the finer points of the craft and adapting them to his own style. Xinhui was a quick learner, but despite his dedication, Lou often scolded him for his mistakes.

He was determined not to fail, and so he kept at it. Eventually, Xinhui mastered the trade and could work on his own. Hanshaw gave him more challenging tasks, and he took on larger projects. He learned to work with a variety of materials, from cast iron to copper, and honed his skills.

IN THE SONORA desert of Mexico, a man stared at his father in their wickiup. He'd seen his father applying war paint, but this time it would be different. Pisago didn't want to go to war, he wanted to sign an armistice with the Mexicans, but his father, the man's grandfather, refused.

Speaking the Athabaskan language of his people, the Tsokanende, the father told his son he may not come back. The man, already taller than his father, did not react. He sat cross-legged, stone faced, as Pisago taught him, but inside he ached.

His father was going to fight the Mexican army with the rest of the menfolk. It saddened Pisago that he must fight for their Chiricahua land after the Mexicans violated the treaty. The army wanted to take the land back from them when his people refused to sign another treaty. But to Pisago, it was an honor to fight. To the North, in America, the Apache, what the white man called his people (for they have no name), were also fighting to take Chiricahua land.

The man, Cochise, watched him go.

Their long practice of sending out raiding parties to capture land, livestock, food, and weapons caught up with them. Cochise, his family, and the rest of the Tsokanende were nomadic by nature. They took only what they needed, and often the lands reverted to the previous owners, or even new owners, once the Chiricahua abandoned them.

But when they homesteaded, his people would fight if need be, to keep what was theirs. Cochise's grandfather was a warrior, as was his father. Pisago himself, while he applied his war paint, reflected on his escape from the ambush set by John Johnson, a mercenary the Mexicans hired for Apache scalps. He prayed Johnson would be in the coming battle. He vowed revenge.

Cochise knew he would soon become a chief, but that was in the future. A future sooner than expected. He begged to go fight with his father, but his father refused.

"Look after your wife, Dos-te-seh, and your son, Taza, and the other womenfolk. It's your duty."

Cochise pleaded, "But I want to be by your side. Please let me go."

His father shook his head. "No, my son. Your place is here. I need you to protect your family and the others. They've attacked a village while we are out fighting before. They have no honor."

Cochise sighed. "Yes, Father. I will."

While it hurt him not to go to war that day. In the future, Cochise's willingness to care for his family and his people made him a great leader. Another great leader his father told him about, Geronimo, a medicine man, would lead the attack. Cochise's father would follow him and another Chief, Miguel Narbona, into the battle.

PISAGO AND GERONIMO'S horses nickered and stepped nervously, standing close to each other. Pisago's horse nipped at the neck of the other horse when Geronimo's mount shifted too near. Neither Apache paid attention.

They focused on the Mexican army across the desert plain, talking in hushed voices and pointing out weaknesses. The other warriors were restless. Eager to fight. Uniformed men of the Mexican army clearly outnumbered them, but that didn't seem to bother them a bit.

Colonel Jose Maria Carrasco viewed the two Apache through his three-draw handheld telescope. The Indians stood apart from the others on the opposing side. He planned to finish what he started in violation of the treaty.

The sun beat down mercilessly. The air filled with the sound of crickets and the smell of dust and sweat. Colonel Carrasco felt a heavy weight of responsibility, knowing that this was the moment he had been preparing for. He wanted Geronimo dead.

Raising the telescope, he focused it on the two Apache. He could see the sweat glistening on their brows, their hands twitching as they sat mounted, ready for battle. Their courage and defiance struck him and the knowledge that he was about to take away their chance for freedom. He lowered the telescope and exhaled slowly, steeling himself for the task ahead.

Pisago was reluctant against such odds, but Geronimo and Narbona wanted this fight. Eight months prior, the army killed twenty warriors and Chief Yrigollen. Geronimo's family also died at the army's hands while he was out in a raiding party. Now he was looking for revenge.

Carrasco ordered the charge, and the battle began. Swords clashed with knives, pistols with rifles, and at first the Apache seemed to win against all odds. Pisago, spotting the colonel, rode headlong toward the monster that massacred their women and children. But he never made it.

A flash of a sword to his left cut him from his horse. Pisago lay on the ground bleeding, but he still had more fight in him. Just as he jumped up, knife in hand, several muskets unloaded balls into him. He died with a war cry on his lips. Geronimo, seeing Pisago fall, retreated on his own, leaving the others. Living to fight another day.

———————◆———————

GERONIMO'S STORIES ARE legendary, but most of his exploits would be lost in the sands of time. Neither Pisago nor Narbona returned from that battle. Shortly thereafter, hearing of their deaths, the village named Cochise chief of the Tsokanende Chiricahua.

Smallpox ravaged the Sonoran Apaches only a few years before Cochise lost his father. The Mexican war and the epidemic led to a reduction of the rations promised to his people by the government. The Chiricahua starved because of these unsustainable levels. Seeing a dark future, Cochise moved the tribe to Arizona, settling in Apache Pass so they would not suffer another massacre at the hands of Carrasco.

Cochise looked back on his time with his father inside the wickiup on the fateful day he died. Cochise kicked the dust in the Arizona desert. His second wife smiled at him, sitting in the women's circle. His two daughters and two sons played with the other kids in the settlement.

Life was good, better than it was for them in Mexico. But somehow he knew it could not last. His relations with other Apache in the region were cordial but not necessarily friendly. He needed to prepare. It was time to make moves to secure their future.

So Cochise arranged a powwow with John Butterfield of the Butterfield Overland Mail Company.

———————————

"SHIN-WEE, WE NEED to adjust the eccentrics so that valve rod rocks back and forth in time with the steam engine. Out of synch and you can't shift the cylinders properly to drive the wheels." Lou looked at his apprentice to see if he was still following him. "What it boils down to is more grease, oil, and hot steam to make this beast go." This was Hanshaw's common refrain.

Xinhui nodded. He actually sweat while concentrating, so focused on learning the ins and outs of maintenance and care. One day soon, he'd go out on the rails by himself, and they'd expect him to fix the locomotive on the fly. Well, not truly by himself, as he'd have a Tong minder to make sure he didn't skip off.

"So, you're saying the eccentrics are like the gears of a watch. The timing has to be perfect. The piston on one side of the train works with, rather than against, the piston on the other side."

"Righty-oh," Lou answered, admiring the speed at which the young Chinaman absorbed information. Since Lou no longer had to struggle through the firebox to get inside the steam engine, it gave him more time to teach the kid. Xinhui was a natural at finding cracks and faults with a hammer. Repairing them only took a little longer. "I think you're getting the hang o' this."

"Hang what? Not me!" Xinhui said, eyes widening.

"There won't be any hanging while I'm around," said the Tong minder. "We've got too much invested in this kid."

"Finally woke up then," Lou noted. Which earned him a snarl from the thug. Hanshaw took a step back. "It's just a saying. Nothing to do with the gallows."

"When he go to work? Too much talk, not enough action."

Before Lou could answer, Xinhui went into a long tirade with the Tong in Mandarin. It included the complexity of the machine, the importance of proper inspection, care, and repair of big locomotives. In seconds, the thug was so far out of his depth he simply stared uncomprehendingly, his previous anger wiped away. Now it was the Tong's turn to step back and let the two of them finish.

"I don't know what you said to him, but it worked," Lou managed.

"I don't think he'll give us any more trouble," Xinhui said.

"Now, where were we? Oh, that's right. The important thing is to know what you can fix while out on the tracks and what needs to be done back here in the rail yard. If a locomotive needs to get towed in for repair, that can cause huge delays. You don't want that."

Xinhui nodded as they continued. He marveled at the ingenuity of a steam engine and thought of ways to improve its efficiency while learning to fix it.

Several months passed, the Tong minder nodding off in the shade while Lou and Xinhui worked. The teaching, learning, and repairing continued. Xinhui found an old toolbox and used it to collect tools he'd need when they sent him out. The time came sooner than expected and not what he planned.

Lou and Xinhui stopped eating when Donahue and his father appeared in the machine shop.. Xinhui stood and shook Peter's hand and bowed to his father.

"How's the Chinaman doing?" the young man's father asked.

"Just about ready to hit the rails. Maybe another month of training," Lou answered. "He's quick. Fastest apprentice I've ever had."

"Well, you're going to have to cut it short. I'm sending him out with a scouting party to investigate routes through Arizona for the transcontinental tomorrow."

"Big plans, Donahue. You've barely got the cash to build the line to San Jose."

"Can't leave it up to the stagecoaches anymore. If we don't think big, we won't get big. How's the wife and kids, Lou?"

"Best as can be expected. Kids in school and all. But she still can't cook to save her life."

They laughed, all except Xinhui. "Still, you are looking mighty prosperous," said Donahue, patting his belly.

"That's from beer, not beef."

"Okay, coolie, come with me. We're having a sit down with the boys in the scouting party this afternoon. Grab what you need, you leave at first light. Can you ride a horse and shoot?"

Xinhui nodded, grabbing his toolbox.

"You won't be needing that where you're going," Peter said. "And you should know, I'm going with ya."

Xinhui gave him a rare smile.

———————◆◇◆———————

NOT USED TO staying put, the Chiricahua were hard pressed to make a life in the desert around Apache Pass. Plus other bands of Apache crowded the region. While Cochise and his band were Tsokanende, his father-in-law, Mangas Coloradas, was chief of the Mimbreno band and cousin to Geronimo.

The third band was the Nednhi, headed by the ruthless Chief Juh. Of the three, Juh did not homestead but continued to raid, creating headaches for Cochise and the others. The white man, not knowing about these distinct bands, considered all Apache dangerous.

Cochise wanted prosperity and peace for his people, therefore the powwow with John Butterfield. Butterfield ran a successful stage-coach mail service that ran through the pass. Cochise allowed him to build an outpost there. But Cochise wanted more. Needing food and weapons, he set up the meeting to negotiate for both.

"How is business, Mister Butterfield?"

"John, please call me John."

Taza, seated at his father's side, listened. Cochise said, "John, how can I help you?"

This took Butterfield by surprise. Indians rarely offered the white man anything. This Cochise was a clever fellow. "And what can you offer, Chief?"

Cochise's eye wandered around the outpost's walls. "We can offer wood. Wood for building, wood for fire. Wood to help your people through the cold winters."

John looked at his hands, saying, "And what would it cost me?"

"I offer more. I offer safe passage for your stagecoaches through the Pass and mountains. No Apache will stop them. For this, we want food, liquor, guns, and ammunition."

"A tall order, Cochise."

"John, you pay us what you feel is fair. I trust you." Cochise would come to regret Butterfield's trust and misread his smile. Only much later would Cochise ever trust a white man again, one Tom Jeffords.

"Then we have an accord. You protect my stagecoaches, provide wood, and I will meet your request." John offered him his hand. Cochise didn't know what to do with the gesture, and after a while, Butterfield dropped his hand. "Let's smoke on it then."

And they did. But when Cochise and Taza were about to leave, John said, "Wait there, Cochise. I have something for you. This just came in from London, and I thought you deserve it."

Butterfield retired to a back room of the outpost and came out with a musket that had a beautifully worked stock. The rifle shined with blue tinted steel. He also carried a pouch filled with bullets. He handed the tooled weapon to the chief.

"That there's the latest rifle made. An 1853 Enfield. Instead of a smooth bore, they rifled through it to put a spin on the bullet. Here, these are French-made mini balls .577 caliber, specially designed for the Enfield. It won't jam, even if you muck up the muzzle with black powder. And a marksman can hit a target with it a half mile away!"

Cochise nodded and cuddled the weapon like a baby. With one hand, he lifted a beaded necklace from around his neck and handed it to Butterfield. Then he put out his hand, palm down, and made a cutting motion. Deal done.

"And if you need more mini balls and black powder, just ask. Next time you bring a wagon-load of wood."

Cochise nodded, and together with his son, they climbed on their horses and rode off.

The arms Cochise received in exchange for firewood and protection would come in handy only a few years later during the Battle of Apache Pass. But before then, conditions improved for Cochise and his people. The food made a difference, but the liquor did not.

One day, sitting in his wickiup with his family, a runner arrived. Cochise heard word from the runner of a scouting party from California. They were railroad men, and thus Cochise knew before John did that life was about to change in Arizona.

"Anything else?" Cochise asked the runner.

"Don't quite know how to say this..."

"Speak up."

"Well, there are two men in the group. Skin like ours, but they are not of any tribe I know of. Certainly not of our people. They speak another language when they talk to each other, but speak English when talking to the white man."

"Hmm," murmured Cochise. "I would like to meet these men."

———————

JUH'S WAR PARTY, however, spotted the railroad men after Cochise's scout left them. They followed the white men, staying hidden, ready to strike.

Peter ordered a halt on that fateful evening, and they proceeded to make camp. Juh waited for nightfall. His war party outnumbered the survey party nearly five to one. But then, the Chief was never one for a fair fight.

Out of hubris, once the braves were in position, Juh fired an arrow into the pig Xinhui was roasting. He wanted to surprise and humiliate the cowboys before killing them. Xinhui was busy turning the pig on the spit when the arrow struck.

With no weapon at his disposal, he was defenseless. This probably saved his life in the gunfight that followed. His Tong minder was overly careful, keeping a derringer on Xinhui as he fought the Indians. Even then, the thug was the first to react, as the Nednhi made their war cries from the dark.

The Tong threw a shuriken, a fighting star, in the direction the arrow came from. Juh, already in motion, saw the glint of silver flying. It struck his cousin in the chest, and the brave screamed.

Juh had never seen a weapon like that, nor an Indian like him that threw it. He looked to be from some unknown tribe. Dressed all in black and firing well-aimed shots despite the veil of darkness, his warriors fell. This strange Indian seemed to see in the dark.

Xinhui hit the ground by the fire pit and stayed there as Donahue and his men fired into the night. Most of their shots hit nothing but air, but they held the Apache at bay. Juh kept the warriors from firing their guns, letting them use their bows instead to not give away their positions to the Tong, as he kept them circling.

Despite his order, and angered by the death of his cousin, Juh lifted his rifle and aimed at the silhouette of this strange Indian. The Tong yelled at Xinhui in a language Juh didn't recognize, as the survey party crouched behind rocks shooting into the dark.

"Stay down, Xinhui, if you get up, I'll kill you myself," the Tong ordered. He threw another shuriken into the night and hit another Apache, hearing a satisfying scream.

Juh gave a signal recognized by the others, and the Nednhi opened fire. Even with poor aim, the overwhelming numbers took the scouting party down. Juh shouted again, this time to cease fire. The only sound remaining was the crackling of the wood in the fire pit.

Xinhui slowly lifted his head from the dust and looked around. Pools of blood appeared around all the men, including Donahue and the Tong. The Nednhi hooted and hollered in their victory, and several charged into the light. Holding pistols, they shot anyone that stirred, so Xinhui lay still.

To Xinhui's amazement, he witnessed the Apache using their knives to finish any who weren't dead. Juh entered the circle of firelight and kicked Donahue and several others. When he got to Xinhui, he kicked him, and the Chinaman grunted. Using a moccasin, Juh flipped him over onto his back and drew down on Xinhui with his pistol, his knife in the other hand.

Xinhui raised his hands. "No, wait! I'm unarmed."

"You speak English?" Juh asked.

Juh's son approached, knife at the ready, and said, "I kill him for you, Father."

"No, wait. What kind of Indian are you? I hear you speak a strange language? Not White-eye speech."

Another brave raised the Tong's weapon over his head, still blood spattered, and gave a victory cry.

Juh, Xinhui, and his son looked at the body of the Tong, and Juh said, "He like you. Why you not fight?"

Xinhui thought how to answer. Something that would make sense to the savage with the bandanna. "I was his prisoner. I was his slave."

"Like squaw. You cook for men?" Juh's son asked.

Xinhui looked at the young brave and nodded.

"Now may I kill him?" The boy took two steps toward the Chinaman, raising his tomahawk.

Just then, two horses entered the circle of light. Both men riding bareback, one carrying an 1853 Enfield. The other was the scout, leading the chief. Pointing at Xinhui, he said, "That's one of them, Cochise."

"Cochise," Juh said, nodding in greeting. "It's been many moons since we last met."

"Leave him be. He is one of us," Cochise answered, speaking Spanish. "Let him speak."

"He is my prize. I'll do with him what I want," Juh answered defiantly. "And I don't like him. He's better off dead, like the other one."

Cochise lowered his rifle, leveling it on Juh. A new silence fell in the firelight. The scout drew his bow, nocked an arrow, and in one smooth move, swept it back and forth over the Nednhi warriors panting at the edge of the circle. Juh's men aimed their pistols at Cochise.

Cochise spoke up. "Rather than killing him, let's question him. His people could be our allies. People we can use against our enemies if we need them." He kept his gun steady, beads dangling from the rifle stock.

Juh ground his teeth but saw merit in the idea. He gestured to his warriors to lower their weapons. Cochise and his scout followed, after all the guns were no longer pointed at them. Everyone turned to Xinhui.

Since the last thing Cochise said was in English, the boilermaker responded in English, hoping to save his skin and scalp. "I, uh, I not Indian. I Chinese fella. Man from China. From other side of world."

"China? Other side of world?" All Juh knew was the desert.

"Across the big sea. Came to San Francisco. That one, the other Chinese. He Tong, he bad man."

"Not no more," Juh said, smiling. "So, what do we do with this one, Cochise? Me, I want his life."

Xinhui ran over and grabbed Cochise's moccasin while still mounted on his horse, surprising him. "Please don't kill me, Boss. I'm finally free. I can serve you."

Cochise pulled back on the reins and backed up his palomino. "I'm no boss. I'm Chief, Chinaman. Cochise. And you can come and live with my people. Stay as long as you like, go when you want. Not a prisoner or a slave."

Juh was not happy about this. But the Chinaman did not fight, and he had nothing. He could see no benefit in killing him. He would earn no honor by killing him. "You can have him, Cochise," and to his other warriors he said, "Go, take what the white man has. Horses, if nothing else, guns, ammo, and food. Forget that one."

They yelped and hooted, then went through the wagons. They stripped the supplies, tossed their saddles, and led the horses to the Nednhi's side of the circle. Xinhui removed his cowboy hat and bowed over the badly injured Peter Donahue. His friend would survive, rescued by the cavalry only hours later.

"Juh, give him back his horse," ordered Cochise. "The Chinaman will ride with us back to Apache Pass."

"Not your place to give me orders, Cochise."

"I'll make it up to you."

"My name's Xinhui, but you can call me Boilermaker if you prefer. Easier on the tongue."

The interruption broke up the brewing fight between the two chiefs, as they stared each other down. Juh shrugged and directed his eldest son to lead a horse over to Xinhui.

Juh said to Cochise, "I'll come for that horse next time I visit your village and another one."

Cochise presented his hand, palm down, and cut the air. It was agreed but not happily. "You know how to ride, Boilermaker?"

Xinhui nodded and grabbed a discarded saddle, placing it on the horse they gave him. Then he mounted. Cochise, seeing him ready, turned and walked his horse east. The scout followed the boilermaker.

An hour later, Cochise gestured to Xinhui to ride next to him. "Tell me about this China. The place across the big sea."

Xinhui smiled. "China began long ago. We were civilized long before Spain was a country, and...." His story continued all the way back to Apache Pass, and Cochise soaked it up like a thirsty man at an oasis.

QUITE A CROWD gathered as they entered the village, following the three men. Lots of whispering and poking among the women and curious speculation from the Apache warriors. Xinhui's small stature did not invite challenges from the braves, now or later.

"You will stay here, Boilermaker. Until we move on or you do. Learn our ways, do not offend, and we will welcome you," Cochise said and pointed to an empty wickiup.

His heart swelled at being free of the Tong, happy not to have died at the hands of the other chief but sad he lost his friend Peter. Yet these people, these savages, were not ones he would have chosen for himself.

He would stay and learn their ways, but at the first opportunity, he'd return to the railroad. This time to earn rather than be spurned as a coolie. Now he was a boilermaker.

—Dr. Keith Raymond is a Family and Emergency Physician. He practiced in eight countries in four languages and is currently living in Austria with his wife. When not volunteering his practice skills, he is writing, lecturing, or scuba diving. In 2008, he discovered the wreck of a Bulgarian freighter in the Black Sea. He has multiple medical citations, along with publications in Flash Fiction Magazine, Chicago Literati, Blood Moon Rising, Utopia Science Fiction Magazine, *and in Sci-Fi anthologies among others. He is the fiction editor of SavagePlanets magazine.*

The Wolf River, Kansas by Albert Bierstadt

THE WILD ONES

DAN WALKER

JESS PURDY HAD spotted the band of wild ponies several times when working fence with Bart Staples. They were both young fellows, so fence mending often fell to them. "See how that stallion guards his harem?" said Bart. "He's herding the mares away from our ropes." They leaned on their tools and watched the band move like shadows across the rolling horizon, making black silhouettes against the sky, and then disappearing into the country beyond.

"I'd love to get a rope on one of them," said Jess, "bring her home, and have my own horse. That would be somethin' wouldn't it, Bart?"

Bart threw his fencing gloves in the back of the wagon, hobbled over to a rock, and eased himself down. "Well, that'd be fine, all right, but first you gotta get within ropin' distance. Then if you get a rope on one, you gotta get her home without her dragging you and whatever you're ridin' all over hell and half of Mexico. Finally, you gotta break 'er."

"I ain't saying it'd be easy."

"Easy? How do you think I got busted up this way? I put a loop on a young 'un and rode him into the dirt 'til I could get him home. Took a saddle okay, but the first time I put a foot in the stirrup, he threw me into the corral poles then near stomped me to death. Left me like this."

"You can't ride anymore at all?"

"Oh, I reckon I could ride if you picked me up and put me in the saddle, but my parts don't bend the way they used to, and I wouldn't be much good if I was mounted. The boss kept me on out of sympathy, I guess. Nope, it wouldn't be easy."

The boss was Jess's uncle Morris, who took the boy in when he didn't know shit about cows except which end to milk. "You don't know much," Morris said, "but there's wood to chop, barns to clean, and Bart can always use a hand. I owe your daddy that much, I reckon." Jess had lost both parents to influenza, and they didn't leave him much when they passed. He showed up at his uncle's place with nothing but a beat-up saddle and a double-barreled shotgun.

The boss would have left him cleaning the stables or mending fence with Bart, but the hands taught him to ride and work a rope good enough to snag the calves for branding and de-nutting. Eventually, Jess was saddling up and chasing cows with the rest of the crew. He took to working with horses like a hound to hunting. Every chance he got, he was horseback. He traded the shotgun for some patched leather chaps and a pair of spurs.

When the spring rains came and the low country started turning green, the crew moved cattle from the winter range out on the new grass in the creek bottoms. Jess and his uncle were working the wooded shoulder of a ridge that ran down from Morgan's Peak when Jess spotted the wild band of mustangs.

"Ain't that a pretty view," he said, gesturing at the horses grazing in the afternoon sun with their backs to the wind and their manes and tails blowing over them.

"It'd be prettier without those damn mustangs."

"What if we caught 'em up and broke them horses?"

"We're going to round up those wild ones this summer, but we'll be running them straight to the killers. They'll make better dog food than mounts," his uncle said. "I reckon we'll have to shoot that stud to get it done, though. He'll just make trouble otherwise. Yup, put a bullet in him and lace the carcass with strychnine to kill off some wolves and coyotes while we're at it."

"Gotta be a few good ones in the bunch," said Jess. He gestured at the herd with his canteen, then took a swallow. He wished he'd grabbed a couple of biscuits off the breakfast table that morning.

"You want one of them good for nothin' range rats, you help yourself," his uncle said, "but do it on your own time. Right now I want to get these cows headed over the hill to that grass by the creek." He turned his horse and went off at a trot toward the three dozen cows they had spent the morning collecting. Jess shook his head and stared at the man's straight back riding away from him.

"Might have to do that," Jess said to the wind before turning his horse and following his uncle over the hill.

All day, while they pushed the cattle toward the meadows below the mesa, Jess thought about horses, one of his own that was his to raise, train, and ride where he wanted. He imagined his uncle aiming his rifle at the painted stallion while the rest of the band ate their last meal before being herded down the county road to the killer's horse trailer.

Thinking of the horses being canned up for dog food stuck in Jess's craw, and after listening to Bart, he spent a lot of his daydreaming time thinking about catching one and breaking it. He was under no delusion that he could rescue all of them or turn the mind of the boss who spent all his time thinking about grass, cows, and dollar outcomes.

The next Sunday morning, Jess rolled some bacon into a cold pancake, saddled a bay mare he liked, and headed up on the mesa while the rest of the crew were still sleeping off a Saturday night drunk. He wore that mare out working back and forth across the mesa and down Crescent Canyon where riders had spotted the wild band several days before. He went home at dusk without ever getting a look at them. The following Sunday was the same story with a different mount, and the other riders started ribbing him about chasing a ghost herd. He kept his mouth shut and let them think it was the stud he was after. Chasing and roping a pregnant mare didn't sound like a very manly pursuit, and he was already taking enough heat for not getting drunk on Saturday night.

The heat of summer was baking the valley and turning the land brown when Jess rode out on a hot Sunday and finally got close to the band of wild horses. He rode over a ridge with the wind in his face nearly into the middle of the band. The stallion, usually alert, seemed to be napping, and most of the herd was spread out between Jess and the stallion. Some horses were grazing the sparse grass and others lay sprawled in the scant shade with their necks stretched out like they'd been shot.

"We can do this," Jess muttered, patting his horse on the neck. He was mounted on an experienced roping horse named Baker. He shook out a loop and hoped the cinch was tight because he didn't have time to check it. He pushed his feet deeper into the stirrups. The horse felt the pressure and jumped forward toward the sleeping mustangs. Suddenly, he was on them with his loop swinging in a slow circle at the end of his arm. His horse charged forward with its neck stretched, and Jess leaned over it. The sleeping mustangs leaped to their feet, and the grazers broke into a gallop, throwing up a cloud of brown dust. Jess rode into the center of it. The panicked horses were a blur of tail and mane and flying hoofs.

His original plan was to pick a horse and separate it from the others like he was working a herd of cows, but his plan blew away with his hat as he charged down the slope into a patch of pines and out of it then around a rock outcropping. He could feel the mob of ponies pulling away from him, and as they spread across the open ground, he could see individual horses. A small one, maybe a two-year-old, made a sudden turn and crossed in front of Jess. He threw his loop without thinking, a reaction to the surprise of the young horse jumping in front of him that way and the others pulling away out of range. The loop settled neatly over the ears and down the neck. Jess pulled the slack. The roping horse stopped on a dime, squatting on its rear end with its front planted hard. When the slack went out of the rope, Jess's mount was at a full stop, and the mustang was at a full gallop. From the neck up the horse stopped, but the body kept going so that the mustang did a backflip and landed on its spine in the dust with the head twisted back the wrong way and dying, eyes wide and staring at the young rider.

Bart was at the barn when Jess pulled the saddle off and started rubbing down his tired mount. "How'd it go? Looks like you gave this pony a workout."

"Not worth a shit," said Jess. He saw his uncle walking down from the house. "I had one."

"And? Your rope missed?" Bart scratched the horse's ears, then slid his hand down to check its feet.

Jess rubbed at the matted hair where the saddle blanket was. "My rope don't miss. It was a perfect catch. But I broke his damn neck. I wrapped a tight dally and set that horse like yer supposed to." A lump in his throat made it hard to speak. "Baker stopped on a dime, and the other horse was running at full gallop, and I didn't think. It happened too fast. I broke his damn neck. Can you believe that shit?"

"I believe it," said Bart. "Shit like that'll happen."

His uncle leaned on the top log of the horse pen. "You having any luck there, Mustanger?"

Jess turned away and kept rubbing the horse with the burlap.

"He had one," said Bart, "but you know Baker, that horse stopped on a dime and broke that mustang's neck."

"Baker okay?" asked Uncle Morris.

"He's fine," said Jess. "It's my fault."

"I reckon," said the uncle. "There was what? Fifteen in that band?" He patted the top fence rail. "Only fourteen to go."

Jess finally turned and looked at his uncle. "What?"

Bart put his hand on the boy's shoulder. "Don't worry about it."

"One less mustang eating my grass." Uncle Morris turned back toward the house and then stopped. "Tomorrow you two go up and put some strychnine on that carcass."

Bart tightened his grip on the boy's shoulder. "Don't say a word," he muttered. "It is what it is."

A wagon road made the first part of the trip to the dead mustang relatively easy, but when the wagon left the road, they bounced along a cow trail that led to the grove of trees where Jess had found the mustangs. They rode without talking most of the way, with Jess pointing directions and soaking in the sour outcome of his horse hunt.

When they spotted the bloating carcass, Jess bit his lip and shook his head. "Shit, that's a damn fool's shame right there." The vultures bounced away or flew when he spoke, and Bart leaned on his knees. "It's a shame, but this kinda thing happens." He reached under the seat and pulled out a .30-30 carbine. He fired over the heads of the vultures, and they scattered. Jess stepped down from the wagon and walked around the dead animal, studying the tracks of the coyotes that had already gnawed the nose and torn the belly.

Bart dismounted and walked around stiffly trying to stretch his twisted frame. "Damn rough ride, and nasty work to go with it."

"Hell of a deal. First, I kill this poor critter, and now I gotta kill some coyotes and vultures, too."

"Don't see any wolf tracks. Maybe they'll stay away." He pointed down the slope where a pair of coyotes stood watching. "Poor dumb dogs. Let's get this over with."

"So, you going out again this Sunday?" Bart asked. They were back in the wagon and bouncing their way back to the ranch leaving the poisoned carcass behind them.

"Naw, I reckon one dead horse is enough."

"Now, those mustangs got a lot of bottom, and when you jump them they can run well past dark and halfway into next week. But they ain't quick like a cow horse. You gotta jump 'em fast and come at them wide open 'cause your horse will be faster on the short hop. That's the only chance a solo rider's got to get a rope on one."

"You're wasting your breath."

"And don't make a tight dally if you get a rope on one of them. And, for God's sake, remember that you're roping a running horse. You gotta run with them and take them in slow. Can't dump them like a calf."

Jess winced and remembered the mustang's head jerking around and the dying eyes of the mustang staring up at him.

The next Sunday morning, Jess stood in the horse corral shaking out a loop when Bart hobbled up in his long handles, boots, and hat. "Horse huntin' again?" he asked as he leaned to his left and right to stretch his twisted back.

"That's right. I know I said I wouldn't."

"You got nothing to lose and the same goes for the horses. What the hell?"

"I'm going to get me a horse of my own, Bart. And I figure this is the only way that's going to happen. What are you doing up so early?"

"My back don't care what day it is. Standing up hurts less than laying down. You oughta take Kicker, that grey gelding. He's quick off the dime and steady." Kicker got his name from lashing out at dogs, which he didn't like around his feet.

"Shit, Bart. That's the boss's hunting horse. He'd skin me for ridin' it."

Bart walked along the log fence with his hands pressed against the small of his back. "It is the steadiest horse we got. I seen the boss lay the barrel of his Model '96 across the saddle and shoot a coyote at two hundred yards. That grey never twitched a back muscle. Just stood there like he was made of wood."

Jess was impatient to be on his way and was working a position to put a loop on a long neck roan that he had ridden two days ago. "That's what I mean. I can't take the boss's horse."

"Jess, your uncle don't care about horses. They're just transport to him. He'd ride a pig if it got the job done. Take the damn grey. He'll prove out for ya and won't spook when things get tense."

The grey was standing right there like he was waiting to go out, so Jess said, "What the hell," put a loop on him, and saddled up.

Bart was headed to the privy when he turned and said, "And by the way, I saw those mustangs watering at the reservoir on Friday. Guess it slipped my mind to tell the boss." He winked.

Jess smiled. "I know the place," he said as he stepped in the saddle.

"Them's a lot more at the end of a rope than a yearling Hereford. One of them will get you tangled in a juniper tree and bust your goddamn neck if you can't let that rope go when you need to."

"Gotcha, Bart. Go have your morning sit down." Jess rode into the sunrise with the slam of the outhouse door ringing in his ears.

He found the mustangs napping in a stand of pinyon pine on the sunny mesa above Turkey Creek. He rode the grey gelding downwind and studied them from behind a clump of junipers. A pinto stallion with a black mane and tail was grazing uphill from the mares and yearlings, unaware that the cowhand was watching him. The stud was a well-built horse but small and too old to be worth the trouble of breaking—if he could be broken. Jess was more interested in the pregnant mares. If he could catch one of those, he'd have a foal that he could make into something.

Three of the mares had the big bellies of pregnancy. One was a small bay with a dirty coat and U-neck. Another was black and straight-legged with a good head. He spent most of his time looking at a mare that was taller than the others. She stood with her back to him, so all he could see was the rear end and the belly with a foal growing in it.

Jess had seen enough to make him want a closer look and stepped back in the saddle. The gelding was steady and either hadn't smelled the horses yet or was disinterested. Jess turned the grey to his right and walked him slowly through pinyons until the wind was blowing on his left cheek.

She turned and looked in his direction, showing a thick neck and a fine head with strange markings below the eyes. She turned again and pricked her ears, and Jess whispered to his mount. "Steady boy, steady now. She's getting spooky." Then "I'll be damned. That ol' gal has got a halter on her." He thought the mare must have been lured off some ranch by the brash stallion.

Without taking his eyes off the mare, he readied his rope. Bart's words were still on Jess's mind when he shook out a loop and walked his horse toward her. In his mind, he was already working the foal in a round pen. He just had to cast a good loop and run with the mare until he could turn her away from the herd and lead her to the ranch.

He walked the gelding within fifty yards of the mare. Then a gust of wind whirled through the trees, and the mare bobbed her head. Jess gave the gelding the spurs. "Let's go, boy! Let's go." The horse leaped forward and gained twenty yards on the mare by the time she lunged into a run. The whole band was running, kicking up dust and stones into the air around the junipers and pinon trees. For a moment, he was back seven days, but he steadied and began twirling the loop.

Bart had been right. The gelding was quicker off the mark than the mustangs. The mare cut in front of a tree, and Jess cast his loop. The loop settled over her ears and past her nose, then tightened around her neck, but she never broke stride. Jess spurred the gelding and was nearly swept to the ground by the clutching limbs of a pine tree. He kept his seat as the mare broke into the open and ran straight for fifty yards with the gelding right behind and the rope tight between them. Jess's hat brim swept back in the wind, and sand struck him like birdshot.

It was a quiet race with only the muffled thud of the horse's hooves hitting the sandy soil and the breath of the gelding pumping like a bellows. When the tension on the rope slackened a bit, Jess gave Kicker a nudge to turn to the left. "Let's turn this gal," Jess said. He took another wrap around the horn and used the reins and his knees to push his mount to the left.

They had to turn the mare from following the rest of the band and get her following the rope and not the stallion. She'd followed a man with a rope before, but she jerked her head up to fight now. That slowed her and allowed Kicker to steadily force her away from the herd as it galloped over the curve of the hill.

Kicker was running full speed when Jess felt the front end drop from under him, and he tumbled forward past the horse's ear into the sagebrush.

Jess woke on his back with the sun in his eyes and a burning pain running up his arm, the same arm that stretched straight up from his shoulder over his head. He turned and saw that his hand was wrapped in the reins. He could see blood dripping from the tip of Kicker's nose. "Easy, Kicker. Easy boy." He tried to roll that way, but that sent pain up his right arm. That arm was twisted behind him, and the slightest movement set a knife-like pain from the shoulder to the elbow.

He dug his left heel into the ground to take the weight off the trapped arm. Nothing happened. Turning his eyes down, he saw that his left leg was crossed beneath the right knee. Confused, he tried to lift it, but nothing moved. He tried again. His legs wouldn't move. His breath quickened. Using only his shoulder muscles, he rolled onto his right side, screamed, vomited, and passed out.

Morris's grey hunting horse stood on three legs covered in dirt and the saddle hanging off the left side. The lasso still ran out to the pregnant mare. She stood facing the gelding with her sides heaving and her head drooping like she remembered the rope and the folly of fighting it.

Like swimming out of deep water, Jess came to and felt he couldn't breathe. He slowly managed short breaths and started to construct a sense of where he was. He still hung from Kicker's reins, and his right arm was broken. He tried to move his legs again, but they were still tangled and not responding. Again, panic washed through him, making his lungs pump and his chest hurt. He cried out, and the mare spooked. Kicker bobbed his head and tugged at Jess's arm. "No! No!" he whimpered.

He heard the mare whinny off to his left. "You're busted, Jess," he said. "Broke in half, I reckon." It was like everything below his belt was someone else's body. He remembered coming over the horse's head, then the horse rolled over him, crushing him into the earth. An experienced rider would have kicked out of the stirrups and launched himself away, but he wasn't an experienced rider, and he'd taken an extra dally around the saddle horn just like Bart told him not to.

He rolled to his side and could see Kicker's broken foreleg hanging bent and useless. The momentum of the falling horse and rider had snapped it like a piece of kindling. "You're done for, too, old boy. Busted beyond fixing." If he could get to the sheath knife on his belt, he could cut the horse loose, but it would still have a broken leg and a saddle hanging off it tethered to the pregnant mare. He thought if he could let the horse go, it would hobble to the ranch for help, but that wasn't going to happen.

"Okay, boy. We've gotta try something." He gave the reins a gentle tug, and the horse leaned down to him releasing the loop of leather from his wrist. He brought his hand to his mouth and took the reins in his teeth. His arm began to tingle as the feeling returned. He felt the horse's ragged breath and smelled blood, sweat, and fear. He reached down to his belt and found the knife. He reached back to grab the rope stretching from the saddle to the trembling mare.

For a moment, he hesitated. The mare was caught just like he planned. If it hadn't been for one gopher hole, she and the foal inside her would be his. He turned his head for a last look, though it hurt to do it. She was wide-eyed and confused. Long without the feel of the rope, the mare was once again bound to a man, her sides heaving as she breathed for her and the foal inside her. He heard the stallion call somewhere out of his range of vision. Jess laid the blade against the rope, and the mare was gone.

Cutting the rope let the saddle slip farther down. The slicker tied behind the cantle brushed Kicker's legs, and he lashed out. An iron shoe struck Jess above the ear. The crippled horse couldn't kick hard, but it was enough to draw blood. It kicked again and broke bone. The reins slipped out of Jess's slack mouth and dragged along the ground when Kicker hobbled away.

Two ranch hands found the young horse hunter the next day. Bart had told them where to look, and the buzzards pointed him out. One fellow threw a slicker over him and stood guard against the scavengers while the other rode for a wagon. Bart drove the wagon up past the old tank and along the ridge until he could see the crippled horse standing head down among the junipers with the saddle hanging off it. He climbed down and looked at the boy and then approached the horse. The right front leg was swollen to twice its size with blood dried around a split in the skin.

"Let's get this saddle off him," said Bart.

The other hands held the nervous mount while Bart undid the cinch strap and pulled the saddle away. He went to the wagon and removed his .30-30 from the case under the seat.

"Don't you think you should wait until the boss gets here?"

Bart jacked a cartridge into the chamber and raised the rifle. "I'm not waiting for anybody. Won't change anything," he said. When Kicker turned his head, Bart put a bullet right behind the left ear.

Bart was leaning over Jess's body when the boss rode up. Morris looked down from his saddle at the dead face of his nephew with the crescent marks of the horseshoe misshaping the young head. He rode back and forth looking at the tracks and the scuff marks, then at the dead horse with the bullet hole and broken leg. He leaned on his saddle horn and stared down at the valley that fell away below them.

"What the hell was he doing, tryin' to catch that stallion?"

Bart hobbled over to lean against the ranch wagon. "He didn't want that stallion any more than you or me. He was after one of those pregnant mares. He figured to catch one up and raise the foal. Just wanted a horse of his own."

The boss shook his head. "Look at this mess. All to catch a goddamn horse."

"Men have died for less, I figure," said the young cripple. "Shall we
load him up now?"

The boss didn't answer. He just kept walking his horse back and
forth and looking at the ground. One of the riders retrieved the bridle
and blanket, then squatted on his heels and rolled a cigarette. He offered the makings to Bart, but he waved it off.

Finally, the boss stepped down from his horse and knelt at the
boy's feet. He stretched a finger out to trace the edge of a hole worn
in the sole of one boot. The newspaper Jess had lined it with showed
through the hole. He went to the wagon and lifted a shovel out of
the wagon bed like it weighed fifty pounds. "I think we'll bury him
right here. He can keep company with these mustangs, and we can say
howdy every time we ride up this way." He walked a few paces and put
the shovel in the dirt to start digging.

Bart looked at the two ranch hands and dragged a blanket out
from under the wagon seat. "You two gather some rocks, and I'll see
to the boy." He got down on one knee with the other leg stretched out
straight and washed Jess's face with canteen water. He straightened
his shirt and forced the stiff arms to lay flat along his sides. The legs
fought against him, but he managed to get them lying side by side.
He laid out a piece of canvas and the blanket on top of that. Then
he waved the two hands over to lift the body onto the blanket and
wrapped it and the canvas around the dead boy. They found his hat
and laid it on his chest, but the wind came up and blew it off, so it
tumbled through the junipers out of sight.

The last sun of the day was on the four men by the time they had
Jess Purdy covered with a heap of stones. One of the hands grabbed
the saddle and hefted it toward the wagon.

"Leave it," said Morris. "The tree's broke, anyway." He took the saddle by the horn and set it atop the grave. He picked up the shovel as if to put it in the wagon but instead stood leaning on it and staring at the grave. "You boys head on home. You're probably ready for supper. I'll be along."

The hands tightened their cinches and mounted while Bart checked the harness on his team. Before he heaved his twisted body into the wagon, he walked over to Morris, took the shovel, and tossed it in the back of the wagon box.

"Boss," he said, looking out across the mesa, "you're well past late on giving a shit. Don't you think?"

The boss just stood silently looking at the ground with his hat in his hand.

—*Alaska author Dan L. Walker was raised on the Kenai Peninsula and grad-uated from East Anchorage high School, where he was sports editor for the school newspaper and wrote sport stories for the* Anchorage Times *newspa-per. A son of homesteaders and Alaska's Teacher of the Year in 1999, Walker has guided and motivated writers from kindergarten to prison inmates. Walk-er has published in* Last Frontier Magazine, Alaska Magazine, Cirque Literary Journal, *and the* Journal of Geography. *Walker is the author of* Secondhand Summer *and its sequel,* Back Home, *Published by Alaska Northwest Books. Walker's memoir,* Letters from Happy Valley, *uses family letters to tell the story of the Walkers' journey to homestead in the last frontier. The author lives and writes in Seward, Alaska. When he leaves his home on Bear Lake, Walker likes to explore the back trails and landmarks of New Mexico and Arizona.*

A Cree Indian by Charles Marion Russell

PLAYERS AND PRAYERS

DAVID BOWMORE

1881

GRAY, INTELLIGENT EYES swept over the sparsely populated room. Four men at a card table—the bar's only customers—ignored the newcomer. The saloon door squeaked as it swung back to its resting place.

"God bless the corners of this house and all inside," the stranger said with a voice as soft as green Irish linen. He approached the bar, tipped his hat at Lilly McGee who sat on a stool. In return, she smiled and thrust her bosom in his direction, pushing the worn fabric of her dress to the brink of its limits.

"You are blessed, so ye are, ma'am," he said, laying his small, battered top hat on the counter. It wasn't a fancy topper, as might be found on the heads of opera-goers out East, but a dusty old thing somewhere between the color of cracked leather and a winter sunset.

Dropping his carpetbag on the wooden boards, he asked Dougie the bar dog for a beer. Dougie went to the end of the bar and opened the tap of a barrel that stood there. Soon, flat brown liquid filled a glass.

Money changed hands. The newcomer offered to buy Dougie a drink, but the bartender refused. Lilly, being the astute businesswoman she was, recognized that despite this man's well-travelled facade, he could well be made of silver dollars or even copper ore.

"Need a room for the night, big fella?"

"Sure now. 'Tis a kind offer, ma'am, and on any another occasion I'd be delighted to oblige ye, but right now, there's a storm coming," he said, unbuttoning his overcoat and loosening his muffler to reveal a battered dog-collar, "and I don't have the time. Father Brannon Murphy at your service, ma'am, but ye can call me Brannon."

Lilly stepped back, her cheeks burning crimson.

"No harm done," Brannon said.

From the card table, a tall, skinny cowboy let out a guffaw and turned to look at Brannon. "There ain't no God hereabouts."

"Never fear, lads, I'm only passing through."

The card player's eyes flicked to the two-gun belt the preacher wore comfortably low on his thighs before returning his attention to the game.

Brannon turned back to Dougie. "And there I was thinking this place would be heaving."

"Later, when the miners come out of their hole."

"You mean the Copper Queen Mine? Well, at least they'll be safe underground, God willing."

"Whut do ya mean?" Lilly asked.

"I did say there's a storm brewing," Brannon said and took a thirsty swig of his brew. "'Tis a big one, so it is," Brannon said wiping his mouth with the palm of his hand.

As if to reiterate the point, the wind began to rattle the shutters, driving sand through the saloon doors. To the annoyance of the gamblers, their cards and money were disturbed.

Brannon and Dougie stepped out onto the boardwalk together. When Lilly joined them a few seconds later, Dougie was cursing, and his face—underneath a fine sheen of sweat—had turned the color of freshly fallen snow. The thing that had turned her friend so pale could not be missed. Though it wasn't yet two in the afternoon, the sky due south was in total darkness. Obscuring the mountain tops, thick gray-black clouds swirled in and around each other, gathering speed and reaching for the earth with long fingerlike tendrils, alive with the flash of lightning and rumbling thunder. The air tasted of copper and smelled of ice.

"Makes ye think of the Olympian gods, doesn't it?" Brannon said. "Perhaps Zeus and Ares have gone into battle."

Lilly didn't know what he meant, nor did she care, for a pit of fear had grown in her stomach.

"Are ya sure it's headed this way?" she asked.

Brannon nodded.

Other Bisbee residents had also noticed the approaching tempest. In truth, only those up at the graveyard could miss it. Every living soul made haste—men rushed their horses to the relative safety of the nearest corral, businessmen brought signs in and secured shutters, while the women of the dancehalls and whorehouses pushed men out into the streets, leaving them to take their chances finding shelter wherever they could. Not ten feet away, a small black and white dog huddled under the boards of the sidewalk, shuddering with fear.

"I don't suppose there's anywhere to hole up?" Brannon asked.

"There's a cellar behind the bar, but I don't know what Mister Glover will say about it," Dougie said.

"Never mind Mister Glover, now, lad," Brannon said, refusing to hear the opinion of someone who wasn't there. "How many can ye squeeze in?"

"A handful," Lilly said.

"That'll do." Brannon bent down and opened his arms wide, welcoming the stray into them.

"You're not bringing that mangy thing down there with us. Mister Glover wouldn't approve," Dougie said.

"We're all equal in the eyes of the Lord." Brannon rubbed the dog behind an ear as it tried to lick the preacher's face. "Besides, do ye want me to pray for a miracle or not?"

The barman shrugged his skinny shoulders, then unhooked the outer full-length doors, pulled them closed, and bolted them tight, before doing the same with the window shutters, bringing them together in quick movements.

BRANNON HAD BRIEFLY caught the names of the card players as they quickly prepared to descend. Will was obviously a professional gambler, judging by his attire. A short fat man carried not only a pistol but a rifle, too. He spoke with an educated voice, calling himself Lewis. A small, fresh-faced cowhand went by the name of Billy Clanton. The last and most unpleasant of the group was Curly. In Brannon's unspoken opinion, this one badly needed the use of the bathhouse. Cleanliness was, after all, next to godliness.

Carrying the dog under one arm, Brannon was the last to descend the cellar steps. Dougie had already brought the preacher's carpetbag into the hole, while Lilly fetched jugs of water. The ceiling was so low that Curly had to remove his hat, but even then, his hair brushed the ceiling. The room was about one hundred square feet and the walls boarded with wooden planks to keep the dry soil from spilling over the floor. It smelled moist, a pleasant surprise for Brannon who had become used to the arid climate of Arizona in recent months. Importantly, the room housed barrels of beer as well as bottles of gin and whiskey and glasses, too.

"There are worse places to be shut up," Billy said, smiling and looking at the shelves.

Agreeing with him, Curly lifted a bottle of whiskey off a shelf, but Dougie snatched it back before the cork could be pulled. Curly loosened the leather thong on his holster, but Billy touched his friend's arm and shook his head. Curly relaxed but left the thong hanging loose.

"Ain't nothing being drunk down here but water," Dougie said. "Mister Glover won't be pleased if you drink all his liquor."

Will and Lewis rearranged four beer barrels around another, like the five side of a dice.

"We finishin' this game?" Will said.

As the sound of the storm grew overhead, the players took their places. Lilly and Brannon sat on the dusty floor together. He reached into his carpetbag for a flask. The dog skittered around between the inmates. Curly aimed a boot at it, but the animal was too quick. Lilly couldn't help noticing the other odd things inside Brannon's bag and asked about them as she passed the flask back to him.

"They're the tools of my trade. Holy water, sacrament, and holy garments, for it is a sad and evil world we live in, and sometimes I have to see a soul on his way to the next life."

"An' whut about the handcuffs, wooden spikes, an' hatchet."

"Like I said, 'tis a dangerous world. Why do ye think I wear these?" He slapped a hand on one of his guns.

"You're about the strangest preacher I ever seen."

The card game ended with Curly spitting tobacco on the floor after having folded, thus losing his small gain from upstairs. In the poorly lit underworld they temporarily inhabited, even Will, the professional gambler, had lost his appetite for the game. He and Lewis put their feet up on the barrels and rolled cigarettes, talking in quiet tones.

Overhead, the floorboards rattled, dusting them all with sand and dirt. The dog settled his jaw on Brannon's knee, whimpering. Stroking the dog's head, he began to pray.

"Saint Anthony, patron saint of lost souls and miracles, pray for us. Deliver these lost souls and protect them from the beauty and the terror of a storm worthy of the Old Testament. Saint Anthony, pray for us.

"Father, your word declares that you show mercy to as many as loved, serve, and keep your word. I ask that you show the townsfolk of Bisbee mercy, too. I do not pray for me, for I am an unworthy sinner, but for the innocent, the exposed, and the wicked who know not what they do. Give them time to rejoice in your light and salvation. Oh, Lord, have mercy.

"Amen." He crossed himself.

"Amen, *Padre.*"

"Are you a believer, Will?" Brannon opened his eyes.

"I'm not much of a churchgoer, *Padre*, but sometimes it's best to hedge yer bets. I seen a lot of strange things that make ya think."

"What strange things?" Lilly asked.

A burst of thunder silenced everyone, and all eyes turned to the cellar roof as wind and rain howled above them.

"'Bout fifteen years back," Will said, "near the end o' the war, I was cut off from my company. There must o' been a thousand Yankees separatin' us. I spent three days laying low when this Indian found me. I would'a took the top of his head clean off if I had any ammunition left. But he sat down in front of me, and he shared his jerky and water. He didn't speak much English. Then he takes his pipe out of a pouch he wore round his neck and filled it with a tobacco, and we shared that, too, and after a few minutes, I could understand him real good, an' he talked about me traveling the country an' even going over the sea to the lands of my forefathers. An' I had the strangest sensation of flying like a bird. It was real peaceful, an' I remember thinking I must be dead an' that the Indian had tricked me, and I was on my way to heaven or mayhaps Indian heaven if they have such a place. I woke up on the edge of my company's camp with the captain scratchin' his head an' me just standin' there slow as molasses. They was a hundred miles from where I was before I met the Indian. Now explain that."

Curly snorted and turned his head to spit in the corner of the room.

"I'm a tellin' ya, boy, I met an Indian and travelled hundreds o' miles by air."

Something big and heavy clattered on the floorboards above, bringing more dust down upon them. Dougie looked up at the trapdoor, wondering if he should go up to see what was happening to Mr. Glover's Saloon.

Will took a hip flask from his pocket and swallowed a long one.

"From the sound of your accent, Father, you're from the old country," Lewis said.

"That I am, just a poor Irish boy lucky enough to travel to Rome to finish his education."

"Did yuh ever see Paris?" Lilly asked.

"Sure, didn't I see it in all its glory and gore."

"Gore?"

"A city is not made of beautiful frocks and angel cake alone. Its bedrock is filth and dirt and people scraping a living any way they can."

"Much like this place, then," Curly said.

"Much like any place. Those with money will always sit at the top of the heap watching those without scrabble in the dirt doing whatever they can, just to pay for the privilege of being alive."

"You're getting a bit preachy there, *Padre*." Curly said.

"Just an observation, son. But we can't always help what's in our nature, can we?"

The storm above began to abate.

"Has it gone an' finished?" Lilly asked.

"Probably just the eye of the storm," Lewis said.

"What's that mean?" Billy asked.

The others ignored him. The dog wandered over to a barrel, lifted his leg, and added his unique scent to the already pungent room. So many bodies in a small place with nowhere for the heat to go soon stifles a space. The dog continued his patrol, attacking the odor of the individuals with a snuffling nose. Curly's boot connected with the canine's ribs, sending it scuttering across the room to hide behind Brannon.

"There was no need for that, son."

"Keep it away from me. Next time, I'll have a need to clean my gun."

"Ye can tell a lot about a man by the way he treats a dog."

Curly spat again.

Lilly leaned into Brannon's ear. "Careful, *Padre*, that one's mean enough to hook the coins off a dead man's eyes."

Lewis said, "I was with a drive when I was a young man, headed to Mile City, out Montana way, when a Norther came in that froze half the beeves to death in ten minutes flat. We only survived because we had an Indian with us."

"Yeah? What's one of them do against the weather that we can't?" Billy asked.

"Redskin magic," Curly said, sneering.

"Slow Beard travelled with a teepee. It was a tight squeeze, but we lived. When we came out two hours later, icicles were dripping from the longhorns' horns. But we'd all been kept safe, bit like we are now."

"Old timer's yarns," Curly mocked.

The older men shared a knowing look. Billy was green as prairie grass in the springtime, and Curly, well, he was the sort who would never learn.

A silence fell as the wind from above started to pick up again. Lewis pulled his harmonica from his waistcoat pocket and started on a long, slow tune.

"What about you, *Padre?*" Dougie said, "Anything strange ever happen to you?"

Brannon thought back to his days fresh from the seminary, some twenty years earlier, when he had been chosen as a soldier of Saint Michael and His Eternal Army. He could still remember the first time he visited the secret vaults beneath the Vatican, which not even the Holy Father himself was supposed to see, as it was deemed too unholy for his holiness's eyes to behold. The smell of damp and wax hit Brannon's olfactory glands once again. By candlelight he read secret texts written in dead languages, while older, wiser soldiers of God guarded him from the enemies of the Lord. His theological education had advanced far beyond fallen angels and human hearts, into the realms of demons, succubi, and unimaginable monsters in all their various shapes and guises from around the world. Sulphur and smoke swirled to form one of hell's servants. Brannon's spiritual training fled at a crucial moment, and his mentor saved the day, possibly the world.

When Brannon's mind could stand it no longer, the church had cast him adrift. But once something is seen, it cannot be unseen. Once something is learned, it cannot be unlearned. So Brannon traveled, ever vigilant of the evils of the underworld, more forgiving of the follies of men than most preachers.

"Ye wouldn't believe me," he said.

"I reckon Bisbee is done for. Wonder how Tombstone will fare?" Billy said.

"Tombstone'll last forever," Will said. "It's that kinda place."

"When I get out of here, I'm headed straight for California," Lilly said. She said it in time with Lewis's harmonica.

"What for?" Dougie asked.

"They say the winters aren't so cold there. Anyways, yuh think I wanna stay here to help rebuild this place?"

"You don't have to do no rebuilding. Men always need a whore," Curly said.

Brannon's slap was louder than a bullet leaving a barrel.

The harmonica fell silent. All eyes focused on Curly as he grabbed for his pistol. But he found the holster empty. Looking down, he saw his own gun in the preacher's hand. That would teach him to leave it untethered.

"Apologize," Brannon said.

"Whut for?"

"Apologize," Brannon repeated, easing the hammer back with his thumb.

With a glance around the room, Curly realized he was outnumbered. Lewis had readied his rifle, and Will had also drawn his gun.

"Better do as he says," Billy said. He had been too slow. Beads of sweat prickled his forehead.

Curly's gaze flicked at Billy but saw the wisdom in retreating.

"Sorry," he mumbled through gritted teeth.

"Sorry, what?"

"Sorry... ma'am."

"Sit over there, ye ignorant cur, and say the Lord's Prayer."

"I want muh gun back," Curly said, stepping into the corner.

"Later," Brannon said, retreating to the other corner. It was bound to happen. Caged men will always fight, as will tigers or any other male animal. Lilly inched herself closer to Brannon. Will nodding respectfully at the preacher, returned his gun to his holster and placed himself on Brannon's other side.

"Tell me about your dreams of California, Lilly."

"They ain't much, but I'd love a little house all o' muh own, a man to cook for, an' a couple of little ones running around. Somewhere near the ocean."

"'Tis a fine dream, so it is," Brannon said.

She smiled a sad smile and then added with a bitter note, "But the best I can probably hope for is a little bordello of my own."

"I can see it now," Brannon said kindly. "Red drapes and golden brocade, professional girls from Paris, brass beds, and inside privies. You'd make a fine madam, Lilly."

"Visited many whorehouses, have you, *Padre?*" Billy said.

"More than ye, son. And where exactly is the harm in a person having dreams?"

"Yeah, but whores?"

"Do I need to slap ye, too?"

"I still got my gun, *Padre.*"

The lad was right. Best let the situation settle down. There was no point in antagonizing anyone. He shouldn't have lost his temper, but if there was one thing Brannon detested more than seeing a dog get a kicking, it was treating a person like they were only an object. To think, only minutes earlier, he'd been congratulating himself on his forbearance of a man's foibles.

Will you never learn, Brannon?

The minutes turned into hours. The sound of Lewis's harmonica drifted from his corner of the room. Lilly leaned the back of her head against the wall, and soon the heavy breathing of a person at rest followed. Brannon took his Bible from a jacket pocket. It fell open at a folded piece of paper used as a bookmark.

Curly stretched his frame along the farthest wall, while Billy made a bridge of his arms across his knees and then rested his head. Will shuffled a deck of cards. Dougie, fighting to keep his eyes open, finally succumbed to sleep. Brannon supposed he would soon, too. Lewis put his harmonica away and lowered his hat over his eyes. Oxygen levels must have been pretty low in the hole.

By the light of the single flickering lamp, Brannon compared the face with the wanted poster. He sighed and put the paper away.

Lilly stirred and leaned into his ear so as not to disturb the others.

"Whut's that?" she whispered as he placed the paper back inside the Bible.

"What would you say if I told you we had killers and cattle rustlers among us?"

"I'd be more surprised if there wasn't."

Brannon smiled and patted her hand. "Get some rest."

THEY WERE WOKEN by a crashing from above that sounded like the entire building had fallen on top of the trap door. Dougie shared a look with Brannon and then went partway up the steps to push on the trap door.

"It's no good. It's stuck," he said, panic in his voice.

Will and Lewis joined him halfway up the steps, and together they tried to push the door upwards.

They couldn't move it.

"Now whut?" Lilly asked, looking at Brannon.

"We wait," he replied.

"For what?" Curly said.

"Someone will come."

"Like who, your God?" Curly jabbed Brannon in the chest with his forefinger.

"Someone will come," Brannon repeated.

"Like hell they will." Curly's voice filled the cellar. The dog whined, cowering in the corner. "Someone shut that mutt up."

"Leave the dog be. He's not hurting ye," Brannon said.

Curly stepped closer to Brannon, towering over him. A vein in his neck throbbed, and his face had taken on a deep red complexion.

"We'd of had a better chance in the mine than down here, an' I said so. Didn't I say so, Billy?"

"Yeah, Curly, ya said that," Billy said.

"We're all dead, an' it's all yer fault," Curly said, looking Brannon straight in the eye. "We shouldn't o' listened to you, *Padre*. You gone an' killed us all." He jabbed the father's chest again—hard this time—to reiterate the point.

Brannon grabbed the finger and holding the arm at the elbow pushed backward till the finger was almost touching the back of the same wrist, which forced Curly to his knees.

"Do ye want your trigger finger broken?"

Curly shook his head, pleading for Brannon to let go.

"Thought so, now shut the feck up, and stop wasting yer energy. There's a good lad." Brannon pushed Curly back, and he sprawled on the ground nursing his finger.

"MISTER GLOVER WON'T like it."

What Brannon saw as he woke was Dougie falling to the floor and Curly pulling the cork from a bottle of rye.

The other men were standing back watching the situation develop.

After all, they weren't responsible for the stock. The water had long gone, and if Curly was having a drink, then they might as well, too.

Brannon stood up. "Put it back."

"I've a thirst on me. I deserve a shot o' gut warmer."

"Then pay for it."

"Who's gunna make me? You, *Padre*?"

"With God's help, yes."

Slowly, Curly placed the bottle back on the shelf and turned to face his nemesis. Then he ran at Brannon. Ducking under a fist aimed at his chin, Brannon landed a blow to Curly's gut. Soon, the two men were rolling on the hard sand, exchanging blows. They came apart, Brannon staggering to his feet, wiping blood that leaked from a split lip. Curly's sneer returned as Brannon noticed his opponent now had a knife in his hand.

"I've got my guns," Brannon said, as they circled each other, eye to eye.

"I ain't afeared o' you, *Padre*. Ya ain't gonna kill no one. See, a man o' God don't wanna burn in Hell."

Curly slashed the knife left and right. His confidence growing, Curly swiped again, this time with a wicked laugh, forcing Brannon to jump backward.

"Then said Jesus unto him, put up again thy sword into his place, for all they that take the sword shall perish with the sword."

"Whut's that s'posed mean?" Curly swiped again, although nowhere near his target.

"When the Good Book fails, go for your guns," Brannon said. A gun jumped to his hand, but he didn't shoot.

Lilly had her hand over her mouth.

"Why do you hate me so much, son?" Brannon's voice and gun were steady.

"Stop calling me *son!*" Spittle ran down Curly's chin.

"If that's all it takes, you only had to say," Brannon said, carefully putting his gun back in its holster.

Curly sheathed the knife and stepped forward. "Preachers are all the same, always making ya feel guilty 'bout something."

"And I said I was just passing through. I'm not here to change any of ye."

Curly spat and turned away.

"Is that it?" Billy said. "You're letting him tell ya what to do?"

"Shud up. I'm tired."

"Well he ain't tellin' me what I can an' can't do."

Billy drew his gun, but Lilly put herself between him and Brannon. "Don't you dare, Billy Clanton."

"Step aside, Miss Lilly."

"For once in his life, Curly has the right idea," Lilly said. "Why don't you think for a minute? Do ya really want a preacher's blood on your hands?"

Lewis slowly raised his rifle.

"Put your iron away," Will advised, drawing his own gun.

With his eyes flicking round the room, Billy holstered his pistol. The odds were against him. They always had been.

"Yeah, well, Curly was right about one thing. We'd of had a better chance up there. We might be the only people alive in the whole wide world, for all we knows."

Billy and Curly returned to their corner and slumped down onto their haunches.

Will came to sit next to Brannon. "An' I thought preachers didn't believe in violence."

"Growing up on the streets of Dublin, ye learn to fight dirty."

"Ya learn to draw like lightning there, too?"

Brannon took a handkerchief from a pocket and dabbed at his own wounds. "I was always a keen student, and I soon learned that a man with no gun in this country dies quickly, and a man with a slow gun dies even quicker."

And then the flame in the oil burner died.

"HOW LONG WE been down here?" Dougie asked.

Will found a match in his waistcoat pocket, struck it on the rough wooden wall, and held it close to his pocket watch. "'Bout fifteen hours."

"I'm thirsty, damnit," Billy said.

"Stop yer blathering," Brannon said.

A LOUD SCRAPING came from above, waking the docile inmates and causing the dog to grumble.

"Dougie, are you down there?"

"Mister Glover, sir, I sure am. Miss Lilly and some folks, too."

"Hang in there, son."

After more scraping and dirt falling, someone opened the trapdoor, and a round face with a trim mustache looked down upon them.

"Well, what ya'll waiting for?" he said. "Get on up here."

As they gathered at the bottom of the steps waiting for Lilly to ascend, a hand grabbed Brannon's shoulder. He turned to face Curly.

"I want muh gun back."

"Sure." Brannon reached into his carpetbag and handed over the pistol. "Here ya go."

"I'm gunna shoot ya, ya know that, right?"

"And I forgive ye." The others moved aside.

"What's going on down there?"

Curly looked from his gun to the preacher, noticed the preacher's weapons were still holstered, then back at his own gun again.

"Now, lads, I don't want any trouble. Let the man do what he must." This was an instruction to Lewis and Will.

Curly's sneer grew. "Let's see if your God can save you now."

Click.

He squeezed the trigger again, nothing.

"Who is it I remind ye of? Who is it ye hate so much?"

"Son of a gun!" Curly snarled and pushed past the preacher to climb the steps.

The dog looked up at Brannon and wagged its tail.

Minutes later, as the group stood blinking in harsh daylight, open-mouthed, they stared at the destruction around them. Three walls had been completely torn away. The bar lay in pieces, and most of the fourth wall had fallen outwards, bringing the staircase down over the trapdoor. However, what shocked them more than the destruction was that every other building was in perfect habitable condition.

Now free, the dog ran off looking for food or water or a bitch.

"Judas," Brannon said.

The town should have been matchwood, yet only one building on the very edge had been destroyed, and no one had been injured.

Brannon touched his fingers to his forehead, chest, and shoulders.

Maybe you were listening, Lord?

But the Lord did not answer. Instead, Mr. Glover introduced himself to Brannon.

"Dougie tells me you prayed for our salvation, sir. Well, I think I speak for everyone in Bisbee when I say, thank you. The way that cyclone cluster looked, I was sure we were all about to meet the Maker himself. But then it just upped and vanished. It's a miracle, sir. I say it's a miracle no one was hurt."

Brannon laid a hand on Dougie's shoulder. "This good man looked after us like a saint. You should be proud of him, Mister Glover, but he needs work and somewhere to sleep."

"And he'll get it, don't you worry. Say, *Padre*, Bisbee needs a God-fearing preacher-man. How about it?"

"I'm just drifting through."

"Well, if you're sure, but the offer's there if you want it. Good day to you, sir." Mr. Glover put his arm around Dougie's shoulder, as he and his posse, along with Will and Lewis, turned toward town. Billy and Curly had long gone.

"Are yuh really a miracle worker?"

"I'm just as full of sin as anyone else, Lilly. All I wanted was somewhere out of the storm. Those prayers were just payment for safe passage. I didn't expect them to work, may God forgive me."

Brannon sighed. Would his on and off relationship with the Lord ever be the same as it once was?

"Well, Lilly, what will ye do now?" Brannon continued, brightening up and indicating the ruin that had been Lilly's home and workplace.

"There's mighty plenty o' work for a girl like me in a town like this. I guess I'll see if Big Bertha has a spare room."

Together, they walked along the narrow street, passing general stores, saloons, miner's restaurants, a bathhouse, and many other rickety buildings serving the population.

"And what about your Californian dreams?" he asked, as they paused on the boardwalk outside the brothel.

"Whut, and deprive all these men of a good reason to part with their money? I play my cards right, Father, an' I might end up a real Copper Queen."

—*David Bowmore was born on a winter's night with the sound of thunder and the flash of lightning welcoming him into a brightly painted Gypsy caravan. Forty-five years later, he started writing fiction. He tends to write thrillers, mysteries, and the occasional western, as well as stories with a touch of the supernatural about them. He focuses on character and the oddities of being human, sometimes with humour but more often with dark unreality.*

An admirer of authors, which include Agatha Christie, Eric Ambler, Ted Lewis, Patricia Highsmith, Elmore Leonard, Stephen King, and P.G. Wodehouse, David sometimes wonders what he is trying to achieve when he sits at his keyboard every morning.

His first story, "Sins of The Father," was published in 2018. Since then, he has appeared in more than seventy-five short story anthologies, journals, and magazines. He has also published two collections of short stories and two novels set in the fictional coastal town of Deben Market.

In 2020, The Magic of Deben Market *was performed by BookStreamz. com, starring John Hales, Kelli Hollis, and Leslie Ash.*

David has lived here, there, and everywhere but currently dwells in Yorkshire with his wonderful wife and a small whitish poodle.

Assiniboin Indian Medicine Sign by Karl Bodmer

SO FAR FROM GOD

STEVEN McFANN

NO MARKER DISTINGUISHED Sonora from Arizona. The two had been one and the same in their fathers' time. But Miguel could swear to some shift in the air and a change to the Earth's pigment when he and Joaquin crossed *la frontera*. As if the slightest change in the wind warned them that they were no longer in Mexico *lindo,* they were now in the United States.

They followed the American cowboy, Lucky, north along the San Pedro River and watched the shadows of sunset spread across the creosote sea. Lucky was their liaison, a gambling partner of Joaquin's who'd often sold stock stolen from Chihuahuan to Sonoran ranchers. Miguel didn't trust Lucky. He trusted few Anglos, despite Joaquin's reminder that the war ended before they were born. But they had few other options. Their job took them into America, and they needed American protection if they were going to exterminate the terror of the border, the man who ravaged ranchos across Sonora with the Cochise Cowboys and his sons. *El Viejo.* Old Man Clanton.

Joaquin didn't share Miguel's paranoia about the motivations of

their American guide. His worry was spent on Miguel. His recklessness on their last job in Coahuila resulted in Joaquin sparing Miguel
from a lynching with a last-second shot from his Spencer repeater.
Imminent death around his neck did little to tame him.

"You're lucky one of us knows how to shoot," Joaquin said.

"Aim lower next time," Miguel said. "I won't have to listen to your
whining anymore."

Miguel still accompanied Joaquin to Arizona despite their bick-
ering. He didn't do it for the money offered by Don Tomas, whose
son had been a victim of a recent Cowboy raid. He went because he
knew in his heart it would be the last time he would see his friend,
and he refused to renege on their boyhood oath that neither would let
the other rot under any other soil than that which they were raised
on alongside the Rio Magdalena. He refused to allow Joaquin to rot
under an American sun.

He wondered how soon he would regret his decision.

———————✦———————

CASA DE LOS Muertos. That's what he called Beckett's *adobe* when
they entered. Coyotes, *lobos,* pronghorns, cougars, birds, the scalp
of an Apache. All adorned the walls and floors, dead eyes watching
them dine on a meal of chilies and beans prepared by the Cantonese
cook, Ah Lo.

Bill Beckett raised horses in the shadow of the Whetstone Mountains. His dissatisfaction with *El Viejo's* influence over the Cochise Cowboys was their ace in the hole. He considered the Clantons
and sycophants like Bill Brocius liabilities whose raids grew risky.
He wanted them out and wouldn't risk a hanging or exile to do the
job himself. Lucky told him how much Don Tomas was offering for

Clanton and he wanted in. He would convince the old man to meet them alone and be guaranteed an equal share for his efforts. A kick in the toe from Joaquin silenced Miguel's impending objection to letting the *güero* take an equal split.

They celebrated their partnership with aguardiente. Beckett ranted about Clanton, rambled about Bill Brocius, and whined that a marshal named Virgil had a grudge against them while turning a blind eye toward his own brother's sins.

Miguel left them and walked the grounds of the *ranchito*. A mudbrick shed sat twenty feet behind the house, the stables and corral farther still. He leaned against the shed, lit a cigarette and heard the faint sound of a woman weeping. He listened for the source of the unseen Llorona and pressed his ear against the wall. The weeping came from the shed.

The shed had no windows. He checked the door and found it bolted and locked. He tapped the door. The weeping ceased.

He sat across from the shed all night, watching and listening. Ah Lo emerged at dawn with a plate of *tortillas*, keys at his waist. He approached the shed, unlocked the door, and entered. He returned quickly and said nothing to Miguel as he passed him. Ah Lo only frowned, mourning his own morality.

———————

"QUIÉN ES LA mujer?"

Beckett played an ineffective idiot to the question until Miguel insisted he heard her crying. Beckett smirked, sighed, and explained that she was a fugitive. A whore who robbed and killed her john that he was holding prisoner until Pima County authorities could take her to Tucson and reward him for her capture.

Pima County authorities never came. Multiple Cowboys did. Each of them slipped Beckett a two dollar entry fee for access to the shed. Joaquin willfully ignored Miguel's observations.

"If you want to poke in the *güero's* business, do it when we have the money and I'm as far away from you as possible."

"What makes you think he'll follow through?" Miguel asked. "I can't trust a man who sells prisoners for pleasure."

"I can. It means he believes in nothing but the dollar."

"What happens if *El Viejo* offers him more than Don Tomas for our heads?"

Joaquin spat. It was his only answer.

Beckett returned from a ride with news that Clanton rode east to New Mexico and wouldn't be back for a week or two. So they held tight, drinking while more Cowboys came and went. Each Cowboy paid for time in the shed with *La Llorona*. Not once did a sheriff or marshal arrive for the woman. Each night, the same weeping.

He cornered Ah Lo before dawn and asked the truth about the woman. The cook shook his head. Miguel flashed money. The cook shoved it away.

"Outside." He followed Ah Lo toward his shack beside the stables.

Her name was Esperanza. Her father was a drinker and a gambler who cheated Beckett on a job and didn't expect retaliation until it stormed through his house near El Paso. Beckett readied a bullet for the man's brain. A last ditch offer was made, his daughter for his life. He killed her father and took the money and the girl. He sold her out and made her a house pet until an escape attempt ended in a severe beating and a permanent stay in the dark shed.

"And you help keep her there."

"It is because of me she is alive," Ah Lo said. He knew worse punishments awaited women in such conditions. His sister had been sold by his starving family and sent to San Francisco. He sailed to Gold Mountain to find her and instead found a grave.

"I would soon join her if I caused trouble," he said. "What choice do I have?"

"The right choice."

"The right choice." The cook mused over the words like a mantra. He'd lost the luxury of the right choice when he came alone to a new land. Survival was his only choice left.

He and Joaquin rode and surveyed the land that morning. They found an old Spanish *presidio* in ruins, evidence of an empire long gone from the land. They observed Clanton Ranch from distant hills and shot jackrabbits for sport. Joaquin didn't waste a bullet. Miguel wasted most of his. He chose then to tell what he had learned.

"I told you, forget it," Joaquin said.

"Are you really that cold?"

Joaquin aimed his rifle at two jackrabbits rutting and fired. It was his only answer.

"There's more to life than money," Miguel said.

"Yeah, staying alive. I'd like to. I can't help you if you don't."

HE WAITED UNTIL the others slept and swiped away the keys. He clutched them to prevent the jingling from waking up Beckett or his Cowboy guests. His heart pounded and he remained cautious of the sound of his footsteps across the dirt toward the shed. He slipped the key inside and watched the lock open.

He lit his lantern and entered.

She pressed herself against the wall. Her white gown a soiled mess, her brown legs bruised. Her eyes gazed at him with a lack of focus, as if the presence of yet another stranger was of no surprise and of no consequence to her fate.

His voice was calm as he spoke her name. *Esperanza.* He called her Esperanza and assured no more harm would come to her. Tonight she would be free. Her bruised lips failed to form words, language a skill she risked forgetting in the absence of kind words to exchange. Small noises escaped, strained nonsense that carried more meaning than the empty words that most men speak in their lives. He told her to save her words for when she was ready and when the sun would shine upon her skin again.

He readied his mare, Blanca, and tethered one of the corralled horses to her, careful to keep her calm and quiet. He packed his provisions, firearms, water and everything necessary for a long journey. He saw the first sign of light along the blue horizon and re-entered the shed. He held his hand out to her. He told her they could ride wherever she wanted but first they needed to leave. She clasped his hands and walked out with him.

She pulled away. He reached back. Her eyes went wide.

"What's wrong?"

Her lips quivered. She let out a scream that had been waiting weeks for release and she pointed toward the *adobe* and ducked.

The mudbrick exploded behind Miguel as Beckett stumbled down the porch with his shotgun raised. Miguel drew his revolver. He fired in the dark. Another gun blast greeted him. He fired again and watched Beckett's shadow fall. The Cowboy struggled to reload the shotgun and Miguel fired twice more at the man until his fingers ceased fiddling with the shells in his hand and his arm fell limp against the Earth.

Voices rose from inside the *adobe*. Miguel grabbed Esperanza and flung her onto the horse. He ran to take Beckett's shotgun. Footsteps approached. He grabbed the gun and the shells and cocked his revolver. The door opened. He aimed at the stunned face of his oldest friend.

"Miguelito? What is this?"

The American voices grew nearer. Miguel ran back to Blanca without a word to Joaquin, mounted, and pressed his heels against her flanks. He led Esperanza on the other horse out of the ranchito and heard distant men and horses. He knew there would be a pursuit. They would be in full sight of a posse and an easy target come dawn. He rode to find a spot to hide until they were clear. He prayed that Joaquin put as much distance between himself and Cochise County and he prayed that Joaquin would forgive Miguel and understand his actions.

The ruined *presidio* proved an effective place to burrow. He watched dust rise on the western horizon, but the riders never approached. By dawn, they vanished. He led the horses to high brush and a cluster of cottonwoods near the river to conceal them and removed the provisions and saddles. He found Esperanza shaking. She flinched when he reached his hand to offer food. He let her have space and kept watch of the presidio and listened as she broke down. He had seen the same pain in his own mother who had been victimized during border raids. He waited until she was ready to see him.

They shared *carne seca,* and she picked at the jerked meat like a nibbling bird. She said little even when he spoke to her.

"Is there somewhere I can take you?"

"I have nowhere."

"Where would you like to go?"

"Not here."

His mind ran through convents and safe houses far from the reach of the Cowboys. He wished Joaquin was there. Joaquin knew every possible place to shelter someone along the border from Yuma to Matamoros. He turned sour, remembering Joaquin's horror to see the mess Miguel created. He left Joaquin because he needed to flee. He figured Joaquin wouldn't follow. But if Joaquin couldn't flee, they would have captured him and blamed him for Beckett's death. Or else hold him as bait.

He looked west and realized they stopped riding because they expected him to return. That meant Joaquin remained at the *ranchito*. That meant he had to return for him.

He explained everything to Esperanza. The color her face regained under the sun drained.

"You're leaving me?"

"I'll be back before the next morning."

"What if you aren't?"

He left her food and the shotgun and shells and instructed her how to shoot. He resaddled the stolen horse and warned Esperanza to ride as far as she could if anything happened. He took Blanca and rode west, heart torn in two, and with no thought of his future.

HE CHECKED HIS Spencer rifle and the two dragoon Colts his father once carried that hung off his saddle and approached the *adobe*. A rifle emerged from a window.

"Don't move any closer!"

The door opened. Joaquin stepped out, hands above his head, his white shirt stained red. Lucky followed behind and made him kneel.

"Reach for your guns and he dies."

"You kill him, and I'll reach for my guns."

Lucky laughed. "I'm sure you will. Won't take many of us."

Four more Cowboys exited the *adobe*. Another rifle stuck out from the open doorway.

"I'll settle on the girl, though," Lucky said.

"She was Beckett's," Miguel said. "What good is she to you?"

"She was all of ours," Lucky said. "It'd look bad if we started letting people take what's ours. Someone's gotta be made an example of. If it ain't her—"

He cocked his revolver against the back of Joaquin's head.

"Bring her by dawn," Lucky said. "Or else we'll make your friend an example to others not to cross the Cochise Cowboys."

Joaquin steered Blanca around. He turned back until the Cowboys led Joaquin back inside and he rode away, careful to not be followed.

Seven men, maybe more by dawn. Joaquin wouldn't have a chance if he rode in alone. He knew the ranchito enough to risk a sneak rescue but he couldn't fathom an escape while outnumbered. He needed more men in a country where he had no connections.

He remembered Beckett's drunken ramblings about a Yankee lawman named Virgil. An anti-Cowboy lawman. He turned Blanca east and rode for Tombstone and for the marshal.

———————

TOMBSTONE OVERLOOKED THE valley. At sundown the lights of the town flickered like fireflies drawn to the flames of Hell.

He approached the marshal's office alongside a wooden jail. The jailer grunted that Marshal Virgil Earp was away.

"Got a problem?"

Miguel turned toward a man with a brown mustache and a badge over his chest.

"Are you the marshal?"

The lawman laughed. He pointed to the gun in Miguel's belt.

"I wouldn't go looking for him with that at your waist. He takes guns seriously in this town. But you're new, so I'll look the other way right now."

"I need to speak to the marshal."

"You have trouble, you can speak to me. They didn't elect me sheriff to do nothing."

Miguel watched the sun dwindle and saw no other option. He explained the situation, omitting his near involvement in a would-be assassination.

Sheriff Behan nodded slowly. "Those Cowboys are a rough bunch. So where is this girl anyway?"

"She's hidden. She's safe."

"You and I might have different ideas of safety. I hope you didn't hide her in the backcountry somewhere to get mauled by wolves or a renegade band."

Miguel hesitated. Behan's brown eyes flickered and he flashed a soft and sympathetic smile. "The quicker I get her to safety, the better. For all you know, Lucky and the boys are out looking."

Miguel mentioned the *presidio* by the river. Behan clapped his shoulder. "I'll head over there with some men."

"I should go with you. She won't recognize you."

"You need to stay put and get some sleep," Behan said. "Soon as I can, I'm rounding more men up to ride toward Beckett's, and I'll need your help with that to get your friend back."

Behan called the jailer and told him to let Miguel borrow the cot for the night. He slipped Miguel a dollar for a meal and welcomed him to Tombstone.

"Don't you worry," the sheriff said. "It'll all be over in the morning."

HE TOSSED AND turned and woke up bathed in sweat. The jailer was still asleep. He took cold coffee from the pot and checked the clock. An hour after midnight, no sign of the sheriff. No word on Esperanza. No posse outside.

He stepped into the warm night and walked the busy streets. He spotted a man dismounting his horse across the street outside a restaurant and recognized Sheriff Behan. Alone, with neither Esperanza nor posse in tow. He lost Behan before he could confront him and decided he was sick of waiting. Night offered enough cover to sneak into the ranchito, and a knife would keep the evening silent. He unhitched Blanca and raced west to Beckett's.

He slid off Blanca before the sound of an approaching horse alerted anyone inside the *adobe*. He removed his spurs and clutched his knife as he crept toward the house. No candlelight inside. No guards posted. The *ranchito* seemed strangely silent. He peeked around and realized not even horses were hitched to posts. The whole place was empty.

He nudged the door open and waited. No gunshots, no voices. He tiptoed inside and saw Joaquin's hat sticking out over a lump on the bed in Beckett's room. He pulled the sheets away and found a bound body too thin to be Joaquin. He removed the hat and Ah Lo stared at him and squirmed. He removed the gag from his mouth and began untying him.

"Where are they?"

"With Esperanza," Ah Lo said.

His fingers froze over the final knot.

"You should not have trusted the sheriff."

He cut the last bond and ran outside. The cook followed and shouted at him.

"Lucky told me to tell you. They stay alive until you arrive. He told me he will let you choose who pays!"

The cook's words faded in the distance and over his own pounding heartbeat he didn't hear the man's parting words. He swung onto Blanca and rode east to the *presidio* as the first sign of light crept above the horizon to illuminate his path and guide him toward his fate.

———————◆◆◆◆◆◆———————

THE COWBOYS CROWDED around them. Man and woman on horseback, the nooses tied to the cottonwood. They whooped when Miguel arrived.

"Thought you'd never make it," Lucky said. "Wouldn't wanna do this without you."

The Cowboys aimed their guns at Miguel.

"These horses are awfully flighty. Don't give them a reason to take off." Lucky paced the perimeter between the Cowboys and Miguel. "Like I said, an example has to be made. This is your fault, so the way I see it, it's your choice who goes. Don't think you're too high and mighty to choose or else I'll just kill all three of you and you can explain your failure to God."

"You think you won't have to explain yourself to him?"

"I got years to make my peace with him. How long you got?"

Miguel stared into the helpless eyes, the consequences of his heroism. Neither pled their case for the privilege of life. Miguel stared at his saddle, at the loaded Spencer rifle that hung from it, at the Colt Dragoon revolvers his father had left him, and the choice became obvious.

"I'll take Joaquin's place. It would be a shame to waste that rope."

Lucky ordered Joaquin down. The Cowboys marched him forward while Miguel walked toward him. The Cowboys pulled his arms back and began tying. He leaned toward Joaquin and spoke to him in Spanish.

"Do it just like my last hanging. You have one chance, so don't miss."

"Quiet greaser!"

The Cowboy kicked him. They released Joaquin from his bonds. Joaquin followed them as they dragged Miguel to the noose.

"Who do I choose?"

Miguel said, "The right choice."

Lucky stepped between them. "Best get moving."

Joaquin rode the horse from the cottonwood and turned to watch until their attention diverted from himself to the victims. He slid off his horse, grabbed the rifle and hit the dirt between tall brush. He aimed for a clean shot. He peered down the barrel while two Cowboys raised their whips and swung for the horses' rears.

The horses charged. Joaquin prayed and fired.

Esperanza's rope severed before the horse could throw her off and it carried her away in the saddle while her legs clung on. Joaquin cocked and aimed toward a dangling Miguel. He saw Lucky aim his rifle at Esperanza for a clear shot. Joaquin turned his barrel toward Lucky and fired.

Smoke filled the air as Cowboy after Cowboy fired at Esperanza and Joaquin. He pierced the smoke with bullets that drove them back. He watched Miguel's legs kick. He made a final aim for the rope.

Esperanza slid from the saddle. Joaquin caught her and swung onto the horse. Bullets flew past his ear. He kicked the horse's flanks and Blanca followed. Blanca fell back as Joaquin's horse loped across the dirt and the gunshots faded in the distance. Joaquin clung to the horse while Esperanza clung to him and he raced to put distance between himself and the Cowboys without a final glance at Miguel.

HE ARRIVED AT Cananea and learned that *rurales had* killed Old Man Clanton the same week Miguel had died. He was too exhausted to care.

They recovered at the nearby Rancho Madrugada. Esperanza spoke only to the maid for weeks, and she avoided the company of men other than Joaquin. He never asked and she never discussed. Their conversations remained banal, but he often heard her shouting in her sleep from his room and recalled the same haunting screams of his father who survived Mexico's wars in body but not in spirit.

Joaquin was an unfit companion for comfort. His melancholy over Miguel numbed him to the tiniest pleasures in life. Each night he prayed forgiveness for abandoning his *compadre* to rot under the Arizona sun. One night he broke down in his chamber. The door opened and Esperanza watched him.

"Do you wish to talk about it?"

"Would you?"

She closed the door and left him be. It was her only answer.

Esperanza's literacy granted her a job teaching children in town. Joaquin visited and watched her teach letters and envied her that, while her scars would never fully heal, she would have what he had lost years ago, a place to call home.

Miguel cried from the Earth to be buried right and Joaquin finally answered. He left Cananea in October. He watched Esperanza gathering children at the school but could not conjure a parting word. All he could think was that it ought to have been Miguel to watch her smile under a Sonoran sky while Joaquin slept under American soil.

There was no body or noose at the *presidio* when he arrived in late October. He rode to Tombstone to gather information to see if he could discover where or if Miguel had been buried. A large crowd gathered on the streets. He recognized a few of them as the Cowboys

but they paid no attention to the strange Mexican in town. Their rage
was fixed elsewhere. To a more recent and nearby enemy.

He heard his name called across the street and spotted a Chinese
man in the doorway of a restaurant with a dirty apron. He ran to Ah
Lo and embraced him. He asked about the crowd but Ah Lo ignored
his question. He wept with joy for Joaquin's safety. He informed
him that he buried Miguel properly at the *ranchito*. Joaquin thanked
him and asked his help to exhume his friend to be buried back home
along the Rio Magdalena. Ah Lo objected. Let the dead rest. Joaquin
insisted, explained the oath he took as a child. Ah Lo understood.
He had failed the same obligation when he left his sister buried back
in California.

He asked the cook again about the crowd. The cook frowned and
told him bad men had been killed. That they wouldn't be the last. That
he ought to leave before the storm struck.

Joaquin mingled among the growing crowd and migrated toward
the front where three open caskets lay in front of the mourners. All
young men, their names written beside each coffin. A familiar sur-
name drew his eyes to the pale youthful face of Billy Clanton.

An older man with a passing resemblance to the boy wept openly
beside Billy's coffin while Cowboys consoled him. The man spat and
swore revenge for his baby brother. Joaquin found his sympathy for
the man whose father he had almost killed ironic. Despite the border
between them, despite Old Man Clanton's crimes against his country-
men, despite the Cowboys' killing of Miguel, he found a kinship with
the mourning man and his heart went out when the man broke down
and cried that the bastard Earps had killed his baby brother.

—*Steven McFann is a writer born and raised in California. His lifelong passion for the history of the American West was sparked by childhood visits to the Autry Museum, his teenage love for the work of Sergio Leone and Clint Eastwood, and the western-inspired art of his uncle Gary McFann, as well as the art of his grandfather's cousin, celebrated western artist Don Crowley. His work has appeared in* Saddlebag Dispatches, Empyrean Literary Magazine, *and the entertainment website* ScreenRant. *He is also the author of the Substack blog "Fool's Gold," which details the history of California from the Gold Rush to WWI. Counting the likes of James Ellroy, Hubert Selby Jr, and Larry McMurtry as his influences, he is currently working on a novel based on a real team of infamous train robbers in the San Joaquin Valley, an extended blog series on Gold Rush bandit Joaquin Murrieta, as well as a screenplay centered on Los Angeles in the violent days of the Gold Rush. When not writing or working as a stagehand, he loves reading, listening to music, and exploring the southwest's majestic deserts. Find him on Twitter @SadCowboiVibes.*

THE BALLAD ⚜ COCHISE'S GRANDDAUGHTER

P.A. O'NEIL

WE HAD RIDDEN together in the Wells Fargo coach all the way from Tucson. But it wasn't until I helped her out of the rig that I realized I had fallen in love. Her touch was featherlike as she took my hand to help her take her first step onto the streets of Tombstone. If not for her dusky complexion, she was the picture of a lady of distinction and breeding. Her black hair was pulled high on her head in the fashion of the day, a collection of curls rested on her shoulder. The ostrich plume in her hat bounced as her feet hit the ground.

"Thank you, Mister Bruno, I think I have it now." Her voice was clear, without an accent. "My hand, Mister Bruno."

My forehead felt wet. "Oh, I'm sorry." I let go of her long, tapered fingers and chuckled. "Please, call me Chris."

She stepped onto the boardwalk. "All right, Chris. Now, can you direct me to the opera house?"

The coach driver unloaded her trunk and my bag. "Sure, it's the next street over and to the left. The Hotel Americana is just across the street here. I'll make sure your trunk gets over there if you want."

She fluffed out her skirt and tugged on her tunic. "Thank you... *Chris*. That's very kind of you. Please tell the clerk I'll be there shortly to register."

"Certainly, ma'am." She began to walk away. "Oh, Miss Blackwater, may I call you Paulina?"

Her teeth, pearly white, shown in contrast to her dark skin. "Of course. It's good to have at least one friend in Tombstone."

———————◆———————

I DID AS she asked and mentioned to the clerk that she would be coming shortly to take a room. My place was at Ma Kendall's Boarding House, but I carried my bag along with her trunk to the hotel. The place had a small café off to the side where I sat waiting for her to arrive. It couldn't have been a half-hour when she opened the outer door. The smile I had prepared faded as I saw her face. Her demeanor was deliberate as she approached the desk. Her speech, commanding.

"My name is Paulina Blackwater. I believe my trunk was brought here this afternoon."

The clerk's mouth opened but for a moment, yet no sound emerged. "Yes, ma'am. Mister Bruno brought it by saying you would follow. I had it sent up to your room already." He turned the register toward her as he handed her a pen. "Do you know how many days you'll be staying, Miss Blackwater?"

"Not long. I'm going back to Tucson on the next stage."

"Well, that won't be until tomorrow, ma'am."

Her shoulders dropped, and her voice softened. "Well, then at least for tonight."

"Yes, ma'am. I'll get your key."

I felt foolish as I approached, my hat literally in my hand. "Forgive me, Miss Blackwater... Paulina... I couldn't help but overhear what you said about leaving. Earlier, you sounded like you were looking forward to staying in Tombstone, at least for a while."

She dipped her head, eyelashes fluttering as if she were holding back emotion. Lifting her head, she took a deep breath and said, "Well, things just didn't turn out to be what I imagined. I guess there is no place for a woman like me in Tombstone."

The clerk cleared his throat. "Ma'am, here is your key. The room number is on the fob. Since you are staying only the one night, its hotel policy to collect the room fee in advance."

"Oh, yes, of course." She reached into her drawstring purse and removed a twenty dollar gold piece. "Will this be enough?"

The clerk's eyebrows shot up. "Oh, yes, ma'am. In fact, you have change coming back. Iffen you'll just wait here."

This gave me a chance to continue with my mystery lady. "Paulina, just a bit ago you called me your friend. Let me take you out to dinner, and maybe we can talk."

"Talk?"

"Yes, because right now you look like you could use a friend."

Though she was tired, she admitted I was right. We agreed to meet again in the hotel lobby in a couple of hours when I would take her for the best steak dinner in Tombstone. I took my valise back to my room and changed into something less dusty. Looking at myself in the mirror, I realized it would make a greater impression if my scraggly whiskers were gone. Trotting down to Bilsley's Barber Shop, I caught him as he was locking the door. Old Bilsley was a romantic at heart and agreed, even though his wife would be wondering why he was late, to give me a quick shave and comb of my hair.

Smelling of rose water, I felt like a cock-of-the-walk as I moved down the street. *So, she's only going to be here one night,* I thought. *I'm going to make sure she has a memorable time while she is here.* Little did I know, it would be *me* who would have the memories. I hadn't long to wait, as Paulina descended the stairs just as I entered the lobby. Her dress was of a midnight blue satin that shone against her dark-skinned complexion.

"Now, how's that for timing?" she asked, chuckling afterwards. She reached out her hand, like she had that afternoon at the stage.

I draped it over the crook of my arm. "It's almost as if it was meant to be."

She tilted her head and smiled. "What do you mean?"

With a slight cough, I answered, "Just, we must be running on the same timetable. That's all."

As we exited the hotel, she nodded. "Oh, I see. The same timetable."

I DIDN'T KNOW for sure, but walking with Paulina made me feel like every man looking at us was envious for not having her on his arm. We ate at the Continental, and even though it cost me a half a week's wages, the meal was remarkable. Paulina ate like a bird, and when it came to the bottle of wine we shared, she barely finished one glass all night. The waiter offered a dessert while removing our plates. I talked her into sharing a piece of apple pie. While we waited, the conversation began to turn from how fresh the vegetables had been to how she hadn't realized how hungry she was.

"Hungry? You barely ate half of your plate. Didn't you like it?"

The waiter set down the pie slice and two forks. As he left, she smiled. "Oh, no, it was quite delicious. Thank you, again, for asking me to dinner."

I picked up my fork to avoid getting lost in her dark eyes. "Well, I figured you needed to have at least one good memory of Tombstone before you leave tomorrow."

She took a bite of the pie and wiped her mouth. "That's very kind of you." She dipped her head again as she set down her fork.

"Paulina, if you don't mind my asking, why did you come here if only just to turn around and leave?"

She tipped her chin up and inhaled. "In truth, leaving right away wasn't my intention. You see, I was offered a position, but when I arrived here...."

I placed my hand on her shoulder. "It's okay, you can tell me."

She nodded and sniffed. "It seems regardless of my talents, I just wasn't the right color for Mister Napoleon, the man who owns the Tombstone Opera House. He rescinded the invitation on the spot."

Dropping my hand, I tilted my head and furrowed my brow. "The opera house? You came here to work at the opera house?"

"To *sing* at the opera house. I was a soloist with the San Francisco Opera, but when my agent told me there was a position open here, he contacted Mister Napoleon. He said, with my credentials, I would be most welcome to come for an audition." Her words were coming faster than before, stopping only to take a forkful of pie.

My lips parted as my smile grew wider. "Imagine that, a real opera singer."

I must've looked the fool because she pulled her napkin to her mouth and laughed. "Opera singers are people, too, you know."

The evening weather was still pleasant as we walked back to her hotel. The sound of our heels were amplified on the boardwalk. When we came to the bench in front of the dry goods store, I asked if we could sit a spell. Removing my handkerchief and shaking it out square, I laid it down for her to sit on.

We sat in silence for a few minutes.

"Tombstone really is a nice place," she said, finally. "It's actually much bigger than I had imagined."

Glancing around, I nodded, before I turned back to her. "What I don't understand is, why would you leave a place as grand as San Francisco to come to this backwater town?" I quickly followed up with, "You don't have to answer if it's too personal."

Paulina leaned back on the bench. "You're right. I could've stayed there, or gone anywhere for that matter, but I wanted to come to Tombstone because this is where it all began."

"I don't understand. Where all what began?"

"Me—or at least, my father."

I started to nod but switched to shaking my head. "You've got family here in Tombstone?"

She crossed her arms and put her hand to her chin. "I don't think so, at least not anymore. I suppose I came here looking for something my family lost. I think I was looking for our dignity."

I held my hands palms up. "Whoa, now you've lost me. I'm just a country boy. You're talking about something deep."

This time it was she who reached out to take my hand. "Chris, what do you think of Indians?"

I sat up straight and silent, looking for words to not offend her. "They're okay, I guess."

"And Mexicans?"

"We have lots of Mexicans who live here, along with Indians and Chinese, a few Negroes, but mostly Tombstone is populated by Whites."

Paulina nodded as she let go. "Would it shock you to know you just had dinner with Cochise's granddaughter?"

My eyes grew wide as I sucked in a deep breath only to end up coughing. Somehow, I choked out my words, "Who... whose... granddaughter, now?"

She dropped my hand and rose. "See, you are in shock." Paulina turned, and talking more to herself than me, said, "I shouldn't have come to Tombstone."

"No, wait!" I took a couple of steps to follow her down the boardwalk, before turning back for my handkerchief. "Paulina, wait up. I didn't mean there was anything wrong with what you said."

She looked up into my face. Her lips taut, her eyes shone bright in the dim light. "Is that how you respond when someone divulges a secret?"

"No, no, you're right." I placed my hands on her shoulders. "I was in shock, but I handled it wrong. I'm sorry."

I could feel the tension in her shoulders disperse as she slowly nodded. Her head dipping farther and farther down, until at last when she raised it, I could see her eyes were brimming with tears. One drop slowly escaped, and I used the back of my finger to catch it before it fell off her cheek and onto her gown.

Paulina used the heel of her palm to catch the next tear. "I'm sorry. I must look the fool."

"No, not at all. C'mon, let's walk a little more while you tell me all about it. This time, I promise to be more mature with my response." I took her by the elbow as we walked the short distance to her hotel and then past the door farther on the boardwalk.

She sniffed. "I must look a mess. Do you have a handkerchief?"

"I do, but I'm afraid it's a little dusty."

Paulina stopped short and looked at me before she burst out laughing. I joined her. Our laughter filled the empty street, causing people walking on the other side to shake their heads. We moved farther on down the boardwalk until we came to another bench. She giggled when I pulled out my handkerchief.

We sat in silence again, breathing in the evening air. At last, I turned to her and said, "I meant what I said about being your friend. If you'd like, please tell me the rest of your story."

Her eyes softened as a small smile filled her face. "It's true what I said about being Cochise's granddaughter."

"Uh, yes, but I don't see how you can be here now and like this." I waved my hand before her indicating the quality of her dress.

"So you think I should be dressed in buckskins with feathers in my braids?"

"Now, I didn't mean to insult...."

She shook her head and smiled. "I know. I'm kind of used to it by now."

"You said you were from San Francisco. I thought Cochise never left the Arizona Territory."

"No. My mother's family came to southern Arizona with the Gadsden Purchase, when land was being given away to homesteaders. It seemed the settlement between the United States and Mexico suited everyone except the Indians. My great-grandfather's *rancho* was attacked. He was killed, and my grandmother was carried away. Her name was Glory Be, Glory Be Hathaway."

"It's a lovely name."

"I've always thought so. I believe it brought her some renown in years to come." She tilted her head and sighed. "Months went by before she and other captives were rescued by the military. Her brother, Jordan Hathaway, who was not home at the time of the raid, was so ashamed of her, well...."

"Her physical situation?"

Paulina patted my hand and nodded. "Yes, she was expecting my father, you see. Uncle Jordan sold the land and moved him and his sister to Los Angeles. It's where my father was born."

"Wait, how come your name isn't Hathaway?"

"Uncle Jordan refused to allow the baby to carry the Hathaway name. Glory Be had no other choice but to give him another. She named him Paul Blackwater. Blackwater being the translation for a word she remembered from her time in captivity."

"Oh, so you're named after your father." I gently rocked my head. "But, if you don't mind my asking, and I mean this with no disrespect, if you are only a quarter Indian, why are you so dark?"

Paulina began to chuckle. "That's why I asked what you thought of Mexicans."

My eyebrows knitted as I asked, "You mean you're Mexican as well as Indian?"

"If you let me finish my story, it will all be clear."

I snorted. "Clear as mud, probably."

She looked at me with open mouth before she huffed out the breath she had been holding. "I suppose it seems like it." She nodded as she continued. "Uncle Jordan sent Glory Be and the baby to San Francisco to live with relatives. A woman rescued from savage Indians, with a half-breed baby, was an oddity. The more people kept asking her to tell her story, the more famous she became in society. As Paul grew, it became apparent he wasn't going to be as welcome as his mother, so he was sent to live at the mission school. It was there, when asked by the nuns for the name of his father, Glory Be announced for all to hear, Paul's father was none other than Cochise."

"Do you think she was telling the truth?"

Paulina shrugged. "I don't know. It could be the truth or it could be just a ploy to embarrass her brother. Regardless, it's family history now. Papa met a Mexican girl at the school, and when they were teens, they got married."

"And that's where you come into the story. But how do you explain your singing opera?"

Paulina put her knuckles to her mouth as she laughed. "It's where the story gets strange."

I ran my hand through my slicked back hair. "As if it hasn't been strange already?"

This just made her laugh some more. "Without a child around, Glory Be became the darling of San Francisco. She eventually married a man named Will Donovan and had a few more children. Grandpa Will was always nice to Papa and Mama. He was an immigrant from Ireland and understood about how America was a country of many peoples." In a moment, Paulina's expression changed from the bright storyteller to one of melancholy narrator. She sighed and continued. "Grandma Glory and Grandpa Will took me in when the influenza epidemic took my parents. I couldn't have been more than four or so."

"How kind of them."

"Well, I really had no other family."

"No, I meant, with you looking so unlike their other children." I reached for her hand and squeezed it ever so slightly.

She smiled back. "I think Grandma was trying to make up for time she had lost with her son. Grandpa, he was a jolly soul and believed all children were a gift. It's him to thank for my career."

"Your grandfather sang opera?"

"No, but he was a member of the choir at our church. He loved music, and through him, I learned to sing. He recognized my voice held something of worth, and he paid for lessons. I was a teenager when I auditioned for the San Francisco Opera, and I've been there ever since."

I squeezed her hand again. "You're really something, Paulina Blackwater. I think it has been a blessing to get to know you."

And there it was, the smile which had captured my heart, with a row of pearls for teeth. "Thank you, Chris Bruno. Now, I think you owe me the story of your life."

I pushed up my chest and laughed as I stood up. "If you promise not to get on the stage tomorrow, I'll tell you all about my sweet self at dinner tomorrow."

Paulina took my hand as she stood. Looking behind her, she picked up the handkerchief with the other. "I believe this belongs to you."

Evening had turned well into night, as we both started laughing. Across the street, a man raised the window from his second story room and yelled for us to be quiet as he was trying to sleep. We stopped on the spot and looked at each other for guidance, but this only caused us to snicker as I walked her back to her hotel.

THE NEXT MORNING, I arose early to be at Judge Finkle's office before it opened. The judge had been kind enough to leave me the writs which had been enacted while I was in Tucson. When he showed up at about 10:00 a.m., I was well into filing the stack left on my desk.

"Good morning, Christopher. You seem to be in fine spirits this morning." He chuckled.

I stopped humming the tune which had been rolling around my head. "Yes, sir, Judge."

As he hung up his hat and coat, he asked, "I take it the trip to Tucson went well."

"Yes, sir! So well, I met the girl I intend to marry."

The judge stopped at his desk and threw his head back. "My, my, I'm going to have to send you to Tucson more often then."

"No need, sir." Placing files on his desk, I added, "She's right here in Tombstone."

Sitting down, the judge exclaimed, "Well then, you'd better finish your work if you want to take her out while it's still daylight."

I continued humming as I went back to my appointed tasks.

At 4:30 p.m., I asked if I could leave the office. "I'd like to show her some of the town while there's still daylight."

Glancing over at my desk, the judge waved toward the door. "Fine, just remember, once you're married, you don't have to be at her beck and call."

"Yes, sir, I'll remember." I reached for the handle of the office door when the judge called back.

"By the way, when are you planning this wedding?"

"Don't know. I have to ask her first."

I didn't bother going back to Ma Kendall's. I just trotted my way over to the Hotel Americana, tipping my hat to everyone I met along the way. Once there, I asked the desk clerk what room Miss Blackwater was in and took the steps two at a time, up to her floor. Removing my hat, I knocked, not really knowing what to expect. The door opened, and there she was, lovelier than the night before. It was all I could do to keep from blurting out, "It wasn't all a dream."

"Chris, I was wondering when I would see you next. Would you like to come in?"

This caught me off guard. "Uh, no, thank you. Paulina, if you are ready, I'd like to show you some of Tombstone before we get something to eat."

"Yes, of course. Let me get my purse, and I'll be right with you."

Standing in the hallway, I thought about how she looked when the door opened. She was wearing a cream-colored blouse with a skirt made of green plaid. With her hair pulled up into a bun, she looked far from the image of an opera star from San Francisco.

We crossed the street, and I took her the opposite way from the opera house. I pointed out the sheriff's office, the city hall, and the county courthouse. The farther we walked, the more the buildings went from stone construction to wood as we found ourselves in the old part of the town. As we passed saloons and gambling houses, I began to think this was no place for a lady.

"We should turn around. This part of town can be rough."

"But, I find this interesting. You know, San Francisco had its wild places, as well. Tell me, is there really a theatre here in Tombstone?"

"Well, yes, the Birdcage Theatre and Saloon, is the next block over. But I advise against going there."

"Oh, c'mon," she said, while pulling on my hand. "Anyplace with a reputation that reaches as far as San Francisco and beyond is worth seeing at least once."

Shaking my head, I let her lead me across the street to the entrance of the Birdcage. Before entering, I instructed her, "At the first sign of any trouble or disturbance, we're leaving, understand?"

With a mock salute she said, "Anything you say, Commander." Then she winked as we turned to the door.

The space within the room was larger and louder than could be imagined from the outside. To the left was a long bar, typical of most saloons. The right was a raised platform with padded booths held separate with a reserved sign. The center of the area was filled with small tables and chairs, so crowded, the serving girls could barely pass by. Though the chairs were all mingled, they could all be turned to face a large wooden stage. Beyond all this were darkened rooms which held what sounded like gambling tables, poker, faro, and such. Past the bar was a stairway which led to a balcony surrounding the entire building leading to rooms for God only knows what.

We must've looked like babes staring as we took in all the sights and sounds. Finally, a large-breasted woman, her hair dyed an impossible shade of red, approached. I recognized her, not as she was presently attired in a dress of orange silk carrying a fan of ostrich feathers.

She had appeared before Judge Finkle on a noise complaint where she batted her eyelashes and paid a fine before sashaying her way out the door. Miss Molly Woodrow knew how to make an impression.

"Well, hello there. Don't I know you, young man?"

I tipped my hat. "Yes, Miss Molly. I'm Christopher Bruno. I clerk for Judge Finkle." I stepped aside and put my arm around Paulina's shoulders. "This here is my friend, Miss Blackwater. She's from San Francisco and wanted to see the Birdcage."

"San Francisco," the lady exclaimed. "Well, I'll be. Tell me, honey, do you know Blake Carmelo?"

"I'm sure she—" But Paulina put forth her hand.

"Yes, ma'am. Mister Carmelo is a friend of my grandfather."

Molly Woodrow waved her fan and put her arm around Paulina's back. "Well, a friend of Blake's is a friend of mine. Why don't you two take a seat up in the reserved section, and I'll treat you to a drink on the house."

I felt lost as I watched the two women chat their way to the padded booths. Trotting behind them, I promptly took a seat on Paulina's open side. I asked the waiter for beer, but the women ordered sherry. I have to admit, I was in over my head as they discussed other people they might have in common.

Finally, the conversation came around to what Paulina was doing in Tombstone. Without going into deep explanation, she told how she had been invited for an audition but hadn't even had a chance to sing because of her dark skin. Molly slammed her hand down on the table. "Marcus Napoleon is a fool. He wouldn't know a good thing if it were handed to him gift-wrapped and smelling of roses."

Paulina dipped her head. "Thank you, that's kind of you."

Then, as if struck by lightning, Molly threw her head back as her mouth dropped open. "Tell you what, why don't you sing something for us here. Word will get out about your performance, and old man Napoleon will have to hire you."

Paulina shook her head. "I really don't know—"

"Paulina doesn't accept charity," I interceded.

"Oh, hell, it wouldn't be charity. Paulina here is a performer. Since when does a performer pass up on a chance to demonstrate her worth? How 'bout it? Shall I shush the crowd for you?"

"I haven't anything prepared," Paulina said as she slipped out of the booth.

"Oh, it's okay, honey. You can just sing something *acapella*. You do sing *acapella*, don't you?"

Paulina nodded, and I watched as the two stepped down onto the crowded floor. Paulina and Molly took center stage. Molly proceeded to shout, "Quiet down, everyone! Quiet down!" Once she had their attention, she added, "This here is Paulina Blackwater, and she's about to sing for us. So, I expect all of you to shut-up and give her your attention." Molly then winked at her before stepping aside.

I never felt so out of place before in my life.

Paulina looked like a frightened child. Then she took a deep breath, releasing it to bring a calm which showed on her face. The room was strangely hushed as she opened her mouth and brought forth a clear voice in a volume far beyond what her little frame should have held.

Ave Maria
Gratia plena
Maria, gratia plena
Maria, gratia plena....

I was beginning to wonder if Paulina was a magician as the room became deathly still. The bartender stopped pulling taps. The servers sat down at whatever chair available. Men left the darkness of the gambling den to see what was occurring in the hall. Unbelievable as it was, men and women in different states of undress, one woman wearing only a Chenille bedspread and her companion in his long johns, emerged from their rooms to line the balcony railings. I looked over at Miss Molly to see a tear run down her cheek as she held her fan over her heaving breast.

...Et in hora mortis nostrae
Et in hora mortis nostrae
Et in hora mortis nostrae
Ave Maria

When she finished her rendition of "Ave Maria," not a sound could be heard from any place in the building. Pauline stood there, her hands in prayerful motion before her chest, her eyes toward the ceiling. I nearly jumped when a dust-covered cowboy stood up and hollered, "Yee-*haw!*" The Birdcage erupted in rousing applause, with everyone whooping, hollering, and stamping their feet.

Paulina, with her hands still clasped now held down before her, took a bow. First to one side, and then to the other, before she turned to wave to the balcony. I ran up to help her down but threw my arms around her before her feet touched the floor. "Your voice is almost as beautiful as you are, Paulina. Will you marry me?"

Before she could answer, Molly pulled us both back to the booths. Everyone we passed reached out to touch Paulina, congratulating her on her singing. We made it back to our seats to find another round of drinks waiting for all. We laughed and marveled at the performance for several minutes before we were interrupted by a stodgy looking man in a rumpled suit.

"Miss Molly, that was probably the best performance I've ever heard. You must introduce me to this lovely songbird." I recognized his face from being one of the men on the balcony.

Molly flapped her fan. "Marcus, please meet Paulina Blackwater. Paulina, this reprobate is Marcus Napoleon, the owner of the Tombstone Opera House."

"Miss Blackwater,"—he took Paulina's hand—"you sing like an angel. I was wondering if you would like to be a soloist at my opera house."

Paulina looked at me with raised eyebrows. I interjected with, "Miss Blackwater would be glad to. In fact, I believe having her there would be a great benefit to your establishment."

Napoleon seemed taken aback by my intrusion. "And why is that young man?"

I put my arm around Paulina's shoulders. "Think of all the publicity you can achieve with the billing, Paulina Blackwater, Cochise's granddaughter."

———————

—P.A. O'Neil's stories have been featured in over forty anthologies, on-line journals, and magazines. She and her husband reside in Thurston County, Washington. A collection of her stories, Witness Testimony and Other Tales, *is available on Amazon. Her article, "Northwest Passage," about the Ellensburg, Washington Rodeo from the Summer 2022 issue of* Saddlebag Dispatches *won a Will Rogers Medallion Award. For links to books which feature her stories, please visit her Amazon author page: P.A. O'Neil.*

Fight for Water by Charles Schreyvogel

BEAST ❁ BURDEN

JULIANNE METZGER TAYLOR

WEGMAN OPENED ONE eye. Dust floated in morning's beams of light. The windows still lacked glass panes in his apartment above the store. His head throbbed, pain increasing as he recalled the events of the night before. Jimmy sloshing whiskey into his cup. Wegman betting his horse. The smug cattleman across the table laying down his cards. All night Wegman had dreamed of a pig with sad brown eyes. There were many things that Wegman Smith would rather forget.

Wegman heard the scuffle of boots on the porch and the jingle of the front door opening.

"Mornin', Weg!" Jimmy yelled. Jimmy thumped up the stairs, two steps at a time.

"Jimmy, I told you about fifteen times, don't you go barging into my property!" said Wegman. "I'll be down in a minute!" The stomping stopped briefly and then went back down in the same robust fashion as they had come.

A while later, when Wegman descended into the store, Jimmy leaned his torso across the counter, foot on the boot rail. The glaring whitewashed walls in the morning sun did nothing to help his head. Wegman's shop of sparse clapboard walls measured fourteen feet square. It was a big store for a place like Ragtown. Wegman's large cast iron stove sat in the corner. It was now the most expensive thing he owned.

Wegman scratched his eye and sighed. Jimmy's eyes seemed suspiciously cheerful this morning.

"Did you come for coffee," asked Wegman, "or did you come to talk about the fact I lost my horse?"

"Well, I sure as shit isn't going to talk about the horse without coffee," said Jimmy, holding his tin mug out.

Wegman lit the stove. The smell of coffee filled the dusty air.

"I made it weak," said Wegman. "Without my horse, I don't know when I'll be able to get more," he said. The closest railroad station was a two-hour ride away.

Jimmy grasped the mug with both hands, smile fading.

"Well, friend, I feel partly responsible egging you on, but it seemed like you were having a hell of a time, you so rarely partaking of the drink. I thought it my duty as your friend to keep you going,'" said Jimmy. "But what in tarnation were you thinking?"

"It doesn't matter now. It's done," said Wegman. "Unless I can get a horse for my wagon, I can't retrieve supplies at the junction." Wegman turned to the window. In his drunken sadness, or maybe anger, he'd bet all his money and his nag. Everyone who had a horse out here needed it desperately. Getting another without cash was impossible.

"That's why I come over!" Jimmy blurted. "When I went to sweep my porch this morning, my cactus was all ate up."

"What? Ate?" asked Wegman, tilting his head. "Some drunkard from last night probably has needles all over his rear this morning. Wouldn't be the first time a cowboy lost a fight with a cactus."

Jimmy shook his head. "There weren't no boot prints. There were other prints though. Look like that over there," Jimmy pointed to the label on the canned peaches.

Jimmy licked a finger and drew in the dust on a window. Two ovals, longer than they were taller, joined at the side, an indentation where a stem once grew. Wegman furrowed his brow.

"I seent this print before," said Jimmy. "Back in '36, I had this lieutenant who was always talking about how inhospitable this here desert terrain was suited for our horses." Jimmy paused, going for drama.

Wegman pried open a wooden crate. "Out with it, Jim," said Wegman. "Molasses is faster than you telling a story."

"Now, now," said Jimmy. "The point is I heard from a buddy that this here lieutenant of mine got the War Department to send him thirty thousand dollars to fix his problem."

Wegman blinked hard at Jimmy, "And?"

"Camels!" Jimmy smacked the counter. His green eyes danced with mirth. "That lieutenant asked the Army to send him camels! And that there outside my stoop... I reckon was a camel hoof print."

Ignoring the fact that Wegman was now stocking a shelf, he went on. "See, that experiment went belly up what with the War Between the States," explained Jimmy. "But they used them for riding, on the count that camels don't need as much water as horses. When the Army quit on the program, the soldiers just let them go. I suspect there's a camel 'round here, free for them who needs it."

Wegman turned his head slightly in Jimmy's direction.

Jimmy smiled and raised his cup in thanks to Wegman's back. The door jingled as Jimmy went back over to the post office.

Wegman had been a major for the 1st Georgia Sharpshooter Battalion. He was the only child of two Atlanta storekeepers, a happy and loving family. Wegman could still feel the dry lips as his mother kissed his cheek. His battalion marched that day for Savannah. Her swollen brown eyes told him she'd already shed her tears for him. It was the last time he saw her.

Wegman felt awkward among the land-owning gentlemen in the officer corps. Despite their middle-class disdain, the battalion's generals soon found Wegman's mercantile skills useful. It was lack of supply, not the Yankees, beating the Confederacy. While other units starved, Wegman could haul cornmeal and bullets back to outfit his companies. With each procurement, Wegman hated himself, and the Confederacy, more and more.

He valued order. The battlefield had none. The battalion carried the smell of blood and rot wherever they went. Wegman often confiscated supplies from staving families, giving them useless Confederate bonds. He preferred not to remember the more vicious ways they'd had to acquire the things they needed.

The leadership knew the war was over long before the surrender. Killing and suffering dragged on, and the South called it bravery and dedication to the cause. Wegman hated waste. To him that's what this war was.

Wegman ventured home to Atlanta after the surrender. Like all the others in town, ash and rubble filled his street. He hung around, but there was no sign of his parents. He had no other family. He had status, and he had money from the war.

What he didn't have was the will to surround himself with the remnants of the Confederate aristocracy. Any time he heard Gettysburg, Shiloh, or Antietam, all he could smell was blood. The blank vastness of Texas appealed to him.

With a horse and a pack, he set out on the road. His boots were new, a luxury after the war. For weeks alone, he rode toward the sunset. He liked it that way.

Around dusk one night, he stumbled onto a small collection of buildings. He squinted in the darkness. He'd come across a few abandoned towns before. Kneeling down, he ran his forefinger across the porch. It was clean. Whoever lived here was fast asleep. He'd introduce himself in the light of day.

Wegman walked toward some nearby trees. Below the tree line, black water sparkled in the moonlight. Wegman shuffled in the dark, setting up his makeshift camp under a large cedar. His small fire crackled. Wegman's eyelids grew heavy with sleep. This place felt like home.

The small outpost called Ragtown had a post office and not much else. Without a railroad to feed the town, its growth was slow. Wegman befriended the owner of the clean stoop, Jimmy.

Jimmy's face was always red from either drink, desert sun, or both. Wegman wondered how such a friendly man had ended up in such a lonely town. One of the unspoken rules was that you didn't ask about a man's past. If he wanted you to know, he probably wouldn't have ended up here to begin with.

Yesterday, Wegman had received a letter. A farmer had come to his parents' store looking for him. The farmer had found his family's store wagon under a bridge outside of Jonesboro. From the looks of it, they'd been shot in the wagon, wrote the farmer. Wegman tried not to wonder whether the farmer found bodies or just the blood. Most likely, hungry Union soldiers had attacked them when they refused to hand over their wagon filled with food and supplies. His parents had fled Atlanta, only to be run over by Sherman's March to the Sea. Another cruel waste, thought Wegman.

As he closed the letter, an image of his mother reading the Bible came to mind. "Be not deceived; God is not mocked: for whatsoever a man soweth, that shall he also reap," she'd read in her southern drawl.

A man of routine, Wegman waited until the store hours concluded. He calmly locked up the store and walked to the town's brand new saloon. He was going to get drunk.

In yellow paint, the sign out front said Wegmans General Store. Ten years ago, he'd been annoyed at the missing apostrophe. It was Sunday, and the town's new chapel attracted more people than ever. *Good for my business,* thought Wegman. *Unlike that new saloon.*

The door jingled as a man and young woman entered the store. The woman was plain, but the man looked at her lovingly. Newlyweds, thought Wegman.

Wegman collected the items the man requested—cornmeal, coffee, lard.

"It was the strangest horse I've ever seen," said the woman. "It looked half-starved too, poor thing."

"I told you love, I didn't see it," said the man. "I don't think you did either. It must be the desert sun playing tricks on you."

The woman huffed at her husband's dismissal. Wegman heard her say, "I know what I saw," under her breath.

Wegman wrapped the parcels in burlap. He was used to folks talking as if he weren't there.

"Thank you for your business," said Wegman. "Say, if I might ask your wife, where did you see this strange horse?"

The husband rolled his eyes and spoke before she could. "She says it was out by that lake, but I doubt she saw anything. Good day to you." The husband turned to leave, gently steering his wife out of the door.

Again, Wegman waited until store hours concluded. Looking around, his eyes landed on a length of rope. Grabbing it, his pistol, and the store key, he set out to find the camel.

The lake was his favorite place. Cattle raisers, buffalo, and the odd mustang often came here to water. It was the only dependable source for miles, and yellow wildflowers grew plentiful around its waters.

Wegman's feet dragged, and his heart pounded. *Why am I out here?* He stared out at the lake. In his mind, his mother's face merged with the faces of the widows he had stolen supplies from during the war.

He once had to take a pig from a skeletal woman. "We'll die without that," she'd pleaded. "There's nothing else." *We,* she kept saying. She'd clutched to the rope tied to the pig. Even something that small could feed ten soldiers. She was still holding it when she fainted, after Wegman had threatened her with his pistol. He'd left her there. The rope he held now was similar, the plaited fibers rough to the touch.

Just then, he noticed slow, strange movement across the lake.

There it was. A tall horse, drinking from the lake. He blinked. Was this real? The animal lifted its head higher. That long-necked beast was no horse. Wegman shaded his eyes against the setting sun. He squinted in the dusk. A camel. It was *really* a camel.

First walking numbly, Wegman started to run.

About ten feet away, Wegman could see its profile was skinny in the way that all wild things are. It had golden tufts of hair. It drank peacefully from the lake. Wegman's hand reached for his pistol. His heart was beating so fast.

He didn't know what to do. He needed this animal, but he was hardly a cowboy. Even if he were able to get a rope around it, how would he get it home?

Slowly, the camel brought its head around to look at Wegman. Its large brown eyes blinked slowly. If he could just get this one thing, the camel could save his business from ruin. He'd felt this sort of thrill of a challenge before, and with it, sadness flooded his heart.

Wegman turned away. He didn't want to look back. He couldn't take this thing and make it into another beast of burden. It had already escaped that fate once. He didn't want to be haunted by brown eyes. It was starting to get dark, so he headed home.

The next morning, he heard a clatter on his front step. Jimmy again. "Open up, Weg!"

When Wegman came down, Jimmy pressed his red face to the glass. Wegman opened the door to see not just Jimmy, but Wegman's horse tied to the store post.

Jimmy looked proud. "I know you were sad about losing your horse. So I won it back for you last night. That whole camel idea was ridiculous, anyway."

———————

—Julianne Metzger Taylor is a fiction writer originally from Stafford, Virginia. She served in the U.S. Navy for thirteen years as a photographer and public affairs specialist, deploying aboard the USS Iwo Jima (LHD-7), and served at the White House and the Pentagon. She has a master's degree from the University of Maryland University College in management and public relations. She's currently working on a Creative Writing M.F.A. from Kent State University. Julianne currently resides in Ravenna, Ohio, with her husband, Jaymes, stepchildren, Grayson and Ellie, and a very large, unruly Bernese Mountain Dog. This is her first fiction publication.

UNWANTED

ANTHONY WOOD

June 5, 1881
Tombstone, Arizona

I DIDN'T KNOW my name until I saw it on a wanted poster.

"The Notch-Eared Kid? Can't be me." I just stood there—gawking at the picture, marveling at the likeness, wondering at the name—at least until passersby slowed their pace to look at the poster on the wall then back at me with raised eyebrows.

A pesky boy, not ten years old with a mouth full of jawbreakers, yelled, "You sure look a lot like the face on that poster, mister."

"Ain't me, boy. Just looks like me. Go on, now, leave me alone."

I flipped the kid a nickel to quiet him, but it was too late. The boy ran off as a man started across the street, hand on his pistol. Women scurried away, dragging their children behind them.

Everything slowed down. Sounds of the street faded. Nothing moved, like time had stood still—for a moment. I racked my brain searching for anything familiar.

The man headed my way with the gun broke my trance. Halfway across, a stagecoach blocked his path. He yelled above the clattering wheels and horses hooves on the hardpan street, "Hold it there just a minute, son. I just want to ask you a few...." His tin star glinted in the afternoon sun said deputy. I didn't recognize this well-dressed, well-heeled man.

"Time to go." I snatched the poster from the bulletin board, pulled my hat down and jacket collar up, and slipped into the nearest alley. I worked my way through several alleys and sneaked behind a stack of grocery crates underneath a stairwell where I had a full view the street.

It took a minute to catch my breath. I might not have known my name, but I *did* know exactly where I was. The sign at the edge of town read Tombstone. Not the best place to be if you were a wanted man. Too many unemployed lawmen and troublesome outlaws lurking around, trying to make names for themselves. I *did* know that.

Most lawmen are just outlaws dressed up to look respectable, anyway. That one looked to be doin' all right for himself. I wasn't sure where that came from or how I knew it.

I stared at the picture and touched an old scab on my right ear. A tiny speck of blood colored my fingertip. How had I gotten that? It was a perfect semi-circle wound. Bullet must've clipped it. The old man who tried to bring me in had said as much. I put the pistol back in the front of my pants. My brain was still foggy.

I looked into the sky, then back at the poster, trying to remember. "For the life of me I can't... the Notch-Eared Kid?" I felt my ear again. Still hurt a little. Felt like it was maybe about a month old. I flicked the old scab away. No blood this time. Good, almost healed.

I traced the outline of the face on the poster. "So that's what I look like." I squinted at the writing. "Tarleton Griffin. Griffin sounds familiar, but Tarleton? Who'd name their kid *that?*"

A store clerk throwing trash into the alley startled me. I snatched my pistol from my pants, fast, like I knew what I was doing.

I glanced back at the poster.

THE NOTCH-EARED KID
WANTED DEAD OR ALIVE FOR MURDER.
A $500 REWARD WILL BE PAYED FOR
THE CAPTURE OF THIS MURDERER.
SEE MARSHAL BEN SIPPY,
TOMBSTONE, ARIZONA, TO COLLECT.

I shooed a fly away. "Huh, they spelled *paid* wrong." Without thinking, I rattled off a definition of the misspelled word like a preacher reading from the Bible. "Payed means tarring a seam on a ship with hot pitch to keep it from leaking." I shook my head to clear my thinking. "What? How'd I even know that? Why would I even care?"

A woman cried out, "My husband would never do such a thing, and you know it, Marshal Ben Sippy! Where is my dear husband, Tarle?"

The deputy who tried to stop me pointed down the alley where I'd escaped. "He went that way, Marshal."

I stuffed the wanted poster into my shirt.

A familiar voice that hissed like a snake, replied, "Don't worry, Dorcas. I'll take care of you now."

———

Mid-February 1881
Dragoon Mountains, Arizona

I HAD NO time to think. No time to draw my pistol. I was too late.

All I heard was a raspy voice in the dark. "Git 'em, Hound!"

A dog growled, grabbed my pants leg, and shook it like there was no tomorrow. A shot rang out. I grabbed my ear like it was on fire, and then it all went dark.

I woke to the rumbling and rocking of a two-wheeled cart like the Mexicans use. Practical, but the ride's rough as a cob. I don't know how long I was out. I tried to sit up, but the pain in my head put me right back down. I pulled at my ear—dust-caked sweat and blood.

"Dang, that hurts." It must've been a helluva lick. I jerked to get free, but my hands and feet were tied together with a rope that stretched tight against my chest.

Unable to see who was driving the cart and not knowing what else to do, I yelled out, "Hey, what'n the heck's goin' on?"

A cranky old man with a tattered hat turned and spat tobacco down the front of my shirt. He laughed, two of his yellow-stained teeth missing in front.

"Hush up, outlaw, or I'll turn Hound loose on you. Git 'em, Hound!"

A mixed-breed dog with one eye and a notched ear snarled and snapped just out of reach of my head, splattering saliva on my face.

"That's enough, Hound. He'll get his soon enough, heh, heh, heh."

"Who are you, old man?"

"Don't matter none. I'll be able to retire after I turn you over to Marshal Sippy, and my dawg and me'll be eatin' steak and sweet tater pie every night. What'cha say 'bout that, Hound?" The mangy dog howled like he was bayin' a raccoon up a tree.

I was caught and didn't even know what for. Feeling helpless, I kicked at the buckboard seat.

"Easy there, son. Ain't no sense you tryin' to escape." The old man threw his head back laughing. "Just like my old one-eyed dawg, Hound. You both got them notches in your ears."

I had nothing to say. I just stared at the ropes that bound me.

The old man turned and winked. "I guess the name fits. People'd know you anywhere with a mark like that, you murderin' outlaw devil."

"You can shut that up right now." For the life of me I couldn't remember my name or what had happened. "What do they call me, old timer?"

"Heh, heh, you don't know, do you? My bullet must'a sucked your brain to one side. Don't worry, you'll know soon enough when I bring you in for the reward."

"For what? I ain't no outlaw, and I sure as hell ain't no murderer. Who'd I kill?"

"You really don't remember what you did, do you?"

It was easy to see he was having too much fun toying with me. I decided to shut up and think about how I was going to escape without that dog getting at me.

"Yeah, cat's got your tongue now. Don't he? You ain't as smart as you think you are. Well, it don't matter much what you say no ways, boy. You just remember it was this here old man and his one-eyed, notch-eared old dawg who caught you. So you best just simmer down. Once we get through Mule Pass and into Tombstone, it won't take long for Marshal Ben Sippy to put a hanging rope over your head. You'll be the one shuttin' up then for sure. Unless, of course, you have some last words before your neck snaps like a kindlin' stick."

"Why don't you stop talkin'? I don't want to hear it."

The old man cackled again, and Hound howled. "And while you're swingin' in the breeze, I'll be throwing back shots of whiskey, and Hound will be gnawin' on a ham bone."

The old man laughed and slapped the reins on the mule's back. "Git 'em up there, Sally. He craned his neck. "Gettin' on toward nightfall. We'll camp at Sulphur Spring up ahead." The old man stood up and danced again, cackling like an old hen. "Yeah, boy, we'll be in Tombstone by noon tomorrow."

That name—Ben Sippy. For some reason, I could see his face in my mind.

THE OLD MAN'S snoring was atrocious. The dog's was worse. Dead to the world those two, but I was tied up tighter than a bull's behind at fly time.

There had to be a way to escape. I thought for a moment. *Atrocious?* How did I even know such a word?

As the campfire embers faded into the darkness, it came to me. The Confederate belt buckle I wore had a hidden blade. Where I got it, I couldn't remember. I was too young to have fought at Glorietta Pass. "Glorietta Pass," I whispered. A faint image of a gray-bearded man popped into my head. "Pa?"

I shushed myself.

I wrestled my hands to my belt, stretching and straining, but quiet as a field mouse so as not to wake the old man and Hound. With a click, the blade slipped from the buckle easy enough. In seconds, I was free of the ropes.

I rubbed my wrists to get the blood going and pushed with my palms to get up. A gun barrel poked the side of my head, and Hound snarled. I slapped it away quick as a rattler strike. The gun went off just as Hound jumped at me with jaws snapping. He fell dead with a groan. The bullet got him. I lunged at the old man's legs and toppled him. He fell hard and didn't move. His head hit a rock. He was dead.

My only thought was, "That's done. Now I can go find out what this is all about."

———

Noon, June 5, 1881,
Tombstone, Arizona

A WOMAN CRIED out, "You know my husband, Tarleton, ain't no outlaw, Ben Sippy. And he sure ain't no killer, damn you. And to think, you called him your best friend."

"I know that voice." I peeked through the steps of the stairwell. She was the prettiest woman I'd ever seen. I whispered, "She's my wife."

Marshal Sippy patted the air to calm the woman down. "I know, I know, Dorcas, but he *did* do time, and you know what they say—'Once an outlaw, always an outlaw.'"

"You should know, Ben Sippy. You're the worst of the bunch. Yeah, that's right. I done spread it all over town how you been stealin' the town's money. Did you forget I do your book keepin'?"

Sippy scanned the crowd. "That's just hearsay, Dorcas. My books are clean, unless you've been doctorin' them up."

Dorcas spat at the marshal. "You thievin' son of a—"

"Now, Dorcas, there's no need for such words. Your husband killed that old miner so he could take his—"

"He did no such thing, you lyin' devil."

A crowd surrounded Marshal Sippy as he took Dorcas's arm. "Let's talk somewhere quiet."

Dorcas slapped Marshal Sippy's face. "My Tarle ain't no murderer, and you know it. Yeah, he did a stretch at Yuma Prison for holdin' them horses when he was just fourteen. He didn't even know those boys were robbin' the bank. But he's done his time, and now, the whole town knows he's a law abidin' citizen. Good heavens, Ben, Tarle teaches your children at the schoolhouse."

"That don't mean he didn't kill—"

Dorcas whimpered for a moment. "Ben, you know what kind of man Tarle is. You boys hunt and fish together. Our families sit together at church. Our children play together."

Marshal Sippy hung his head. "I'm sorry, Dorcas, but I have to do my duty."

Her face turned red, and she shouted, "You got one damn thing right. You *are* a sorry rascal. You didn't even blink an eye askin' Tarle to stand with you when the lynch mob came for Johnny Behind the Deuce a month ago, did you? And beatin' Virgil Earp for City Marshal don't make you right. The whole town knows you bought and paid for that election. You'll never be half the man Virgil Earp is, or my husband, for that matter. You're just tryin' to make a name for yourself. What you did for Johnny Behind the Deuce don't mean squat. You're cut from the same bolt of cloth as that heathen, and you're both rotten."

Embarrassed, Marshal Sippy grinned at the crowd and clasped his hands together. "Now, Dorcas, you—"

"Don't *Dorcas* me, you adulterous sack of lice. What would your wife say to you carryin' on with me like this? You'll do well to remember who my husband is." Dorcas straightened her blouse and fixed her hair. "Now then, I demand to know where my Tarle is, Marshal Sippy."

Marshal Sippy sighed. "He's a wanted man on the run, Dorcas, and we're fixin' to catch him."

"Well, you better make him *un*wanted, Ben Sippy. He's only runnin' because you lied." Dorcas wiped the sweat from her brow and squinted. Not because of the glaring sun but from a realization. "My goodness, now I get it. Old Sam struck pay dirt just before he was found dead." Dorcas stepped back. "You had Old Sam killed so you could take his silver mine."

Marshal Sippy fanned his hands around at the crowd, looking for support. "We found blood on a McGuffey's Reader in the woods next to his body."

Dorcas growled like a she bear, "Yeah, the one you *stole* and put out there to be found."

"It was Tarle's book, after all." Sippy looked around at the crowd again, smiling.

"Yes, it was, but you ain't foolin' nobody, fool. He was teachin' Old Sam how to read. Do you want to know how I know that? I was there. My husband was teachin' me right alongside Old Sam the night you had him murdered."

"No two ways about it, Dorcas. Tarle will hang when we catch him." Sippy wrapped his arm around Dorcas, feigning sympathy. "It's okay, baby, I'm here. I'll take care of you now."

She snatched her shoulder away and spat. "Touch me again and you will lose that hand. What do you mean, 'baby?' You will address me as Missus Tarleton Griffin. Do you understand? I want my husband's name cleared, and now!"

My face flushed hot as a blacksmith's fire. I snatched the pistol from the front of my pants and aimed it at Sippy's head. I started for the marshal when a vise-like hand seized my shoulder.

"Hold on, Tarle." I turned to see the weathered face of a man I immediately recognized.

Virgil Earp.

"You know me?"

Earp grinned. "I do. Just be patient and let him sink his own boat, son. His time's been comin'."

Sippy carried on like a camp meeting preacher, but Dorcas refuted his every claim with the truth. It became clear that Sippy was in trouble, and he moved away from the crowd toward a backstreet.

Virgil barked, "All right, that ought to about do it. His time is up. Stay behind me."

Sippy turned to run, but Earp stepped from behind the stairwell where we'd been listening.

"That's far enough, Sippy. You're coming with me."

Sippy's deputy rushed across the street to aid, pulling his pistol. Earp jerked his revolver and planted it on the man's chest. "Just you move." The deputy took another step forward. Earp cocked the hammer on his Colt. "Please move again. It'll save Cochise County time and the cost of a court case." Earp turned to me. "Help me take these dirty rotten sacks of snakes down to the marshal's office, will you, Tarle?" I took the deputy's pistol, turned him around, and stuck his own gun in his back.

Sippy screamed, "You can't do this, Earp. You ain't the law."

"I will be by the time the door slams on your jail cell."

EARP PATTED ME on the back as I left the marshal's office. "I may call on you sometime, son."

The prettiest and toughest woman I'd ever seen waited for me across the street, tapping her foot.

I grinned. "Not before I get ahold of my wife, Mister Earp."

He laughed. "Good 'nough. See you when I see you."

The shock of the past hour's happenings brought memories back like a spring flashflood. It all came back to me. I remembered who I was. Dorcas met me in the middle of the street and threw her arms around my neck.

I stroked her silky auburn hair. "I guess now I'm unwanted, like you said."

Dorcas pulled me close for a kiss. "You'll always be a wanted man in my book, Tarle Griffin."

———◆———

—*Anthony grew up in historic Natchez, Mississippi, fueling a life-long love of history. Not long after high school, he lived and worked in Alaska for several years. He returned to the South and ministered for nearly three decades among the poor, homeless, and incarcerated before retiring to become a full-time author. His first novel, the critically-acclaimed Civil War epic* White & Black, *hit the shelves in 2021. Four sequels have followed, with two more scheduled for 2024.*

When not writing, Anthony enjoys roaming and researching historical sites, camping and kayaking on the Mississippi River, and being with family. Anthony and his wife, Lisa, live in Conway, Arkansas.

Cowboy by Frank Tenney Johnson

THE HUNT FOR AUGUSTINE CHACON

RICKEY PITTMAN

"Those whom life does not cure, death will."
—Cormac McCarthy

AFTER HE FINISHED his day's duties on the Ollney Ranch, Augustine Chacon rode to his employer's house. Ben Ollney, a prosperous Arizona rancher, sat in a rocker on the porch smoking a pipe. He studied Chacon for a moment and then said, "Nelly's not here, Augustine, if that's why you're here."

Chacon dismounted and walked toward the rancher. "I didn't come to see your daughter. I'm here to collect the wages you owe me."

"I'm glad you didn't come to see Nelly. I don't cotton to you seeing her. As far as your wages, you were paid last week."

"You or your foreman shorted me, Ben." Chacon took off his hat and ran his hands through his long dark hair. "I want the wages you promised when you hired me. Three months' worth."

"I wouldn't hold your breath waiting for any money from me. I can see you're liquored up again."

Chacon lifted his rawhide whip from the saddle's pommel. "You're going to pay me if I have to take it out of your hide."

"You ought to know better than to threaten me, Chacon." Ollney reached for his shotgun leaning on the wall next to him.

Chacon dropped the whip, drew his pistol, and shot the rancher dead. Five cowboys working in the barn and at the corral rushed over, each drawing his revolver, but Chacon calmly and deliberately raised his pistol and dropped all five one at a time. He mounted his horse and headed toward the border. After an hour's ride, he entered a canyon where he could water and rest his horse.

He had not been in the canyon long when he heard a voice shouting, "Augustine Chacon! This is Will Ollney, the brother of Ben Ollney—the man you killed today. I've got six men with me, and we've got you boxed in that canyon. We're going to take you back."

Chacon quickly considered his options. If he surrendered and they took him back, he knew he would hang. Also, Ollney's brother was angry enough that he would shoot him on sight, even if he did surrender. He decided to not make his capture easy for them. He mounted his horse—reins in his teeth and an extra pistol in his other hand. Securing his sombrero on his back with the stampede strap, he bent down over his horse and charged the posse. The cowboys were on foot in a group outside the canyon and started shooting. He shot down four of them before one bullet ripped through his left arm. Chacon rode on till dark when he stopped to tend to his arm and get some rest.

Two days later, the entire Ollney family was murdered in their sleep. Folks were sure that Chacon had committed this horrible crime.

They were right.

From the Ollney ranch, Chacon rode to his home in Sonora. There, he nursed his anger toward the *gringos* who had first tried to cheat him and then tried to kill him. "I will make them pay!" he said out loud. "The border will know the name and the anger of Augustine Chacon!"

The outlaw soon recruited others from both sides of the border to help him. There was no shortage of men who rode the owl hoot trail and were eager to work with him. He found Burt Alvord and Billy Stiles, both of whom, like Chacon himself, had once been peace officers. Joining him, too, were several Mexican *banditos*—Pilar Franco, Leonardo Morales, Pedro Lucero, and Francisco Blumna.

Chacon unleashed his gang upon the ranches and people on both sides of the border, rustling cattle and stealing horses in Arizona and selling them in Mexico or stealing stock in Mexico and selling it in Arizona. As their reputation grew, so did the violence of their crimes. Numerous rapes, robberies, and trafficking of stolen goods were attributed to the Chacon gang. The gang was lucky and always managed to avoid capture. Even the notorious man-hunter, Sheriff John Horton Slaughter, with his famous ten-gauge shotgun, had failed to catch them. Success fed their hubris, and their crimes became careless and blatant.

For a while, the gang established themselves in a cabin near the mining town of Morenci, Arizona. One cold December night, Chacon and two gang members were drunker than usual, and they had a notion that they needed some excitement and supplies. They jimmied open the door of McCormack's store. The outlaws silently moved through the store to the manager's sleeping area. Chacon looked at the sleeping Paul Becker and then stabbed him with his Bowie knife.

After he took the money from the store's moneybox, he said to his men, "That was easy. I thought he'd put up more of a fight. Gather all you want, and let's get back to our cabin."

AFTER THE OUTLAWS left, Paul Becker groaned and pressed his hand against the knife wound in his chest. He sat up, rose to his feet, and staggered through the store to the door still in his nightshirt. He could see lights in the saloon, so he staggered across the road and entered. Sheriff Davis sat at a table with two of his deputies. When the sheriff saw his bloodied nightshirt, he said, "Lord sakes, Paul! What happened to you?" They helped Becker into a chair, and one pressed a rag against the knife wound. Another deputy brought him a cup of water.

"Chacon and his men broke into my store, stabbed me, and robbed me. I let them think I was dead. I waited till they were gone before I got up. God, I'm losing blood, and I think I'm going to pass out."

"You just hang on," Wilson said. "My deputies will get you to the doctor."

The next morning, Sheriff Davis organized a posse, and they followed the bandits' trail to their cabin. When the posse neared the cabin, Chacon and his men burst out, took cover behind some rocks, and began firing their rifles and pistols.

The posse also took cover and returned the fire. One of the deputies, Pablo Salcido said, "Sheriff, let me go talk to Chacon and see if I can convince him to surrender. You know I worked with him at the Greene Ranch."

"Pablo, go ahead and try."

"*Augustine!*" Salcido called out. "It's Pablo Salcido. Hold your fire. I'm coming closer to talk to you. Don't shoot."

"Come closer, Pablo, my friend! Step out where I can see you."

When Deputy Salcido rose and moved closer, Chacon shot Salcido in the head, killing him instantly. The posse then rained a hailstorm of lead upon the desperados. One of the deputies later said he guessed they fired over three hundred rounds. Sheriff Wilson managed to shoot Chacon twice.

In the thick, acrid black powder smoke, Franco said to Morales, "I've only a few bullets left. Let's get to the horses and get out of here."

"What about Chacon?" Morales asked.

"Augustine took a couple of bullets. Look at him. I don't think he can ride."

The two rushed behind the cabin where their horses were tied and managed to ride around the posse.

When Sheriff Wilson saw the two outlaws fleeing, he said to his two remaining deputies, "Go get them. I'll watch for Chacon."

The fleeing bandits had not gone very far before the pursuing deputies shot them off their horses. After ensuring the outlaws were dead, the deputies slung the bodies across the outlaws' horses and returned. Finally, the posse moved in on the wounded Chacon and took him into custody.

"Sheriff Wilson," Chacon said weakly, "you are lucky that I could not hold my rifle, or you would be dead. My two *compadres* will come back for me."

"Not hardly, Chacon. My deputies killed them. Shot them down like the dogs they were. There's nothing waiting for you but the end of a rope."

"*Quizás.* We shall see, Sheriff. We shall see."

Sheriff Wilson reached down for Chacon's Colt. He spun the empty chamber, noticing the notches on its handle.

Chacon laughed. "It is a fine *pistola*, Sheriff. Take it as a gift from me. You see the thirty notches on the handle. Each one is for a *gringo*. On my next pistol I will have more. Who knows, you may have your own notch one day."

One of the deputies muttered, "One of those notches is for my friend Ben Ollney. I think we should just hang him now."

The sheriff spat. "You'll keep such thoughts to yourself. We'll take him to the Clifton jail. He'll hang as soon as we can find a judge."

———————

FROM THE CLIFTON jail, Chacon was taken to Solomonville to be tried for robbery, assault, and the murder of Pablo Salcido. Chacon claimed to be innocent of Salcido's murder. "He was my friend," he said. "How could I murder my friend? We were *vaqueros* together at a ranch for many years."

A Mexican citizen from Clifton testified on Chacon's behalf. *"El Peludo* is a good man, *señor.* He is generous and has helped the poor miners of our village and the mining camps many times."

Judge Owen T. Rouse dismissed the Mexican's testimony. "Mister Chacon is no Robin Hood. We know for a fact that he and his gang have committed many crimes against the Mexican people as well as against us in Arizona. And because of the eyewitnesses, Mister Chacon's plea of innocence is ridiculous. Augustine Chacon, you are sentenced to be hanged on June 18, 1897. Take the prisoner away." He stood as he pounded the table with his gavel.

The arresting sheriff and his deputies returned to Morenci, leaving Chacon and his destiny in the care of the town marshal.

Chacon's jail was built of ten-inch-thick *adobe* bricks with a double layer of two-inch pine boards, held together with five-inch nails. There was one barred window in his cell. Admirers gathered daily outside his cell window to talk with him. A *mariachi* group sang corridos in his honor as they strolled around town. Tall and thin, and a charmer, Chacon attracted throngs of female admirers who revered his looks and long dark hair. One lovely *senorita*, Alejandra, was especially attentive.

He called her close to the window and looked into her brown eyes with all the sincerity he could muster. "Alejandra, you are so beautiful! I thank you for seeing me. I need to ask you for a small favor."

"Anything, *Peludo*."

"Do you know what a hacksaw is?"

"*Sí, yo sé.*" She placed her small hands on the cell bars.

Chacon wrapped his hands around hers. "I need you to find a saw blade and bring it to me. Hide it inside something."

Later, Alejandra returned with a large family Bible, turned it sideways, and slipped it into his hands. "For you, *Peludo.*"

"*Gracias. Dame un beso.*"

Alejandra closed her eyes and rose up on her tiptoes and kissed him.

As soon as he was sure his jailer was asleep, Chacon went to work. As his musical entourage played loudly on into the night, he sawed on in the darkness of his cell.

Alejandra returned the next afternoon. "Ah, my love," Chacon said, "You are lovelier every time I see you. I am soon to be gone from here, but I will come back for you soon. I need one more favor. You know the night jailer?"

Alejandra nodded.

"He is a *gringo,* but he is not ugly. He will like you. Come back later tonight. Enter the jail and see if you can convince him to go with you into the back room for a while. I will soon be finished, but I cannot take the chance that he will hear me as I leave. Can you get me a horse?"

When Alejandra left the jail late that night, she walked by Chacon's cell window. The bars were on the ground, the cell was empty, and the horse she had left there was gone.

Chacon never saw or spoke to her again.

AFTER A SHORT enlistment in the *Rurales,* Chacon returned to his thievery, murder, robbery, rapes, and other crimes against Arizona citizens with a new gang, once again using his home, Sonora, as a base. Some of his crimes included the robbery of the casino in Jerome, the robbery of a stagecoach outside Phoenix, and the murder of various sheep shearers, hunters, and miners. There was also one botched train robbery that cost him one of his men.

Three years after Chacon's escape from the Solomonville jail, Territorial Governor Oakes Murphy directed Arizona Ranger Captain Burt Mossman to bring Chacon to justice. "He must no longer be allowed to enter Arizona and commit his crimes with impunity," the governor said. "Bring this villain in by any means. He must face Arizona justice and the sooner the better. I hear he and his band are in the Sierra Madre in Sonora. Go there and drag his ass back to Arizona. The Mexican authorities may put up a fight, but I'll deal with that. I know he has eluded you a few times, but enough is enough. I charge you to get him this time."

Mossman replied, "I will, Governor."

Mossman interviewed citizens, border residents, and even other outlaws who might know where Chacon's exact hideout was. Two outlaws who had ridden with Chacon agreed to help Mossman in exchange for a cash payment and help in having the charges against them lessened or dropped.

One of the outlaws was Burt Alvord.

With the help of his bribed outlaws, he and a deputy passed themselves off as outlaws and met with Chacon and Alvord at the Socorro

Mountain Springs in Sonora. They met on the pretense of helping Chacon steal horses from Greene's Ranch, just across the border.

Early the next morning at breakfast, Alvord whispered to Mossman, "I brought Chacon to you, but unless you act soon, you won't be able to take him. He's able to sense when something is wrong. I've done my share, and I don't want him to suspect me. Remember that if you take him, you have promised that the reward shall go to me and that you'll stand by me at my trial if I surrender. You sure want to be mighty careful, or he'll kill you. So long."

With that, he mounted his horse and left.

Chacon woke and asked Mossman, "Where is Alvord?"

"He went on ahead to take a look at Greene's Ranch. A cigarette, *por favor?*"

Chacon had just rolled a cornhusk cigarette. He handed it to Mossman and started to roll another. Mossman pulled a burning twig from the campfire and lit his cigarette. *"Gracias.* Are you ready to go after those horses on the Greene Ranch?"

"I've changed my mind. I'm going home. We will raid the ranch another time."

Then Mossman pulled out his Colt revolver. "You best put your hands in the air, Chacon."

Chacon said, "You make a joke, *un broma?*"

"No, I'm not joking. I'm a captain with the Arizona Rangers, and I'm bringing you back to the jail you broke out of. Now, throw your hands up or you're a dead man."

Chacon, with his customary coolness, smoked his cigarette and said, "I don't see as it makes any difference after he is dead whether a man's hands are up or down. You're going to kill me, anyway. Why don't you shoot?"

"Deputy, take his pistol and knife." After Chacon had been disarmed, Mossman said, "You can just sit there while the deputy saddles your horse. Get that lariat over there, Deputy. We're going to hog-tie him to the horse. Chacon, I wish I could say it will be comfortable, but I don't think you'll enjoy the ride."

Chacon was delivered once again to the Solomonville jail. He was still popular in the town, and a group of citizens petitioned the judge to have his hanging reduced to life in prison. Their request was denied, and he was sentenced to be hanged at 2:00 p.m. on November 21, 1902. He was kept under heavy guard this time, and there were no musicians or pretty *señoritas* allowed near the jail.

On the day of his execution, he enjoyed a good breakfast and a visit from a priest and from two friends. He was given a shave and a new black suit to wear.

Chacon strolled out of the jail calmly. A high *adobe* wall had been erected around the scaffold that had been built for him in 1897. About fifty people who had been invited to the event, waited for him.

Chacon ascended the gallows, shaking hands with some of his friends as if he were a folk hero. He then addressed his executioner. "*Señor,* as a last request before my death, may I have a cigarette and a cup of coffee?"

As soon as he drank down the coffee, he spoke in Spanish with an English interpreter, saying, "My good friends, *mis amigos!* I am innocent of the murder of my friend Pablo Salcido, though certainly, I have committed many other crimes." His speech went on for thirty minutes. Then, Chacon asked for and received another cigarette and cup of coffee. He addressed the judge saying, "*Gracias,* my friends. Now, may I please be allowed to live until three o'clock?"

The judge answered him curtly, "No." He motioned to the executioner with his hand. "Get on with it."

The executioner slipped the noose around Chacon's neck and

tightened it. Chacon scanned the faces of those invited to his hanging. *"Adios, todos mis amigos.* I hope you will see to the care of my wife and son."

His family later carved these words on his tombstone.

AUGUSTINE CHACON
1861 - 1902
HE LIVED LIFE WITHOUT FEAR,
HE FACED DEATH WITHOUT FEAR.
HOMBRE MUY BRAVO

———————————

—*Rickey Pittman, the Bard of the South, is a storyteller, author, songwriter, and folksinger. This Dallas native was the Grand Prize Winner of the 1998 Ernest Hemingway Short Story Competition. Pittman presents his historical songs and stories presentations at schools, libraries, museums, and Celtic festivals throughout the South.*

Pointing Out the Trail by Charles Marion Russell

JOHNNY REB AND THE GUNFIGHT AT THE O.K. CORRAL

JAMES A. TWEEDIE

IF HE WAS the real deal, I should win a Pulitzer Prize for the story, a Nobel prize for the medical implications of my encounter, and an entry in the *Guinness Book of World Records* for having stumbled across the oldest man in the world. If he wasn't the real deal, then I should at least win a Spur award from the Western Writers of America—and maybe even a Hugo for the fantasy and science fiction parts woven into the story.

He said his name was Johnny. If he had a last name, he never let on what it was.

When I first met him in May of 2021, he was drunk and puking on a sidewalk in downtown Portland, Oregon—the gauntest, longest-bearded, grayest, most wizened, shriveled up, emaciated bag of human bones I had ever seen.

"You all right?" I asked as my shadow stretched across his back in the late afternoon sunlight.

The question was inane, of course, because whether he was willing to fess up to it or not, the man was clearly not "all right."

But I meant well, and my concern for his health was sincere since he looked to be as close to death as a person can get without actually being stretched out on a cold slab at the morgue.

The man rolled over onto his back and stared up at me with two pale eyes that sent a chill down my spine.

"Blue or Gray?" he asked with a voice that rasped like a hacksaw cutting through a piece of galvanized steel pipe.

I ignored the question and asked if he would be able to stand up and walk with me to the Starbucks across the street.

"Knew a man named Starbuck during the war," he groaned as he stood up. "Bragged that Melville borrowed his daddy's name for the First Mate in *Moby Dick*."

I'm not the smartest cookie in the jar, but I knew that *Moby Dick* was published in the 1850s, and if Melville....

The dates did not match up with the man who was now standing next to me, swaying back and forth as if he were about fall back onto the sidewalk.

My brain started working like a calculator.

Let's see, I thought, *if the son's father knew Herman Melville in the 1840s and if Johnny knew the son... uh... that would make Johnny at least....*

The answer I came up with didn't make sense, so I asked the first question that came to mind.

"What war are you talking about?"

Johnny slowly stretched himself as ram-rod straight as he could and said, "'War between the States,' whats the Northern folks call the 'Civil War.'"

Without checking for traffic, he stepped off the curb and began staggering across the street through the tail-end of the afternoon rush hour.

As I followed alongside, he kept talking.

"Hell," he spat, "that war was the most *un*Civil war ever dreamed up by the Devil hisself. More of a nightmare than a dream. Blood, bodies, and parts of bodies lying everywhere after a battle... and the screams... and the smell of black powder and death all mixed together...."

When we reached the other side of the street, he stopped and looked me in the eye. "That's why I like the wine. It's cheaper than the whiskey, and it takes away the smell just the same... and sometimes the memories...."

Now, I happen to love tall tales, and this one had already started to grow taller than Pinocchio's nose was long. I had some time to spare and figured spending two fifty to buy Johnny a cup of coffee might turn out to be a bargain if he was able to stay awake long enough to keep spinning the yarn.

"Lost the big toe on my right foot in defense of Petersburg on July 30, 1864," he continued as we sat at a table waiting for my name to be called by the barista. "General Lee and the rest of us boys knocked them Union bastards back on their heels, but when my toe came off, my foot turned green, and that near put me in the grave for the next eight months of the siege."

As he paused, he looked across the table, pulled his earlobe, and asked if I wanted to see where his toe used to be.

"Tito!" the barista called, which saved me from answering the question. But as I stood to collect our coffee, Johnny grabbed my sleeve.

"Folks think I'm drunk," he whispered in a voice loud enough for nearly everyone in the room to hear, "and I reckon you do, too, 'cause I stagger when I walk. But it ain't the wine—at least not always. Most times it's because of the toe. I haven't walked in a straight line since...."

When I came back with the coffee, Johnny was snoring with his head lying on the table and his beard hanging half-way to the floor. I poked him in the shoulder and he woke up quicker than I had expected. He sat up, grabbed the coffee out of my hand, and started gulping it down as if his life depended on it. My coffee was too hot for me to take anything but a stray sip or two, but the old man didn't seem to suffer any ill effects.

"Where was I?" he mumbled as he looked across the table and seemed to remember why he was sitting in Starbucks drinking coffee with a stranger named Tito.

For some reason that I can't explain, he looked and sounded younger than before, less gaunt, with hints of the young man he must have once been.

"You were telling me about your toe and Petersburg," I said.

With that prompt, he started talking as quick as a sprinter leaving the blocks when the starting gun goes off. "After General Lee quit Petersburg and Richmond, we slogged south a ways until there was nowhere else to go, and then the world that me and the boys had been fighting and dying for came to an end. Just like that... it was gone."

He paused as if he was fishing for a piece of memory that didn't want to take the bait.

After several moments, he tipped his head to the side.

"I heard Grant wouldn't take his sword—General Lee's, I mean. Gave it right back and then that was the end of it—the end of the war and the way of life we'd known since we were pups.

"It was all gone when I got home. Sheridan had burned it to the ground, crops and all. We never had no slaves and worked the farm ourselves, but it was no use to pick up where we left off. Big brother, Robbie, was dead at Fredericksburg, and Pa was too old to hold a plow. So I kissed Ma goodbye and headed west, thinking I'd hook up with one of the irregular boys I heard about in Missouri named Clement, who'd fought with Anderson and mebbe Quantrill a'fore that. It was all just rumors and word of mouth back then.

"It took me nearly two years to get there, and by the time I did, Clement was dead, but the gang he'd started after the war was still there with the James boys and Younger brothers still angry at what the Union folks had done to their families and wanting to get revenge. I felt the same and joined the gang just before they robbed a bank in Richmond, Missouri.

"We took four thousand dollars, but some poor kid was shot in the head, and Jesse or one of the others shot the boy's father dead when he ran over to hold his dying son in his arms. None of it seemed right to me, but I didn't say anything, and I didn't get any share in the loot, either. After that, they went on to rob trains and such, but I didn't like the killing and the way they went about things, so I quit and left Missouri for Kansas."

With that, he abruptly stood up and said, "Gotta pee."

On his way back to the table, he picked up a scone and a second cup of coffee, all the while pointing across the room, as if telling the barista that I was going to pay for it.

When he sat down, he looked younger than ever, with his face all fleshed out and his beard looking like he'd rubbed in a tube of Grecian Formula and given it a trim while he was in the restroom.

I met with Johnny at least a dozen times over the next three months, and I never saw him as an old man again. From then on, he never looked a day older or a day younger than he looked when he came out of that Starbucks men's room.

As I sat and listened to him over the following weeks, I began taking notes as he told story after story of where he'd been and what he'd done since April 6, 1843, the day and year he claimed to have been born on a farm near Rincon, Georgia, twenty miles north of Savannah.

He said that over the years he changed his mind about slavery and the South, but, even so, he was still proud of what he'd done as a Reb.

"For most folks the war was about slavery, no doubt about it," he said. "But for me it was about Ma and Pa, our home, and the farm. That's all I was fightin' for, and when we lost that, I guess—at the time—it didn't matter to me one way or the other what happened to the slaves.

"But," he added, "during the Civil Rights days in the 1960s, I took a bus down South and marched in some of them demonstrations. Got my picture in *Life* magazine with me in the background during a sit-in at a Woolworth's lunch counter. 'Course, I looked younger then and didn't have a beard...."

As he talked, it turned out he had met more people and been present at more historical events than Forest Gump.

"After Missouri," he said, "I spent thirteen years herding cattle back and forth across Kansas until 1880 when I got tired of the dust and bought a one-way ticket on the first train to travel straight through from Kansas City to Santa Fe.

"As I recall," he continued, "Santa Fe was a crowded stinkhole swarming with dirt poor Indians selling pots and baskets and Spanish ladies parading about in long, embroidered dresses and shawls. And there were cattlemen, too, and cowboys—not the kind in the movies, but what we called cowboys back then were the rustlers, robbers, and cheats—murdering thugs who controlled just about everything outside of the cities and towns that were springing up everywhere like weeds— places like Las Vegas, New Mexico, and newer towns like Tombstone, Arizona, where someone discovered enough silver to trigger a stampede of miners, prospectors, businessmen... and cowboys.

"When I heard that Wyatt Earp and his brothers had gone down to Tombstone to clean the place up, I knew I had to see it for myself. I'd first met Wyatt in the Long Branch Saloon in Dodge City when he was a deputy marshal or some such thing that gave him a badge and a license to carry a gun wherever he went. But he wasn't a shooter like Luke Short, the man who owned the saloon, or even his brother, Virgil, who had a reputation bigger than Wyatt's at the time.

"I'd heard about there being a friction of sorts between Virgil, who was the Tombstone town marshal, and the county sheriff whose name was Behan, or some such. Virgil protected the town from the cowboys, and Behan was partial to them for some reason.

"Anyways, when I get into town on October 25, 1881, the friction is heating up with Ike Clanton and some of the other cowboys threatening to kill Virgil and his brothers the next time they get them out in the open. Clanton says he's going to kill their friend, Doc Holliday, too, and when I walk into the Alhambra Saloon around midnight, I see Morgan trying to keep Holliday and Clanton from going after each other right then and there.

"Holliday, now he's a dandy, or acts like one. But he's mean and drunk, and I get the feeling that if they both have guns, old Doc shoots Ike down like a dog without giving him a chance to draw. At least that's how I see it at the time.

"I find out later that the Earps are enforcing a law that says folks staying in town have to check their weapons at a hotel or with the sheriff until they're fixin' to leave, so I guess that's the only thing that keeps Doc and Ike from shooting each other on the spot.

"I don't talk to Morgan that night, and since Wyatt walks Doc back to his room and then goes home to his own bed, I don't get to talk to him either. But Ike and Virgil walk across the street and spend the rest of the night playing cards at the Occidental Saloon. I sit in for a few hands and talk with both of them, and although Ike is drunker than a pickled pepper, they seem to have set aside the bad feelings, at least for the cards. As I'm getting up to leave, Ike says something about someone named Benton or Benson, or some such, and Virgil, he stands up and tells Ike that if he wants to live till morning, he'd best be keeping his mouth shut.

"The next morning things go from bad to worse when Ike picks up his pistol and rifle from where he's checked them in and staggers around town telling folks he's going to shoot Holliday and take out an Earp the next time he sees one.

"Just before one o'clock p.m., I catch up with Wyatt. He's acting all distracted like, and we're talking about Dodge City, when Morgan and Virgil see Ike breaking the rule by wearing his pistol. So Virgil comes up from behind and hits Ike over the head with his Smith & Wesson and Wyatt's called over to take him to the local court where Ike pays a hefty fine before the judge lets him go.

"I'm waiting outside the court for Wyatt to come out, and when he does, before I can restart our conversation, he walks straight into some cowboy named Tom McLaury, and they get into an argument over whether Tom's armed or not. But after Wyatt sees him wearing a gun, he pistol whips him to the ground and tells him to turn in his gun someplace like he's supposed to do.

"After this, Wyatt tells me that no good is going to come of it, and he has a bad feeling that things are going to get hotter before they cool off.

"Right about then Tom's brother, Frank, rides into town with Ike's little brother, Billy. When they hear about how their brothers were pistol whipped by the Earps, they get to steaming and meet up with Ike and Tom at the O.K. Corral without turning in their guns.

"While we're talking, word comes to Wyatt that Ike still has his guns and is still swearing that he's going to kill Doc and all three of the Earp brothers.

"About two thirty, Wyatt sends me over to Fly's Boarding House to fetch Holliday, but when I gets there, he's already gone. When I come out, I see the Clanton and McLaury brothers and two other cowboys standing in a narrow empty lot next door, along with a couple of horses. Ike is still drunk and acting mean. As I walk past on my way to find Wyatt, Sheriff Behan walks up and has a few words with the boys before he turns and joins me in walking west on Fremont Street where we run into Doc Holliday and the three Earps coming from the opposite direction.

"We meet in front of the O.K. Corral, and Virgil tells Behan that he's on his way to tell the cowboys to turn in their guns.

"I hear the sheriff say, 'I just met up to disarm them' or words to that effect. I take it to mean he tried to do it but hadn't had much success in the matter.

"But Wyatt and the others take it to mean that the sheriff has actually disarmed them, so when they walk up to the Clantons and Mc-Laurys, they aren't expecting them to be armed. But they are, and just like Wyatt said, 'No good' was what came of it.

"As the sheriff disappears down the street, Wyatt waves me away, as if to warn me to stand back, which I do.

"What happens next happens so fast it's hard to keep up, especially from a distance.

"The men aren't more than ten feet apart from each other, and words are said, but I can't hear what they are. I see Billy throw his right arm up in the air, and Frank goes for his gun, and Virgil's arm goes up, and I hear him yell, "No, I don't mean that!" And then Wyatt makes a move, and I hear at least two gunshots go off at the same time with black powder smoke rising from where Wyatt and Billy Clanton are standing. There is a pause for a second as Frank McLaury doubles over, and then, as all hell breaks loose, Ike runs up to Wyatt who pushes him away, and then Ike runs off and disappears into the boarding house without firing a shot. The other two cowboys run off in the other direction, and Tom McLaury runs behind his horse—I can't tell if he is shooting or not or if he even has a gun—but it looks like he is reaching for the rifle sheathed next to his saddle when Doc steps around the horse and blows him to hell with a close-up blast from a short-barrel shotgun aimed directly below his upraised arm. Tom then staggers across the street and drops dead. Frank backs off shooting until he falls dead on the street with a bullet in his head.

"I can't tell if Billy Clanton fires the first shot along with Wyatt or not, but I see him holding a gun in his left hand after his right hand and arm are hit. He falls against the wall, which props him up until he stops shooting and slides to the ground, not yet dead, but dying.

"The whole thing takes less than thirty seconds, and when it's over, Billy Clanton and Tom and Frank McLaury are dead. Virgil is still standing but with a hole in his leg, and Morgan, who went down with a wound that crossed his back chipping off a bit of his backbone and both shoulder blades, ends the fight back on his feet emptying his gun into Billy. Doc's holster and hip are grazed by a bullet, and Wyatt turns out to be the only one not hit and unhurt.

"The next morning, as soon as I hear the Earps are going to live, I say goodbye to Wyatt. There's no reason for me to stay, and Tombstone doesn't look like a place where I want to settle.

"Years later, I meet up with Wyatt in San Francisco, and we compare notes about the fight. Ike Clanton give one version of what happened, and Wyatt give another, and it turned out that Wyatt and me had seen it the same way, except for me not being sure if Tom McLaury had taken any pistol shots before Doc finished him off. If he had a gun, someone must have taken it because it wasn't found after the fight.

"When I ask him about why Virgil had gotten all riled up when Ike mentioned the word Benson or Benton, Wyatt pulled his watch out of his pocket and said, 'Nice seein' you again, Johnny, but I gotta go.'

"Later, I got upset when a book called it the 'Gunfight at the O.K. Corral' because the fight didn't take place there at all. The movies kept up the lie, but history seems to have finally got it right—although with all the black powder smoke, not even the men doing the shooting could see everything that happened while it was going on.

"And in any case, Wyatt wasn't the hero. He wasn't even the marshal. Virgil was the marshal, and Morgan, Wyatt, and Doc were just sworn deputies."

The next time I met up with Johnny, he started off by saying how he happened to be at the Lakehurst Naval Air Station in New Jersey on May 6, 1937, when the *Hindenburg* caught fire.

I wanted to hear more, but Johnny didn't show up for our next meeting, and I haven't seen him since.

Who he is, or was, and where he is now, I have no idea.

At the end of the summer, I took the time and trouble to fly back to Savannah where I found a church baptismal record for a baby named John Creigh McNaughton, born in Rincon, Georgia, on April 6, 1843.

I also found the name Robert McNaughton on a list of Confederate war dead from Fredericksburg.

But all of that could have just been a coincidence.

———————————————

—James A. Tweedie has lived in California, Utah, Scotland, Australia, Hawaii, and presently next to a Pacific Ocean beach in southwest Washington. He has published six novels, three collections of poetry, and one collection of short stories with Dunecrest Press. His western stories and poetry have appeared in both print and online media. He claims to be an optimist.

Indian Maid at Stockade by Frederic Remington

TALES ⚜ PADRE ROJO

BARBARA L. CLOUSE

THE NIGHT WAS was cold and quiet. Blackness surrounded him like a heavy blanket. Thick clouds hiding the moon suddenly drifted away, and the golden ball brightened up the desert landscape.

Slowly, on all fours, the boy crept down the dry riverbed, gravel crunching softly beneath his touch. Low growing palo verde trees, hugging the riverbank, loomed ahead, and he scampered up the side of the ravine and hid under the twisted branches.

He searched the darkness as he rose to his feet, peering into the shadows of the night. The lad sensed movement in the brush on the far hillside, so he crouched low again.

Then he felt it—the tremor shaking the earth and the green branches of the tree above, then lightning from a cloudless sky, booming over the desert, getting closer—coming his way.

Grasping the spear and bow at his side, the youngster rushed from the cover of the tree and jumped into the arroyo. The sand grabbed at his feet as he scurried wildly to the opposite bank and climbed swiftly to the top.

Perched on the rocky edge of the cliff, he stood frozen, searching for the moving shadow. He sniffed the cool, dry air and caught the strong odor of the approaching animal and quickly placed an arrow in his bow.

Suddenly, roaring thunder shook the ground once more, and the black spirit was before him. The large, ferocious beast was running, charging under the moon's light. Black as midnight, he was breathing hard, his breath foggy in the chilly night.

Surprised, the boy stepped backward and stumbled over his spear, dropping his drawn bow. Frantically, he tried to regain his footing, then he fell into oblivion... falling... falling... falling.

GABRIEL SAT UP with a jerk, perspiration covering his face as he trembled on the bed. Blinking and rubbing his brown eyes, he looked around the small room, and the familiar objects came into focus.

He sighed deeply and lay back against the pillow. "So real, this time," he mumbled. Pushing a lock of dark hair from his forehead, the boy stared at the log ceiling above and tried to remember details of the vision. Several times in his life, the thundering beast had returned to haunt him. Even at fourteen years, he continued to fear the black thunder in his dreams. It was time to find out the reason why.

He turned over and yanked the quilts up around his chin. "I'm going to visit *Padre Rojo*," he said softly into the pillow.

LEAVING SPAIN WAS easy for Father Frederick Rhedd. He traveled to the west coast of the Americas to the Spanish Colony called

California. He had studied history with a church elder in Pamplona, plus languages and horticulture. At an early age, the young man had shown great interest in farming and ranching. He made a vow to himself that he would pursue this dream and maybe even become a priest or teacher himself.

Those years long ago had passed by quickly. Now as an old man, the Catholic priest recalled his youth was always in service to others. He became a builder of *adobe* missions and a teacher for children orphaned during the Civil War. He avoided the political desire of many in the clergy. Instead of pursuing status in the hierarchy of the church, he spent his time helping to find families for the homeless.

That is how Father Frederick Rhedd discovered the old *adobe* chapel in the desert community of Elfrida, located in the southeast corner of Arizona Territory. Close to the Mexican border, the nuns and priests who tended the orphanage in this forgotten place were dedicated to teaching and healing the broken children in their care. His friends called him *Padre Rojo*.

GABRIEL VANN BECAME an orphan at age seven. He lived with his family in Indian Territory when the War of the States began. Men in gray uniforms came to their tribal village on the banks of the Arkansas River. They ordered all the men in the little community of Gritts to find a horse and follow them. All the children were gathered with the women in the small rural church. The Confederate soldiers locked the door and told them to stay inside, or they would shoot them.

Gabriel remembered the sound of men outside shouting to the gray suits. A few guns fired quickly, and the women screamed in fear.

Quietness fell over the assembled crowd inside the church, as they all went to their knees in prayer. No sounds came from their men. Evening came, and the children fell asleep in the pews. A loud thunderstorm in the middle of the night woke the children. The women soothed their fears, and Gabriel's newly adopted mother comforted him. The woman was Mrs. Vann, the pastor's wife. After the storm passed, she walked up to the front door of the church and turned the handle. The wide door opened slowly, and she peeked outside.

"Praise the Lord," Mrs. Vann whispered. "They're all gone."

The women and their children dispersed and cautiously exited the old building. There were no bodies outside, and murmurs of thankfulness echoed in the cool night air.

Gabriel thought about that night often and the terror of the loud storm in the darkness of the church. The image of all the soldiers with guns ordering the men around sent memories of confusion through the young boy's heart and soul. His nightmares began that night, in the beginning of his seventh year.

THE SMALL COMMUNITY in Bonita Canyon, in the Arizona Territory, was home to the relocated families from that frightening night in Gritts. Pastor John Vann's brother, Simon, had organized a wagon train to head westward, away from the looters and thieves that began to raid and pilfer in the area known as Indian Territory.

Within the month of preparation for their departure, the women rejoiced at the return of their husbands. Pastor Vann had accompanied the men to the little church, still standing unharmed from the cruelty of the warring groups around them. Most buildings, and especially churches, were often burned and never rebuilt. The Gritts

Indian Baptist Church was spared, so prayers of thankfulness blessed the small congregation.

While returning home after the encampment with the gray coats, Pastor John and his flock of Christian Indians met two traveling priests. Father Frederick Rhedd and Father Antonio Vega spent several nights with the group. The two men told Pastor John about the need for farmers and ranchers to help feed the soldiers who helped keep the peace in the treacherous Arizona Territory.

Forts had already been built in those areas housing the mounted armies to protect the residents and settlers from the raids of the Apache and Comanche Indian tribes. Wars with the tribal populations plus the threat of Mexican thieves and rustlers had subsided. A plan for settlements in the Sulphur Springs Valley was an invitation to those interested in bringing their ranching and farming skills to help provide the resources for the multiple soldiers still located in the Bonita Canyon.

Father Rhedd and Father Vega agreed to accompany the congregation from Indian Territory to their new home in the west. The priests bragged about the abundant acreage of native grasses and rivers teeming with fish. They shared their knowledge of the pleasant climate in the remote area of the Territory of Arizona.

———◆———

AT FOURTEEN, GABRIEL Vann was a tall, lanky boy, well-versed in working with horses and cattle, repairing fences, cutting wood, and plowing fields. After the families from Indian Territory arrived and set up camp in their new location in the Sulphur Springs Valley, the men gathered to make the plans in their farming venture come true.

"Gentlemen and friends," Pastor John began, "we have praised the

Lord for our successful journey to this new land and pray that the seasons of this dry place will cooperate with our efforts."

"Amen," the crowd mumbled.

"If the rains do not come, as we have planned, we have men here who are skilled in farming by irrigation canals and ditches," added Pastor John.

"Amen," the men echoed.

"Excuse me, Brother," said Simon, "is this a prayer meeting or a discussion about what crops we're going to plant?"

"Thank you, Simon," said John. "We've mapped out this valley and have chosen the vegetables, grains, and fruit trees that we brought with us to plant. Everyone has chosen the fields of their interest and drawn lots on our choices. Well, that's enough for today. Looks like Missus Vann has the picnic ready. Let's eat!"

Gabriel helped the older travelers find a place to sit and helped carry their food. He finally got a chance to eat and joined Pastor John's older brother Simon.

"Uncle Simon, ain't I old enough to get a job in the mines at Bisbee? We sure need the money around here. All the men have important jobs to do, keeping the farming done and the crops watered."

"Gabriel, you're just as important as they are. Your skills with the horses and mules keep my old bones from getting cracked, son. You have become our best hunter of all the small game and occasional deer that wander into this valley. Also, you catch more fish in the Bonita River than any of us old timers." He laughed and patted the boy on the back.

"May I go to Elfrida to visit with Father Rhedd? Since he returned to his church, I have missed our talks about his travels around the world."

"I don't see why not, but that's a long journey for someone so young, Gabriel. However, we did promise his church that we would share our seeds for winter crops. I'll help you pack the wagon."

Gabriel was excited about the short trip away from his daily chores at the ranch and in the fields, even if for only a few days and nights. The Sulphur Springs Valley felt like a safe camp in the wilderness of Bonita Canyon. Simon insisted that Father Antonio Vega accompany Gabriel to the *adobe* village of Elfrida, which was close to the Mexican border. The priest had been a welcome visitor to their farms and knew the winding paths of the area. Gabriel called him *Padre Tonito*, which caused a smile to brighten his somber face.

FATHER VEGA DROVE the wagon into the *adobe* walled grounds of the old mission chapel in the small community. He tied the mules to the hitching post and began unpacking the burlap bags in the wagon.

Father Rhedd walked across the tiled courtyard to greet them.

Gabriel lifted several parcels from the supplies and handed them to the priest. "I kept my promise of bringing you these seeds from our farms, *Padre*."

The grey-haired man hugged the boy, his face filled with a huge smile. *"Gracias,* Gabriel!"

"Muchas gracias, Padre Rojo, for your friendship and guidance."

Gabriel handed over the last sack and smiled at the old man. He turned to the sound of laughter and screams nearby. He looked behind him and saw a group of young children walking from the chapel to a playground area.

"Who are they?"

The priest handed the supplies in his arms to Father Vega, who nodded and walked into the building.

"These are the orphans who attend classes at our school," explained the priest. "They were brought here from our mission in Mexico, just across the border."

"So, they live here with you, go to school, and then what?"

"Hopefully, they will be adopted by a local family. Their parents were killed in the Indian wars or by other conflicts in their country. They had no family members to take care of them."

"Just like me," whispered Gabriel.

"Yes, just like you."

"Do you think they have bad dreams like I do?" asked Gabriel.

"I'm sorry to say, they do, my son. That's why we are here, to share the stories of the Bible to encourage them. We provide a safe and peaceful place with the love and joy they need."

"Sounds like a good home to have until they find their own."

"We hope so, Gabriel," he said.

They walked across the graveled yard to a shady arbor of vines and flowers growing next to the chapel's side doors.

"We are grateful for your gifts of seed plus all the vegetables and fruits you have provided, but that's not the real reason you made the dusty trip, is it?" asked *Padre Rojo.*

"No, sir," said Gabriel, "the black thunder has returned to my dreams, *Padre.*"

"Shall we sit for a while?"

THE FOLLOWING DAY, *Padre Rojo* joined *Padre Tonito* and Gabriel on their slow trip back to the Vann encampment in Bonita Canyon. That first evening, with their campfire secure, the three rested on their bedrolls and stared into the night sky.

"I know this beast of your dreams," said *Padre Rojo*. "I've known him since I was your age, Gabriel. He comes like a phantom in the night—trying to rob us of our rest, our peace, and our faith. He is called Fear—crawling into our minds with untruths, taking the smiles out of our days, and saddening our hearts to the joy in life. But Fear is a coward.

"I have lived with this kind of darkness my whole life. My father was a tortured man, and as a result, caused those around him much anger. Like those in my father's culture, he demanded seven sons from his wife, mi madre. He wanted the status of royalty in the village, where horned animals were guided down the cobblestone streets, to chase the young men in a frightening maze of fear and blood, all the way to the bull ring. There the *matadors* would dance with the angry bulls until the animals were maimed and killed in front of an audience.

"*Sí*, it was a blood bath in our small village, covering the ancient stones with the scent of blood and fear—not only from the bulls, but from those young boys who ran for their lives."

"Thundering black beasts, causing fear in your dreams."

"*Sí*, for both of us."

"Did your mother have seven sons?" asked Gabriel.

The priest tossed another piece of wood on the campfire and smiled. "She certainly tried, *mi amigo.*"

"Tell me about your family," urged Gabriel.

The man glanced over at his old friend, who had waited patiently across the flames of the fire.

"Most men who are called to wear these robes want to forget their past," said *Padre Tonito*. "Some hide from their memories, their homes, and their families."

"Forgive me," whispered Gabriel.

"Maybe another time, Gabriel. Get some sleep," added *Padre Rojo*.

The second evening of their journey, *Padre Rojo* looked westward as they rested the two mules pulling the wagon and made camp for the night. The small stream nearby was unusually full of rolling, muddy water. The three travelers knew what that meant on the desert floor—storms in the mountains.

"*Padre Rojo*, should we seek higher ground?" asked Gabriel.

The two priests nodded at the same time and hurried to relocate their gear and the animals. A bluff to the east was a short distance away, and they urged the mules to climb the slanted ground to the top of the overlooking cliffs.

"Let's set up our tent, in case the rains come this way," suggested *Padre Rojo*.

"I'll look for firewood for our campfire," added Gabriel.

The three worked silently, as they prepared for the possibility of a storm in the night. As the sun was setting, far away to the west, the sky changed from a golden yellow to a deep orange, then plunged the desert into darkness. The rumblings of thunder miles away echoed across the dry ground, and the smell of rain filled the air.

Gabriel sat by the campfire, staring into the flames. "*Padre Rojo*, I've been scared of storms since I was a young boy. I guess it's the loud sound of thunder and lightning. Do you think it's because of what happened at our old church back home?"

Padre Rojo looked over at *Padre Tonito*, who nodded.

"I believe so, Gabriel. You had just lost your parents, relocated to another home, and then your community was raided by the gray coats."

"Even though you had others to comfort you," added *Padre Tonito*, "the traumatic events of that night were made worse because of the storm."

"In my case," *Padre Rojo* shared, "my father's insistence that his sons participate in the running of the bulls caused such terror in young men. It's difficult to admit how afraid I was, Gabriel. That's why I understand your fears."

"Some of us were spared the humiliation," said *Padre Tonito*. "My father believed the whole tradition was foolish. He took me, as a young boy, to pray in the chapel for those who were forced to take part."

"Those were the horned animals used in the bull ring for the *matadors?*" asked Gabriel.

"*Sí*, who's behavior is just like the black bulls of Mexico—fierce, violent and deadly," explained *Padre Rojo*.

"*Ay, Dios mio,*" said Gabriel.

"Amen!" replied the priests.

The campfire was only glowing embers, and the coffee was cold, but the trio remained alert. They lay in their bedrolls and waited for the anticipated storm. A slight breeze brought another smell in the dark to the men poised on the bluff above the creek below. The pungent odor of animals and stockyards filled the cool air, and the men stood up quickly.

"I can smell them," said Gabriel.

"Yes. They're not very far away," said *Padre Rojo*.

"Who would be herding steers in the dark?" asked *Padre Tonito*.

"Besides thieves?" replied *Padre Rojo*.

A large streak of lightning flashed across the sky above their camp. The thunder boomed overhead soon after the bright yellow light. The spooked herd shrieked, and their cries echoed in the desert stillness.

"Over there." *Padre Rojo* shouted to be heard. "It could be the herd of cattle from Mexico."

"I heard about that. Camp Supply at Elfrida bought them," said *Padre Tonito*.

"What are they doing this far north?" asked Gabriel.

"They must have been scattered by the storms," said *Padre Rojo*.

"*Padre*, we need to turn them, or they will drown," hollered Gabriel. "Look down there, the creek is over its banks."

Gabriel knew what to do. He had been working on ranches long enough to know how to handle horses or cattle. He untied one of the mules from their tether at the wagon. He rigged a bridle and reins for the mule from the rope and reached for *Padre Tonito*'s large straw hat. "I'm going to turn the herd, *Padre*! I know what to do!"

Padre Rojo and *Padre Tonito* hollered at the boy. The rolling thunder and flashing lightning in the night sky did not faze Gabriel. He rode toward the huge horned bulls, waving the straw hat, and yelling at the animals to stop.

The priests grabbed their ponchos from the wagon and waited near their campfire at the edge of the bluff. If the steers did not stop or curve around the dangerous cliff, they would surely fall into the raging waters below and drown.

Gabriel rode fast and caught up to the bull leading the animals to their death. The black beast of his dreams looked his way, but Gabriel did not fear the animal. He yelled at the bull, and the others began to follow the mule.

Padre Rojo and *Padre Tonito* added more sticks to the campfire until it was blazing. The priests stood their ground, flapping their ponchos toward the bulls, waving them like *matadors* in the bull rings of Spain.

The thunder stopped, the lightning ceased, and the herd of frightened cattle calmed and turned as a light sprinkling rain began. Gabriel followed the largest bull until he stopped.

"I will call you Black Thunder, since you are the largest, blackest, Mexican bull I ever saw in my life. I hope you are thankful that we saved you and your friends from drowning. *Adios, amigo.*"

THE NEXT DAY, the weary trio returned to the Vann community in Bonita Canyon.

"Father Rhedd," said Pastor John, "It's so good to see you again. Welcome."

"Something smells very good, my friend."

"Missus Vann has made a feast for us tonight," said Pastor John.

After the meal, the travelers shared the story of the bulls and their efforts to save the herd and the boy's bravery during the storm.

"Well done, Gabriel," Pastor John said. "By the way, while you were at the Elfrida mission, the Pony Express rider dropped off mail today. The note attached said it was for John Vann's son, Gabriel."

The boy looked at the man with a questioning gaze. "But I don't know anyone, Pastor John."

"Well, shall we open it to see who sent this envelope?" asked Father Rhedd.

Pastor John passed the long brown envelope to Gabriel. "That looks like a strange name to me. I can't even read it."

"We couldn't read it, either," replied Pastor John.

Father Rhedd looked at Father Vega and passed the envelope to him. "It's from Pamplona," he said in a whisper.

The priest held the package close to his face in the fading light, then moved closer to the lantern. "Gabriel, have you ever been to the country of Spain?"

"No, he has not," Pastor John replied.

"He came to live with us at seven years old," said Mrs. Vann. "All the children we have adopted came from Indian Territory."

"What does the envelope say?" asked Gabriel.

Father Rhedd opened the glued ends of the envelope and removed the contents. He laid them carefully on the table. "The envelope is addressed to Gabriel Blue Feather Estrada."

Father Vega picked up the document and read it to the assembled group. When he finished, he carefully laid the document on the tablecloth covering the old wood surface. He glanced at his *compadre*, Father Rhedd. They both were wiping away tears.

"*Padre Rojo*, what does this mean?" asked Gabriel. The crowd around the table were scratching their heads in confusion and surprise.

"Would you mind explaining the contents of the mail?" asked Pastor Vann. "It sounds very important."

The priests, in a cloud of astonishment, finally smiled. "Pastor John and dear friends, we have confessions to make to you and our great company of fellow travelers in this world," said Father Rhedd.

"Confessions, gentlemen?" asked Pastor John.

Both priests stood up, and the crowd around the table took a few steps back, away from the two men.

"We must first ask for your forgiveness in the lies we have told you through the years, as to our identities and real names," said Father Rhedd. "We were afraid that we would bring harm to you, during the Civil War, and even now to this day."

"You mean you have different names?" asked Gabriel. "I changed your name, *Padre*."

Everyone chuckled and looked at each other, not realizing the importance of the statements being made.

"Gentlemen and ladies, may I introduce to you my cousin, Father Antonio Vega," said Father Rhedd, "who is from the country of Spain and is known there as Marco Guadalupe Estrada."

Marco nodded and waved his arm in the air. "And I must ask for your forgiveness as well, in introducing my cousin, the Spanish priest Fernando Pisano Estrada."

"I don't get it," said Gabriel, "what's the difference here?"

Everybody laughed, and Mrs. Vann brought out a small wooden

box and set it in the middle of the table. She slowly opened it and reached inside for the documents enclosed.

"Father Fernando and Father Marco," she said, "we have welcomed you into our homes and family and have trusted your words and advice through the years. Just because we may now call you a different name does not make you less than our good friends."

"Amen," added Pastor John. "I had no idea you were residents of Spain, but that hardly matters to us."

Mrs. Vann waved at the boy to come closer to the table. "Gabriel, when we adopted you, we put the information about your mother and father in this little cedar chest."

The boy looked at the folded paper and sat down beside her. "This is written in fancy words. What does it say?"

The woman handed the little box of papers to Father Fernando, who carefully spread them across the table.

"My friends, this is the documentation that we hoped would be possible to find. Here in this vast desert of the Arizona Territory, we have found the last piece of a very intricate puzzle of how our lives and those of yours, Gabriel, have intertwined until we now know, without a doubt, that we are family."

Father Marco took the pages of the long official document from Spain and laid it beside Gabriel's records of birth. "What a miracle that the man who brought this mail survived his fast ride across this savage land, but he did and gave us a most valuable and treasured gift."

"Gabriel, this box of papers Missus Vann has saved for you says that your father was Carlos Sandoval Estrada, from Spain," Father Fernando read. "Your mother was Vina Blue Feather of Gritts."

He passed the paper to Gabriel who could read the printed information. "Imagine that," said the boy, "from the country of Spain. That means I'm half Indian and half Spanish, doesn't it, *Padre Rojo?*"

The assembled group around the table chuckled, and everyone's spirits were lightened by the surprising news.

"Yes, son, it does." The priest laughed, and the crowd began to relax.

Father Marco stood up to get everyone's attention. "Excuse me, my friends, but the most important revelation of all has yet to be revealed." He held up the official Spanish document titled the *Last Will and Testament of the Estrada Family, from Pamplona, Spain.*

"This paper says that Ricardo Santiago Estrada and Antonietta Pisano Estrada had three sons—Orlando, Alejandro, and Fernando." He pointed at *Padre Rojo* and smiled. "That's their youngest son there, who is my cousin, and Gabriel's great-uncle."

"You are my family?" asked Gabriel.

Mrs. Vann began to cry, dabbing her eyes with her handkerchief.

"Hallelujah, praise the Lord," shouted Pastor John.

The assembled crowd around the campfire table began to applaud. Smiling faces and a pat on Gabriel's back closed the evening as everyone dispersed to their own tents.

"So, Uncle, what do I call you now?" asked Gabriel. "And Cousin?" He looked at both men and began to laugh. "I have changed your names again!"

"Yes, but you can still call me *Padre Rojo*." The priest laughed.

Laughing and crying, the trio could not stop the joy in the moment of revelation.

THEY ENDED UP around the campfire, talking into the night about the possibilities of the future. Gabriel wanted to know everything about their lives in Spain, their childhoods, and their travels which caused them to be here to complete the circle of reunion.

MORNING CAME EARLY for the Estrada family. Mrs. Vann was up early to start the breakfast meal. "Coffee's ready!" she said.

"Thank you," said Gabriel.

He watched as the woman poured three cups of coffee and set them on the nearby table. "Just because we have two more members of 'our' family, does not mean I will leave and never return."

"You read my mind, boy," said Mrs. Vann, wiping her weepy eyes. "Please forgive my tears. They are not of sadness but of joy, son."

"Mine, as well," whispered Pastor John. He stood beside his wife, and they both hugged Gabriel between them.

"We have prayed that you would someday find your relatives," said Pastor John. "We had heard rumors about your father being from Spain, but we had no way to verify that notion."

Father Fernando picked up his coffee and nodded toward Mrs. Vann. "Much appreciated, señora."

"You're welcome, Father," she replied. "I just want to know if you two are taking our boy back to Spain with you."

"How did you know we had been planning a trip such as that?" asked Father Marco. He laughed at her clever deduction of the situation.

"Women have an uncanny intuition," said Pastor John.

"We had a discussion about what the future may hold for Gabriel," said Father Fernando, "but we need to travel back to Pamplona to legalize the transfer of estates."

"You mean I'm going with you?" asked Gabriel.

The priests stood on either side of the boy. "We will take the stagecoach to Wilcox, where we will board the train," said Father Fernando. "We will travel to the east coast, where we then take a ship to Spain. It is a long journey but one that we must make together."

"The mission at Elfrida will be well supported by our staff. Also, the soldiers at Camp Supply offered their assistance, anytime we need to be away," said Father Marco.

"Looks like I'm going to Spain," said Gabriel. "And that old Mexican bull, Black Thunder, won't be able to follow me."

"*Sí*, that is true, my nephew," said Father Fernando. "However, the dark beast of my dreams will be waiting for me. Watching how you faced your fears has helped me, Gabriel. Now I know that I can do it, too."

"Thank you, Uncle *Padre Rojo*," said Gabriel. "Thank you for showing me the way."

———

—*Barbara L. Clouse is a retired federal paralegal, lives on a farm in Muskogee, Oklahoma, with her husband Jerry. When not helping with the gardening, she enjoys teaching art, sewing, genealogy, and research of her Cherokee heritage. She has been a Sunday school teacher for many years, working with children of all ages. Hosting family gatherings and helping with projects for their grandchildren keeps the Clouse country home busy and blessed.*

UNTIL THEN

MEGAN McCAIN

I FIRST MET Joaquin Carillo, robber and murderer extraordinaire, just outside of Tombstone. Although I was a marshal at the time, under the badge I was the same wild youth whose very familiarity with the rough side of life had interested me in the law. My father encouraged the interest, hoping to keep me from trouble, while I hoped to make a name for myself. William Beaker, famous throughout Cochise County and a terror to bandits everywhere. But deep down, I knew that romance lies with the outlaw, not the lawman. I never quite settled into my new role.

Carillo and I crossed paths after a tavern gambling dispute ended in hot gunfire and another dead fool. As marshal, I chased Carillo out of town and cornered him. At the critical moment when I could have taken him, instead I offered a deal. I would help him get out clear and free. He would take me along with him out in the mesa, far from the eyes of the law, and I'd begin my new life as an outlaw, no constraints.

Nothing came so easy, though. Not in that place, or that time, and especially not in the company I'd chosen. It took months to feel easy in the company of Carillo and his men, knowing that our partnership was based entirely upon convenience, and that at the slightest whim, Carillo could take me down. Whenever I did sleep, I slept lightly, hand on the gun under my pillow, and praying to the devil to stay away for just one more night.

Carillo boasted of murdering dozens of white men and natives, both for greed and pleasure. Although he had rightly earned a reputation for violence and brutality, I was astonished at his casual cruelty. His disregard for human life and honor was one aspect of our partnership I could never handle with ease, often averting my gaze as he and his compadres mutilated their victims.

Carillo took it too far one night after a feud, murdering an entire family. Unfortunately for him, one child escaped, severely wounded, and reported the atrocity to local authorities, causing us to take flight once again, this time to the mountains of Mexico far from the vengeful David Ward, county sheriff with a hound-like nose for retribution. Even then, I went along with Carillo, never daring to cross a man with deadly fingers always close to his trigger. I turned more toward drink than ever, trying to forget. But that night set the stage for the end of Joaquin Carillo.

Carillo and our group of bastards stayed up in the mountains but still ventured into the local village for a good time. I went for the drinks, unable as I was to communicate between my awkward tongue and guilty conscience. Carillo went for the cards and women, always popular with his handsome face and wild black hair. Many evenings were spent in a little *cantina* down at the base of the mountains, whiling away the nights with mezcal.

I found myself drinking almost to incoherence, head lying on the table, seeing images of my former life with more clarity than I saw the *cantina*. My wife, still living in Tombstone, God knows how. My father, dead in a grave out in the desert, dust mingling with the remnants of my mother. My associates in the law, my favorite saloon back home, where I could hold an easy conversation and look my fellow men in the eye without shame.

It was on one of these nights that Sheriff Ward approached. He came in disguise, a clever disguise at that, but I recognized his face as he sat on a stool next to me. Ward grabbed my hand as it flew to my holster and leaned over as he whispered, "Don't even try, Becker. This affair will be easier on the both of us if you act natural."

Carillo was in the backrooms with some woman. I had no worries as to our other associates, who held me in disdain as both a traitor to my call and a *gringo*. It was just me and Ward, who had straightened himself up and ordered a drink but kept a close watch on me, wary of every move. He didn't need to worry. Without Carillo, I had no nerve to stand up to the sheriff. My courage had shrunk with every step away from Tombstone.

Ward clapped my back, trying to look companionable as he began a conversation and pulled out a deck of cards, passing my hand for a game of twenty-one. He kept up a steady stream of conversation, if conversation is a fitting word for one man speaking at another. I was drunk enough by then that a facade was above my abilities, while Ward sat sober and assured, ready to spring his trap.

Quietly, Ward asked me when my friend would be back. I shook my head. Ward put an arm around me and guided me into a corner farther from the bar, ostensibly to continue our game. As we sat down, he looked around the room and then whispered, "Becker, you know why I'm here. Unlike yourself, a place like this isn't my first choice of establishment. Help me bag Carillo, and I can get out."

His directness penetrated the fog of my mind, just enough to elicit an answer.

"Why would I do that?"

"Because you miss home, and you never meant to let it get this far. You want to go back to your wife and sort yourself out."

"It's too late for that, Ward," I said.

"We all know this started with Carillo. It can end with him, too. Come home. I can guarantee your freedom and reputation. All you have to do is help me catch Carillo," Ward replied.

"What do you want with him?"

"Carillo chose his path long ago—heading straight for the gallows."

"And if I refuse?" I asked with a low laugh.

"Do you think I hold you in such esteem that I'd regret our friendship's sudden, violent end?" He briefly revealed a gun under his poncho.

"Give me time," I said. He had my attention, but capturing Carillo on a moment's notice? Impossible. The man had achieved his reputation for a reason. My near-capture had been sheer luck, perhaps by fate's hand or perhaps by the devil's.

"I know where you've been hiding, Becker. You have two days to return with a complete plan to capture Carillo, tied up with a bow. I'd have him already if he weren't so damned slippery. Two days."

I nodded, and Ward slammed his cards on the table, proclaiming me the winner. He shook my hand, leaving a slip of paper indicating where to find him, and left me to make my choice. Betray Carillo and go home? Or betray Ward yet again and continue my descent to hell?

The plan I devised was simple. Two days following, I'd make sure we came out to the *cantina*. Carillo had a robbery planned for the next afternoon, some unwary travelers or some such, so it would be simple enough to convince him to celebrate. Ward would be waiting in the *cantina* and catch Carillo by surprise, by the aid of revelry. If Ward couldn't manage the capture, I'd take it as a sign from destiny.

The next night, Carillo was gone again on some errand. I made my way into town, careful to watch for any sign of suspicion from the men. Ward wasn't hard to find in a little *adobe* hut on the outskirts of town. I looked through the window, careful to ensure it was the right home before walking in.

Ward slept lightly in a little wooden chair and sat upright immediately upon hearing the soft rustle of my footsteps. Moonlight poured in from the doorway, illuminating the sandy floor, and making my old companion look more like a specter than a man, eye-hollows looking black in the white glow of his skin. Thankful for the flask at my side, I took a swig of courage. I remained in the doorway, still unwilling to move closer to the ghost.

"What's the plan?" Ward asked quietly.

"We'll be at the *cantina*. Talk to the owner, talk to the señorita, you can work that out. I know that Carillo will be drinking," I told him. "I will make sure of that. But any further... my hands are clean."

"Clean," Ward agreed. He smiled slightly, cheeks shadowed.

I didn't wait to converse further but turned and walked out of the door, fairly running, once I was out of sight. The white glow of Ward's face haunted my journey back to camp, as I contemplated whether the man was more angel come to save me or demon sent to finish my journey to hell.

Next day, everything played out exactly as Carillo had planned, much to his elation. I strove for normalcy, but perhaps it was just as well that my nerves were always high after a job anyway. Carillo seemed to notice nothing, at any rate. His demeanor toward me remained the same as usual, that is, as a dog that had performed well and avoided a beating.

At the *cantina*, I gave Carillo his first drink of the evening, insisting that he'd earned it. Perhaps I was too jovial, but he accepted drink after drink, anyway, more than I'd ever seen him consume in one evening. Some of his compadres began to dance with local women, and Carillo joined in, charming as always. Lithe, nimble, moving as if on air instead of his own two feet. I sat watching and saw Ward sidle in, whispering something to the man behind the bar, who nodded grimly, and brought Ward to a backroom. Ward looked at me, but I looked down into my drink, unwilling to involve myself any further.

Done with dancing, Carillo made his way into a private room with a girl on his arm, escorted by the man Ward had spoken to. Despite my hesitation to be involved either way, I felt compelled to follow. As the door shut, I ambled over, ready to listen and step in if so prompted.

The affair was brief. A girl screamed. Somebody muffled the sound. I heard the clink of cuffs and Ward's low voice. Then Carillo's higher voice, quick, but still calm. A scuffle and the sound of something heavy being dragged out the back door concluded the whole business.

It was time for me to leave. If Carillo was captured, I dreaded his men's revenge. I, as Ward's former friend, would be implicated whether the attempt succeeded or not. Either way, I had little interest in waiting to find out. I wove in between dancing couples and ran straight to Ward's hideout.

I sat alone in the little hut, again illuminated only by a little moonlight. Minutes passed. A dull thud outside was followed by Ward walking in, dragging Carillo limp and unconscious behind him. Ward and I made no delay in starting the journey back to Tombstone, traveling by night to avoid the heat of the day, always watching for any rescue attempts. As none came, I began to question the loyalty of Carillo's men. Carillo himself was well-secured and stripped of every one of his weapons. Ward had made very sure of that.

Through the long journey, Carillo never spoke. But he watched me. He avoided Ward's questions and attempts to converse, but even when I could not see his eyes, I could feel them on me, burning me.

Often the only sounds would be the trot of the mules, our own footsteps, and Ward perversely whistling a cheerful tune.

Our journey came to an end in Tombstone just before sunrise. Carillo, as famous as he was, endured only a short trial before his sentence. The execution would take place the following morning.

Men and women crowded around Carillo before the execution the next morning, curious to see the famous outlaw. Carillo walked to the gallows, tall and proud as ever despite the rope around his hands. I shrunk into the buzzing mass behind me as he approached, unwilling to feel that gaze upon me one more time.

The sun sat high in the east, silhouetting Carillo at the awful contraption. If Ward, illuminated in the moonlight that night in Mexico, resembled either a twisted angel or a demon of light, so Carillo bore a counter-resemblance of either a singularly noble demon or a dark angel, standing against the bright sun preparing for his next journey. According to tradition, he was offered a final word, and in true Carillo-fashion, his words were casual. *Hasta entonces.* Although it may seem ludicrous amidst the crowd, I swear that his last look was at my face.

I could not bear to meet that stare and turned around, going to my old home. I had not returned there last night, instead spending the day drinking and the night prowling the streets under cover of darkness. I returned to much the same home I'd left. Starkly bare, quiet. My wife was home. I had no concept of what she must have done to survive while I was gone, but I seemed to be an unwelcome sight as she gasped and shrank into her chair at the sight of me.

After a moment, she asked me where I'd been. I shook my head, unwilling to flesh out whatever story she'd formed in my absence. The reality must be worse than even the rumors she'd have heard.

Toward evening, I headed to the saloon. I had no idea if the extent or nature of my crimes had become public knowledge, but nobody solicited my company. Cold nods and hushed voices replaced what had once been companionship. I drank into the night, heading out somewhere around three in the morning.

No clouds hid the sky, which seemed more cavernous than ever. I headed toward the gallows where Carillo still hung, limp as the night Ward had dragged him through the doorway. In my head, I heard him like the echoes of a cave repeating over and over until the words blended together, *hasta entonces.* Until then.

Until when, my companion? My leader? His body swayed slightly in the wind, and I chuckled slightly at the attempted answer to my unspoken question. Hell. Of course, I knew.

Turning away, with the familiar prickling feeling of Carillo watching me, but this time from eyes that could not see, I began to walk toward Ward's home. All was quiet in his dark windows, and I had become proficient enough at the art of horse theft to manage a simple mule. His pack lay in the fenced yard, still laden with essentials from yesterday's trip. My wife would hardly miss me after learning to live without me so long. The company of honest, unashamed men was no longer mine to keep. So, I made no delay heading south, into the desert. After all, I had an appointment to keep.

———————

—*Megan McCain grew up on her great-grandparents' homestead in Washington State, learning to love the wild and outdoors. She currently lives in Southeast Idaho with her husband and three children, striving to raise her children with a similar love of the outdoors despite the challenges of urban life. She can usually be found hunting bugs, curating her children's rock collection, taming the wilderness of her garden, or hiking scenic Idaho. As a storyteller and a musician, Megan's greatest inspiration is to explore what it means to be human, whether in the old Western frontier or more modern frontiers.*

DESERT FISH

MICHAEL WOODS

SAND LOST OVER sand, the men scraped craters into the tanned earth. Their metal spades rang out as they threw beds of sand over their shoulders onto freshly engraved headstones. With every strike of his tool, one man's leathered palms tore little by little. The first hundred blows were numb—comforting and natural against his calloused hands, too used to this kind of work. It wasn't until the perspiration from his furred wrists leaked into his cuts that his body acknowledged the wear. He snapped out of his tunneling fervor to catch a few dusted breaths. Broad daylight stared down at him in his sinful act. Islands of clouds strolled across the blaze in the sky, giving him shade in his pause.

A silence fell as the thuds of his partner's shovel ceased as well. Across a few other exhumed sites, a smooth forehead gleamed toward the sky with relief. The pale face turned to the man, his Danish blues peered above the overturned rocks and dirt. A breeze rolled through, dusting sand into their damp scalps, wetting a layer of mud on their skin.

A door whipped about. They darted their attention to the back of the church. The man clutched his shovel, blood twisting into the grain of its handle.

"It's just the wind," the boy said, muffled behind a bandana tied around his head. They watched as the lime-washed backdoor rattled against the exterior of the building.

"Told you, ain't a soul within jailin' distance," the man said. He stroked his beard, long but not grayed. He spoke as if he was the boy's father yet wasn't a decade and a half his senior. His wife always told him he'd look much younger if he quit this "bounty job" and came back to tending the soil God gave them.

He flung himself out of his current "bounty" and gave the boy his hand. Their palms grasped one another, and the wound between his thumb and index widened.

Along the edge of the graveyard, two horses grazed on wheat-grass, letting out a cordial neigh as the man approached. He retrieved hollowed gourds from the saddles, giving one to his partner, who finally removed his mask. The water smelled sweet, cool from its river and refreshing amongst the necropolis.

"You ought to wear one of these, Enoch," the younger man said, gesturing to the bandana he stuffed in his pocket. "It's bad air," he continued. "Surgeons, they wear a barrier when working on the afflicted. Marie told me all about it."

"I ain't never fell more ill than a sneeze when I was five, and I'm sure not gonna get sick at thirty-five. Esbon, I'm built like the iron on them railroads. Quicker than the locomotives on 'em, too." He smirked, mimicking a speedy draw from the revolver hanging at his hip.

Eventually, their shade sailed away, ending their respite and deserting them to their work.

Esbon reached his goal first. He beckoned Enoch over, and together they heaved a casket out of the ground. It was young, rushed, and produced quickly for the sudden surplus of tragedy. They leveled the pine and studied its edges. Enoch ran his fingers along the lid, feeling the bumps of the nail heads that sealed it.

He readied the crowbar, but fatigue convinced him to try an alternative. He motioned Esbon back, withdrawing his revolver and pulling the hammer back six times—shattering six nail heads with a series of dramatic booms.

Esbon flung the lid off to unveil their prize. The stench from within knotted their stomachs like the tumbleweeds around them. Enoch patted the bloated flesh to recover a silver pocket watch, a silver wedding band, and two golden teeth. Enoch wiped each of the items clean before moving on to the next one. Years of this type of work had numbed his brain. A job was a job. Shoveling manure or graves—both were dirty. One just paid a lot more.

After each dig, Esbon propped the lid back on the coffin and slid it back into its resting place. Acknowledging that reburying it took too much energy, he at least replaced its initial layer of stones so scavenging animals wouldn't disturb it.

The process repeated itself twenty-two more times until their cache was sufficient and the sun had left the sky to a bitter black.

Once they had ten miles between them and their depleted target, the hunters rested on their backs, soaking their blisters in wet fabric.

Esbon attempted to grip a pencil, but his sore fingers cramped after the first sentence in his journal.

Ma cherie, night is dark because the light you emit is absent.

The flames licked shadows over Enoch's grinning face, the band of his hat lay low over his caked forehead. He whittled away at a piece of mesquite. Esbon felt his eyes on him and would have been self-conscious if Enoch was literate. However, he made it very clear that the only thing worth knowing how to read was "me and my family's names."

"How much more do you need?" Enoch asked.

"More what?"

"Money."

"For what?"

"Don't play dumb, Esby. Your sister told me what you're doing. It's the only reason she lets you come out here with me."

He closed the journal, thinking of his purpose, the kick behind his heart, and the poetry that looped in his mind about her. He pictured brunette hair curled over her *café au lait* eyes. The way she tended to break a gaze, always accompanied by her natural raspberry blush. For a moment, he thought he saw her there through the dancing flames, instead of his brother-in-law, slumped back, drying his damp feet by the fire.

"Not sure," he finally answered. "I reckon I'll see what her city in Quebec is like. If that doesn't suit our fancy, a plot on Arizona soil will."

"Friend," the man said, now beginning to doze with slowed speech. "Go back to school. School will get the girl and a house on soil, not sand."

"Well, why do you think I'm out here? I don't have enough to pay through school, and by the time I do save up, it'll be years before I finish. All years I could have had with her. I'd be lost in books while she's across the country fending off suitors. I assume one can only go so long before you're worn down. I'm not sayin' she won't—" The boy cut his feelings short as he noticed Enoch's eyes fell to rest. He clutched his journal to his chest and brushed the edges, letting the corners frill through his fingertip like a deck of playing cards.

The next morning, they woke before the rays above did. Coffee brewed, and its caffeinated aroma paired well with two slices of bread and some jerky split between them. They rode off with satchels weighing down their saddles, overflowing with unearthed objects. Enoch decided to take a detour through a small mining town called Tombstone. In it, there was a grocer well acquainted with Enoch. He sold anything from carrots to hand cannons. More importantly, he would buy any form of precious metal with cold hard cash, no questions asked.

Enoch dumped the satchels on the counter like marbles from a boy's toy bag. The grocer eyed each item, determining what was worth his time. He took it all except a pen and a brooch he lobbed back at Enoch.

The scavengers left happy with a roll of United States legal tender, a sack of coffee beans, and two peppermint sticks.

As Esbon mounted his saddle, he asked if they were cheated. Surely the amount they brought was worth a bit more. Enoch placed the peppermint between his lips as if it were a cigarette, ignoring the sharp pains the sugar sent through all twenty-four of his teeth. He explained that discretion is heavily taxed in their line of work. Esbon swallowed this, chomping through his candy.

After half a day's travel, they arrived at a homestead. At its fence, they heard the waters tumble from a running creek and at an equal distance away caught the pleasant wind of the blooming peaches. Riding up the hill, they removed their hats to show their faces to the lady and toddler perched on the edge of the porch.

The blonde woman instantly lifted her dress to sprint barefoot across the lawn, and the equally golden-haired boy rushed close behind. Her lips met Enoch's with the passion and frustration that distance builds between a couple. The little boy tumbled and slobbered until his pudgy arms wrapped around his father's thigh. His crystal eyes smiled up at him.

"Enoch Blackredge," his wife said, "you was a night later than expected. You know what today is? Monday, you was"—Enoch pecked her on the lips—"supposed to be here before church, before that sun fell over that creek, and you wasn't."

Another kiss.

"But I'm here now, Sarah. Lawbreakers don't exactly abide to being taken in, do they, Esbon?"

"No, they do not," he said, avoiding eye contact with his sister, lifting his nephew up over his shoulders. The child, dressed in patched overalls, giggled and drooled a bullet past Esbon's face. Laughing, he handed Enoch his son, who brushed his beard against his youngin's plump, doughy cheeks. To sense his tiny heart thump against his shoulder and to feel his miniature breaths were almost enough to make him settle back at the farm.

Sarah hugged her brother and led them inside. Stew boiled over the oven, vegetables and herbs dried over the counters, the fireplace fought the oncoming dimness of sunset, and Sarah's elderly mother sat in the corner mending one of Enoch's shirts.

At dinner, the adults drank cider and ate savory beef stew—with extra carrot and little on the beef. Sarah interviewed her brother on his latest adventure. With each answer, she would shame Enoch for dragging him into the bounty world, only for Esbon to defend himself and say it was of his own accord.

"That Canadian girl ain't worth blood, you know? Ain't no woman."

"Young love. Don't you remember? It's what made li'l Abraham here," Enoch said, pointing to the toddler mushing a carrot between his fingers.

"I met you when you was cuttin' crops, not turning in killers."

She trailed off as she stared at the worn hands the two of them brought back to the table. Questions dodged around her mind. She thought of yesterday at church when she asked Deputy Tyre about the current bounties set near Cochise and how he told her there weren't any he knew about. She pondered why they left with two shovels, why there was a woman's broach in her husband's breast pocket, and why blisters littered his palms. She swallowed her curiosities with a chug of cider.

Later that night when candles ate wax and lanterns burnt oil, Enoch edged Esbon out of the house near the pig pen close to the creek and told him to grab a shovel. Their lanterns cast exaggerated shadows of the men over the dumb eyes of the spectating hogs. At a yard's depth, they hit a walnut chest. Instead of a decayed body, this time, Enoch revealed it to be filled with cash, guns, silver, trinkets, heirlooms, gold, and rolls of cash he "earned" after the war.

"How much do you need?" Enoch said, sharing the view.

"Good God, I didn't know you had it like this. I know you must've had a bit to buy the property so quick... but not like this."

"Esbon."

"I can't take any. I'll earn my way north. I can't take this... this is—"

"Then don't take all of it, brother. Just some. I'm doing this for Sarah and well.... Imma just saying, this occupation I've fostered upon you, it's not exactly Christian, is it? I thank you for your help, but this job is a hook, kid. It's gonna reel ya in until the fisherman chops yer head off. Please take this at least."

Enoch retrieved a roll of a hundred dollars, then another, and then a handful of gold eagles. Esbon lost words as the weight compounded in his hand. Enoch pushed his brother-in-law's fingers closed and refused a thank you. He just told Esbon to go back to the house and leave him to do some inventory.

He began to dig even further. Soon he fell upon another trunk, twice the width. He uncovered it enough to lift the lid. Inside was all the evidence that chronicled his first heists when he started the outlaw business. He didn't return to his house for another hour. Instead, he bathed in the filth of that hole. His eyes watered over this work. He sifted through it a dozen times under the choir of pigs above. How at home he was in his bed.

FOUR DAYS LATER, an associate, called Peter Clariborne, walked onto Enoch's property with a rumor he overheard at a bar. He was a tall, thin man in a torn suit, and if you didn't hear him speak, you would think he was an animated effigy meant to scare crows away.

Years ago, Peter informed Enoch about a train crossing New Mexico—and years ago, Enoch and three other men robbed a train for all it was worth. He told him of several other fiscal opportunities since then, including their most recent involving a quiet town wiped out by a strain of influenza. Never was his information a blunder. All he asked for in return was a small cut when Enoch had a payday.

Enoch rolled a cigarette for the man, and they discussed business near the outhouse, away from feminine and adolescent ears.

Peter took a draw of tobacco. "Cattle drive."

Enoch let that filter through his brain. He inhaled his nicotine and responded with one word. "Where?"

"Prescott."

Enoch nodded.

"All right, Petey. When they sellin'?"

"I'm estimatin' they'll get there in two nights, so you'll have to get there in one." Enoch licked the smoke residue from his teeth, then spat.

"Sounds like I can do that," he said, patting him on the shoulder and leading him to his hitched horse.

As he settled on his saddle, he held his hand out.

Enoch smirked, surprised it took him this long. He skinned three ten-dollar bills and handed them to his informant.

"Was a good haul, huh?"

"Was okay, I suppose. Done broke my back over it."

Then a sudden break from the front door cued Peter to take off.

"Get that sunnuva bitch outta here," shrilled Sarah, armed with a double-barrel.

"Farewell to you, Nucky," the sunnuva bitch said before his horse's hooves kicked a storm up as he galloped out of lethal range.

"Don't you do it!" Sarah tossed the gun to the side and rushing to her husband. "I hate that ugly man! Every time he shows, you go!"

Enoch was about to give a rehearsed excuse when the outhouse door swung open, adding Esbon into the fray.

"I'll help. Promise I will," he said.

"What?" Sarah protested. "You better not!"

"She's right," Enoch grunted. "Your cut was good enough, wasn't it?"

"Of course it was, but I owe you... for housing me and all, don't I, Sarah? Don't you want your husband to be safe out there? I'll have his back."

Despite his sister's protests, the men gathered their gear to look for a nonexistent man wanted for murder near Phoenix. Before they left with fully loaded gun belts and provisions, Enoch had *deja vu* from the scene of his boy and wife moping on the porch. Enoch handed his son a sculpture he'd been working on.

"You know what this is?" Enoch asked the boy.

He answered with a shake of his head, bringing it close to his face. "It's a whale, son."

The toddler echoed the word in two syllables.

"Yeah, bud, they live in the ocean. May not know what that is livin' in our landlocked state, but you will. I'll show you California when I get back, okay? We'll fish for a whale—pry Jonah out its mouth."

Soon they saddled up, and Enoch took one last look at his family, then toward the sun reflecting on the creek. Under the disturbed patch of dirt lay his treasure, soaking in the setting sun, waiting for his return.

A NIGHT PASSED, and they found themselves in a bar amongst swirling smoke, sticky floorboards, a Spanish argument, and the savory smell of a medium-rare steak sizzling under their noses.

"I do love cattle towns," Enoch said, disappearing a chunk of meat under his mustache.

Esbon leaned an elbow on his knee, his steak uncut.

"I can't find the appetite I thought I had," he grunted.

"What's the matter?"

"Think it's all the smoke. Or the noise. Shit, I dunno."

Then he threw up what little he had in his stomach.

"Jesus, Esby," Enoch said, pulling the perfect sirloin away from the mess. He handed him his handkerchief.

"I'm all right. It's dandy."

Esbon shifted all his weight into the back of his chair and let his eyes rest while Enoch had both steaks and a bottle of beer. They stayed within those walls until a subtle rumble quaked the glass panes.

"Seems they're right on time," Enoch said, leading them out the saloon doors. On the outskirts of town, a blur of a thousand head of cattle washed over the muted colors of the dusty landscape, beaten by four thousand hooves. The pair of men leaned against the building, watching the dust flow behind the stock on its way to the market. "How many you count?" asked Enoch.

Esbon peered through the cloud. "Thinkin'... five or six on horse-back... and one fella on the chuckwagon near the rear. Can't really get a good look, though."

"Don't need to. As of now, we just gotta wait. Maybe it'll be good if we washed up in the meantime, friend."

While the ground thumped beneath their boots, the men journeyed to the humble two-story hotel. Entering, Esbon whispered with urgency, "If we don't have eyes on them, they're gonna slip away."

His partner waved him off and said to the man behind the counter, "Ready my pal here a cold bath. Soap, towel, maybe even a lady to help him. He's feelin' under."

"Of course," the suited man said, adjusting his glasses. "It'll take some time if that's all right. I'll have to ready the bath myself."

"Not a problem. We have all the time in the world," Enoch winked at a disheveled Esbon. "Just relax, clean up, you'll see."

———————◆◆◆◆◆———————

ENOCH SMOKED NEXT to his hitched horse while Esbon bathed. The stampede in the background whimpered out as the cattle dispersed within the gates of the market. Soon, all the moos and bawls of the cows would be carried northward.

He was already in the perfect spot to stakeout. By the time his cigarette singed his fingers, seven cowboys brushed his shoulders and passed Esbon, exiting the hotel.

Esbon wide-eyed his brother, pointing by his hip at the men.

Enoch nodded.

They listened to the conversation inside—the owner was inform-
ing them that used water was at the ready, but fresh and warm would
cost twice as much and take twice as long to prepare. A few stayed
while the others departed.

"Come on, kid," Enoch instructed. "Stay close."

The cowmen traveled in a herd like the one they sold. As they
walked, Enoch noticed how each checked their pocket subconscious-
ly, making sure their payday was still there.

Three veered off into the local gunsmith, while the last two became silhouettes in the distance toward the saloon.

"Found your appetite?" Enoch asked, implying their destination.

Esbon shook his head.

"No. Give me a break before we continue this marathon."

He leaned against Enoch. His skin was clear, and he smelled of lye
soap, yet he grew fatigued and his breaths quick. His brother helped
him hobble his way into the same chairs they had left hours ago.

Details emerged from the silhouettes inside. Enoch studied them
a few tables over. One was young, maybe younger than Esbon, but his
labored skin gave him seniority. The other man mirrored Enoch, similar age, roughed beard, and a squinted expression. With those eyes,
he locked onto Enoch's, who snapped away from the cowboy's gaze.

Esbon leaned toward him. "So when do we... you know?"

"We wait. Enjoy the night. It'll be dark soon."

"Why?" Esbon questioned, followed by a cough that had worsened
over the past few days. "We wait till they turn over for the night?"

"No, just listen to me. We may wait nights."

And nights did pass, lodged in the room next to the cattlemen,
collecting information. Every morning, each cowhand emerged dif-
ferently than when they rode in.

Once a pair of cracked brown boots were replaced with shiny black ones adorned with gold spurs. Others had freshly oiled handguns, while some had entirely new models. All bandoliers were stocked with new brass that caught the light like a lady's diamond. Every cowboy, save two, acquired new outfits—freshly-dyed jeans and button-up shirts that were tossed to the bedposts nightly at the hen house. Enoch focused on the less lavish pair—the same he saw in the saloon.

One morning when Esbon was particularly slow to stir and nearly impossible to drag out of bed, they overheard the men talk about leaving Prescott at noon. Enoch managed to get him down to the lobby with the promise of cold water. Soon enough, the cowboys descended the stairs.

"Go ahead, Boss," said a jovial hand to the bearded man. "But I think I need to hear more ladies in this town say my name." He left the hotel with spurs rattling in the distance, passing Esbon huddled in a Mexican blanket.

The cow boss sighed and told the kid beside him to tell the cook to restock and be prepared to ride at noon.

"So, we finally doin' it?" Esbon shivered.

Enoch weighed his options. That man was managing the drive. He'd have the fattest cut along with the goods carried in the chuck. And from the looks of it, the others spent most of their earnings on women and gear.

"We ride, but after... we'll call in the doctor if you're still feelin' low, but I think the night sky on the way back home will clear you up."

THREE MILES EAST, they perched atop a plateau like vultures seeking out scraps on the desert ground. A little after noon, two horses and a coach wheeled their way over the horizon.

"Know the plan?" Enoch asked.

Esbon nodded and trudged down to the side of the road.

Enoch followed behind but stopped behind a boulder. He pulled a black bandana over his face and lowered the brim of his hat above his eyebrows.

Enoch collapsed, his face buried in the dirt, inhaling hot sand while his elbow dug into a wiry weed. On his knees, he gave a forced cough that evolved genuine as the caravan approached.

The hooves ceased, and the wooden wheels halted.

"Feller," said the bearded man on his stallion. "You all right?" He leaned back to the pear-shaped cook. "Get this man some water."

The cook reached into the shadows of the wagon and handed a canteen to the young cowman who dismounted and approached Esbon, whose curled body produced sandy puffs under his shirtsleeves.

"Friend," said the boyish face, "can you hear us?"

The cow boss stood nearby, his attention on the landscape. Many miles he endured, his pistol grip worn, the tip of his index callused. The geography rose high around them, creating a hallway with Esbon blocking their path forward and the chuck blocking their exit. Hair straightened on his neck, he noticed the sick man's holster was empty. Before he could grip his own sidearm, a masked man rolled around a boulder with a barrel aimed at his eye socket.

The cow boss froze, but the young cowboy watered the ground with the canteen and withdrew from his firearm.

Esbon then rose with a covered face and death aimed at his peer. The cowboy, now jittery, aimed his six-shooter between the robbers, unsure of the consequence that would ensue if he pulled the trigger.

"Put it down, Ben!" the rugged cow boss said. He didn't break eye contact with Enoch. He wondered about those eyes and what face he saw them attached to. Still, he raised his hands in surrender, knowing the labors of life and all the joys it had to offer—if you could stay living. And although he endured months to receive the money in his pocket, he knew none of it was worth the blood of his nephew in front of him. "Benjamin," he said.

The boy shook his head. "Not fair," he mumbled. "Not fair... we was working on this drive since March, and now we gon' lose it all?"

"Benjamin," he said again with sadness in his voice.

He lowered his weapon, but he did not holster it.

Esbon attempted to tell him to drop it but speaking made him fall into a fit of coughs.

"Aw, hell," grumbled the cook. "The kid's right. I ain't gonna lose my life to this!"

"Shut up!" interrupted Enoch. "Throw your irons on the ground, or I'll let you hear mine sing!"

The crackles and hacks of Esbon continued.

A double-barreled shotgun rattled at the feet of the cook.

"Down or I'll spill ya here!" warned Enoch.

"Don't put it down," grumbled the cook, whose face turned barn red with rage. His eyes darted down toward the shotgun.

"Shut up!" Enoch repeated.

"Listen to the man," advised his uncle.

Tears formed in Esbon's eyes as he heaved to catch his breath. His ribs burned, his body convulsed, and his iron sights wavered from its target.

The cook took the opportunity, jerking downward. His boss was unaware of his action until an explosion went off behind his head—quickly followed by two blasts from Enoch.

One round entered the shotgun wielder's chest, the other in one of the chuck's horse's skull, punching a blowhole through the back of its head, misting the wagon's canvas red.

Amongst the firefight, a defeated *"No!"* escaped the cow boss's lips. The living horse shot forward in panic, tossing the dead man over. The sunken weight of the dead stallion overturned the wagon onto the cowman, then Enoch. The impact knocked him unconscious, where one last gunshot sounded before everything went dark.

He awoke minutes later to the thrashing of the remaining horse tied to the chuck, desperately trying to stand but to no avail. Enoch studied the scene. The cook was face down, his shirt wet with a river of red mud flowing from his chest. Near the wreck, the bearded man was mangled on the ground, his expression wide with blood tearing down his eyes. His skull gashed, he did not stir.

Quickly, Enoch was reminded of his brother and yelled for him. He turned over to see the boyish cowboy instead. He was on his side as if asleep. He had a dime-sized entry wound in his forehead.

Yards away, a gurgle sounded. Esbon lay supine. Enoch struggled to his feet, stumbling to him, feeling his body for injuries. He ripped the buttons off his shirt to reveal three pellet wounds in between his ribs. The blood bubbled with each exhale like a boiling stew. "I was quick," Esbon mumbled. His eyes grew weak.

Enoch wrapped the punctures with his bandana, applying pressure. He whistled for his horse. Familiar hooves stomped near, and Enoch sat his brother upright in front of his saddle. He pulled the reins back toward Prescott, but all rationality left. Fear sunk into him, afraid that they would leave the doctors in silver cuffs.

He veered around and headed straight home. For the first hundred feet, Enoch tried to recall what little French Esbon taught him. He tried to say "let's go" but mumbled stupidly. He asked Esbon what it was in French, but the breathing slowed. He asked about Canada. He asked about snow.

Soon the gurgles stopped entirely.

At the first campfire, Esbon lay with his jacket over his face. Enoch held his knees to his chest on the other side of the flames. He watched the shadows flicker over the body, playing tricks on his eyes as the light seemed to reanimate the corpse. Enoch curled into the fetal position, tears muddied cracked sand beneath him.

At dawn, he stowed Esbon on the back of the horse the rest of the way. The nightmare numbed Enoch's subconscious. Imagining his wife's response was impossible. The emotional fatigue would not allow it.

The sun began to make its golden descent when he entered his property's gate. His hat low in shame, his horse slowed to a creep. His journey up to the house was eternity. He met with no one at the porch. Wind buckled a rocking chair, he called for his family, but no one answered. Entering, he heard his mother-in-law coughing and hacking in the corner, her crochet sprawled at her feet. Her face sunken, pale, struck with illness—the very same Enoch and Esbon had unknowingly brought from the ghost town and into the walls of his own home.

Behind her, the creek reflected the sun through the window. He could not process what he saw. In disbelief, he burst through the backdoor and fumbled across the lawn until his feet gave way.

Crosses marked two graves.

Under the disturbed patches of dirt lay his treasures, soaking in the setting sun, waiting for his return. On each marker were two of the few names he knew how to read. "Sarah" and "Abraham."

—*Michael Woods was raised in a small town in North Florida. Although nostalgic for Spanish moss, he fell in love with all things western watching old spaghettis with his father. He aims to pass the tradition down to his son when they find spare time from swimming and hunting for buried treasure. Prior to becoming a librarian, he went to Florida State University where he indulged in all things literature and poetry. While tending to his librarian duties, he has the habit of jotting down ideas in the corners of paperbacks and scrap pieces of paper.*

In his free time, he likes to study history and French, although his American accent is impossible to get rid of. He will always aim to improve his writing whether through poetry or prose. As of now, he is on the millionth draft of his first manuscript.

NO TOMORROW

LEIGH ALVER

The self-inflicted consequence of a youthful disregard for the law.

1888

Gallup, New Mexico Territory

SHERIFF HARRY CARTER had pulled the kid off the 4:15 Atlantic and Pacific after a formal complaint to the station master by a nettled conductor. The allegation was one of violent disruption. A physical altercation had occurred between a cocksure adolescent sporting an arrogant attitude, while smelling strongly of liquor, and two peaceable passengers.

The sheriff had arrived within minutes of the call, while there was still heat in the excitement, and his presence helped to calm the hoopla. He'd seen it all before and could have laid a charge of disorderly conduct there and then. But he chose to give the youth a second chance. Carter was a church-going Methodist who practiced his faith through deed and an even temperament. Originally from the Ozarks, he had been drawn to the clear, wide open vistas of the southwest after witnessing the loss and butchery of war. However, there had been no escape from these personal demons. The wanton waste of life had followed him, and as a lawman, he could only shake his head at the folly of wild adolescents looking for a fight. A pull of the trigger in a moment of foolish pique often led to instant regret. Especially, when the kinfolk took to the saddle to settle the score.

His plan was to hold the offender overnight, let him sober up, and see if he showed any remorse in the morning. If he did, he would put him back on tomorrow's 4:15, but only after he'd paid retribution for his sins by scrubbing out the cells and whitewashing the front fence and hitching rail.

However, none of that happened.

When signing him in, his charge gave a false name. Carter didn't know of the deception until it became clear that the kid couldn't spell the name he'd just given. He said he was Ralph Raymond but wrote *Ralf Raymon*. Even the unschooled knew all the letters to their own name. This feeble fabrication annoyed the sheriff. It had been a long day. Yet, he constrained his irritation and asked again. This time, the name presented exhausted all patience. John Smith was not only unimaginative but too much to bear for one day. Smith was escorted downstairs to the cells and locked up for the night without another word being uttered by the sheriff.

As the key turned in the lock, the kid demanded to know, "What are you holding me on? You have no measure against me."

The sheriff had three signed witness statements. However, he let it go and still said nothing.

"Need a blanket here, Sheriff, a headrest, too," came the demand.

The sheriff remained mute.

"Damn and hell, are you listening to me, Sheriff?"

He wasn't. Instead, he just turned away to climb the stairs back up to the office to finish off the day's paperwork.

Gallup was no metropolis, but it did have a second lawman, a deputy, only he was down Red Rock way looking into a dispute over water being drawn from a well by a neighbor who had failed to ask permission. So, short staffed, Sheriff Harry Carter sat down at the office table and pulled out all the wanted posters on file and went looking for the true identity of the prisoner he was holding in the cells. Experience told him, when someone tries to hide their name, they are usually wanted for something, somewhere.

Yet, he found nothing.

Rita, who had come from El Paso the previous year to live with her sister, cleaned the office once a week and had neatly filed all the wanted posters just the week before. When she saw the scattered jumble on the table, she asked why. Harry told her. Without saying a word, Rita went downstairs to the cells, looked at the prisoner, returned, and said she had seen his face on one of the posters.

Harry said, "Well, damned if I can find it," only to quickly apologize for his intemperate language and ask if she would take a look.

It took Rita ten minutes to identify the kid.

He was William Travis Lithgow, wanted on an outstanding warrant for two counts of aggravated assault, suspected horse thieving, and threatening violence against a prominent person. For one who looked so young, he had certainly matured his charge sheet in quick fashion.

The prominent person that Lithgow had threatened was a district judge from Peralta. This was significant as that particular offense fell outside his jurisdiction. It was covered under a federal statute and required notification to the U.S. deputy marshal in Albuquerque.

His name was Leon Ryan.

Ryan was a softly spoken left-hander in his mid-forties who had never married. To some, his appearance and polite manner was perceived as a weakness, but they were wrong. Below this exterior was a hard edge. Some knew of it—most didn't. Those who had experienced it were sometimes startled. One was fellow Deputy Marshal Ben Rollins from Tucson who witnessed Ryan shoot two men in what seemed to be cold blood. It had happened in an instant during a brief confrontation where Rollins saw no imminent danger, as he believed both men to be unarmed.

Inspection of the bodies revealed a concealed truth. Two hidden .44 Webley pocket pistols and two Spanish switchblade knives were found in their possession, along with a pocketbook spelling out a plan to holdup the Catalina branch of the First National. The chilling part, however, was a signed oath on the last page by both men, cousins, to kill anyone who tried to arrest them.

Rollins asked, "How did you know of their intent or that they were even armed?"

Ryan replied, "It was just a feeling."

"What sort of feeling, exactly?" quizzed Rollins.

"That you and I were not going to have a tomorrow."

When Marshal Ryan arrived in Gallup to pick up Lithgow three days after Carter had sent his telegram to Albuquerque, his opening words to the prisoner were, "Billy, do you want to see tomorrow?"

Lithgow's reply was, "What? See tomorrow? Of course, I want to see tomorrow. And what's that to you anyway?"

"Absolutely nothing," said Ryan, "but if you were to ask what it meant to me to see tomorrow, I'd say absolutely everything."

Billy had no idea what the marshal was talking about. He'd grown up without a solitary thought to rattle around in his head, and he wasn't about to get one anytime soon. When Ryan applied the shackles, he noticed the smooth soft hands of someone who had never done a day's hard work in their life. It caused him to shake his head. The youth of today had all been born after the end of the war in '65 and had no idea of the sacrifice or the treasure that had been expended to forge the nation that he now wanted to take for a free ride.

The two boarded the noon train back to Albuquerque and took up a position in the right rear of the last carriage, next to the guard and luggage cars. The marshal sat on the aisle, his gun away from Billy who sat against the window. No tickets were required, and on sighting the cuffs on Billy, just as Ryan showed his badge, the conductor asked if any assistance was required. Ryan shook his head.

The train left on time and arrived on schedule at Grants Depot for a water stop. Billy advised that he needed to relieve himself. Ryan eased out into the aisle and took his charge to the gentlemen's facility and asked for the courtesy of waiting until the train got moving. Clutching at his crotch, the response was an emphatic no. Ryan pressed his lips in annoyance and opened the door, telling Billy to whistle while alleviating himself.

"Why?" came the response from a curled lip of resentment.

"So I know that you haven't left by the window."

The sheriff remained directly outside the door in the narrow corridor and waited. When the train received a heavy jolt due to a miscalculation by a brakeman when hooking up four flat beds, baggage tumbled from the overhead racks in the passenger cars, and the marshal was thrown forward against the wood paneled passageway, knocking off his hat. When he retrieved it from the floor and returned it to his head, he noticed that Billy had stopped whistling.

The door remained locked.

The train was in motion when the conductor finally unlocked the door.

Billy was gone, and the small window was open.

Ryan rushed to the back of the train, through the luggage compartment and into the guard's cabin. The conductor followed and unlocked the door to the rear platform. The marshal looked back over the empty flatbeds seeking to locate Billy.

He couldn't be seen.

"Maybe, he's up on top," suggested the conductor.

Ryan stepped up onto the handrail, then onto the rungs of the vertical iron ladder. He climbed until he could see over the tops of the three passenger cars as they swayed to the pull of the locomotive now travelling at speed. He went to climb up further, but the conductor pulled on his trouser leg. "Too dangerous," he called. "If you can't see him, maybe he's hiding between the carriages. We can check from inside."

The search revealed nothing. It was as if the kid had vanished into thin air, until the conductor pointed to the shadow being cast by the train as it turned south just near Cubero. The silhouette of a reclining body could be seen below the carriage.

"How the hell did he get down there?" said Ryan in amazement.

The conductor shrugged. "Got me. Somehow he's climbed down under the car."

"What's he holding on to?" queried Ryan above the rattle and hum of the rolling stock as they stood on the steel plates between the carriages.

"I think he wedged himself in between the bearers. Do you want me to stop the train so you can get him out?"

"When's the next stop?" asked the marshal while having to speak directly into the conductor's ear over the noise of the train.

"Mesita, in less than an hour, to pick up the mail."

"I'll wait."

"Be mighty uncomfortable under there."

"Sure hope so," said Ryan.

The conductor kept looking down at the shadow as if mesmerized, watching as the silhouette darted and jumped over the tuffs of feathergrass. "What's he up for?" he asked, lifting his voice but not turning his head.

"With parole for good behavior, I'd say five. But he hasn't learnt to behave, so probably eight."

"Long time for someone so young. What is he, sixteen, seventeen?"

"Eighteen, but yeah, still young."

"But old enough to know better," offered the conductor.

"That, too," said Ryan, "but nowadays they breed them ill-mannered and dangerous."

"Tell me about it. Getting so you can't order some of these young bucks to take their boots off the back of the seat without having a gun pulled on you."

Ryan was about to agree when the shadow of Billy disappeared. "Hell! He's fallen off. Stop the train."

The conductor swung around and hurried forward, his girth bouncing off the sides of the corridor. The marshal rushed back to the rear platform of the guard's compartment. Standing on the railing to get a better view over the flatbeds, he caught sight of a body lying beside the tracks.

When the train's speed slowed to a quick walking pace, Ryan alighted and began to run back toward Billy, now some three hundred yards away. When he got close, he could see the mess. Billy's foot had been severed at the ankle, an upright boot sitting in the middle of the tracks. The young man's face was as white as a sheet with a look of disbelief as he repeated, "Oh, God. Oh, God. Oh, God."

Ryan pulled the belt from his trousers, crouched down, and

looped it below the knee. He pulled it tight to allay the flow of blood then lifted the leg in the air.

From this position, Billy could now see the full extent of his injury. "Oh, God, my foot's been taken clean off." The words came out pitched high in astonishment and between gasps of breath. "I can't live with only one foot."

"Sure you can. Lots of men lost limbs in the war and survived."

"I've seen them pitiful characters," mocked Billy, "I don't want to be like them."

The marshal kept the leg elevated. "Them? They seek neither pity nor a handout. They just get on with life and make the best of it, like we all do."

"They become maimed beggars. I've seen. I'd rather shoot myself before that happened to me." And with that pronouncement, Billy rolled to his right and with his hands still cuffed, seized the marshal's pistol, and pulled it from the holster.

Ryan's head had been turned as he looked back toward the train as it slowly backed up, the conductor hanging from the side with a red flag to signal to the engineer. He felt the Colt leave its holster and jerked his head back to look at Billy, the barrel pushed up under his chin, tears streaming from his eyes.

The marshal's shout of, "No," was the last word Billy was to hear as the sound of the pistol shot punched through the still dry air, just as a long spray of steam vented from the engine.

The train was now less than twenty yards away as it slowly came to a halt, the conductor stepping down and hurrying to the marshal's side. "Good Lord, what's he gone and done?"

Ryan was still holding Billy's leg aloft. "This is all my fault. You asked me if I wanted the train stopped to get him out, and I left him hanging there."

The conductor seemed to dismiss the marshal's omission, just shaking his head in disbelief. "Ain't never," he said quietly as his gaze shifted from Billy's face to the severed ankle and then to the boot in the middle of the tracks. "What do you make of something like that?"

The marshal lowered the leg back down gently to rest the stump upon the end of a sleeper. "I don't. I used to think I knew what made people tick. Not sure anymore."

"Maybe the loss of a foot and going to prison was just too much for him to contemplate. Guess he saw no future, no tomorrow."

Marshal Leon Ryan took his pistol back from the lifeless hands of William Travis Lithgow and returned it to its holster. "If that was so," he said softly, "then maybe the kid was way smarter than I gave him credit."

—*Lee Alver is an Australian writer with ten Western novels published under the pen name of Lee Clinton in the Black Horse Western (BHW) series. The UK publishing house responsible for the BHW series has now discontinued that line of books, however, the author's novels remain available worldwide in digital form via Amazon. In the meantime, he has now turned his hand to short stories as he continues with his love of the American Western. Lee is based in one of the most isolated cities in the world, in Western Australia, the largest of the Australian states, which is mostly arid desert but rich in minerals and home to some two million head of beef cattle. He is now retired after a career in the military, which saw service in Vietnam, the U.S., and UK. His Western titles include* Raking Hell, The Mexican, Coyote, *and* Animal Instinct.

The Horse Thief by Frank Tenney Johnson

THE
PACKAGE

DENNIS DOTY

THE SENTRIES AT Camp Huachuca came to a relaxed attention and gave a casual wave as the dusty rider on the trail-worn grulla mare passed what served as a gate. Ignoring the hustle and bustle of a military post, he rode straight to the stables. There, he allowed the mare a drink from the trough while he stepped down and loosened his girth. When she'd had enough, but far less than she wanted, he led her into the corral, removed his hull and slung it on a fence rail, then slipped the bridle off and let her go for a good roll in the dirt.

Satisfied that his horse was taken care of, he slung his saddlebags over his shoulder and pulled his Winchester '66 from the saddle scabbard. Turning, he walked with a tired sort of shuffle to the Sutler's tent.

"Can a man get a drink somewhere around this rat-infested pile of discarded googaws and moldy yardage?" He watched the big man behind the counter stiffen and turn before breaking out in a wide grin.

"Why, Jefferson Riley, I see you've still got your ha'r. Thought you'd be all settled on that Wyoming horse ranch you've been talking about for years. Rye?" He reached for a bottle and a glass.

"Thanks. You know my preferences."

"So does the captain. He said I wasn't to serve you a drop until you reported to him," the big man said as he poured.

"Sounds like ol' Samuel Marmaduke Whitside. Lucky for us we aren't in his army. Ten days out in that desert and I've built a powerful thirst." He tossed back three fingers of the amber liquid. "Was he wanting my report, or does he have another bee in his bonnet?"

"You'll have to ask him, and it looks like you'll get your chance. Here comes the first sergeant."

Jeff glanced over his shoulder, then grabbed the bottle and poured another. He'd just raised the glass to his lips when First Sergeant Brown stomped in.

"Riley. Captain wants to see you, and right now, he says."

"Now, First Sergeant, doesn't the captain put on his trousers just like you do of a morning? Surely he'll allow you a moment to share a drink with an old friend."

"Not this time, Jefferson. He's been pacing a hole in the floorboards of his office waiting for you."

"Well then, we shouldn't keep the gentleman waiting. Lead on, First Sergeant." Jeff placed a coin on the bar and followed the sergeant out.

They crossed the parade ground and climbed the stairs to the porch of the commanding officer's quarters and one of the few adobe buildings in the mostly tent camp. The first sergeant knocked twice, then opened the door and reported, "Sir, Mister Riley to see the captain, sir." He waved Riley in and closed the door behind him.

"Well, Mister Riley," said Captain Whitside, "what do you have for me?"

"Not a lot, sir. There are numerous fresh trails south and east of us. They're all small bands. No more than five or six warriors in each. All of them headed to Mexico."

"How fresh were they?"

"Some a few hours. Others a day or two."

"Can we catch any of them?"

"Not a chance, sir. They'd spot a patrol a day off and disappear into the rocks and prickly pear."

"Well, that's just as well, I suppose. I have another job for you."

"Sir, I just got in from ten days on scout. I need a shave, and my belly needs something besides hardtack and coffee."

"I understand, but I have an important package that needs to be delivered to Tombstone. Rest up today. You'll leave out first thing in the morning."

"Sir, doesn't the Army have regular couriers for parcels?"

"It does. But this one is special." He raised his voice. "First Sergeant Brown."

The first sergeant opened the door and entered pulling an unwilling young girl by the hand. Her hair was long and matted. Everything about her except the shift she wore was filthy. She was barefoot and looked very angry.

"What in the—" Jeff started.

"Mister Riley, may I present Miss Abigail Withers."

"Now, Captain, I ain't no wet nurse. I can't be draggin' a young'un like this around these parts. You know that."

"Jefferson, Miss Withers has been a guest of the Apache for the last four years. One of our patrols recaptured her two days ago. She's ten years old and doesn't speak a word of English. Her father is one James Livingston Withers whose last known location was Tombstone. Mother, deceased. I need a man I can trust to not bother the girl and get her safely to her father. That man is you."

"Kee-rist, Captain. You don't know what you're asking. It's two days to Tombstone, and the country is crawling with hostiles."

"I wouldn't ask it if I had another choice, Jeff. You have my complete confidence. Draw whatever you need from the quartermaster and be ready to leave at first light."

"Has she said anything since you got her?"

"Not a word."

"Is she eating?"

"She ate part of a small bowl of *frijoles* and a tortilla yesterday afternoon and immediately soiled herself. That's how we got her to put on that shift. We burned her old rags."

"Sam, if you were anyone else, I'd tell you to go to hell."

"I know, Jeff. Better get a good night's sleep."

Jeff stared at him for a long moment, then glanced down at the dirty-faced little urchin. She stared back at him, her deep blue eyes unblinking. He had a suspicion.

"Kee-rist!" Jeff knelt and took the little girl's hand.

"Cómo te llamas?"

"Mi nombre es Nascha."

"Well, she speaks some Spanish. She says her name is Nasha."

Turning to the girl again, he asked, "Nasha?"

She nodded and repeated, "Nascha." Then she did a perfect imitation of a barn owl.

"I reckon that's the Apache word for owl, huh?" asked the captain.

"Seems like. I don't speak the lingo, but I've got enough Mexican to get by."

"All right, then. Will you be wanting a wagon or a buckboard?"

"Neither. I'll need two good fast horses. The Apache teach their kids to ride before they can hardly walk. We wouldn't have a prayer of getting through in a wagon. I'll draw what supplies we need. Have them horses outside here at sunup."

"You heard the man, First Sergeant. See to it."

"Sir, yes, sir."

Jeff turned to the girl again. "Nascha, *vendrás conmigo?*"

She hesitated a moment, then nodded, *"Sí. Iré contigo."* She held out her hand, and he took it.

"She says she'll go with me. That's a start. We'll be here at daybreak." With that, he rose and led the girl out. They crossed the parade ground to a large stone and adobe building marked Quartermaster. He drew two blankets, four canteens, an extra tin cup, a sack of grain, a box of .44 Henry shells for the rifle and pistol, and two days rations. As an afterthought, he picked up a short-handled stiff brush.

Leaving the Quartermaster's, they caught the first sergeant on the parade ground.

"Sergeant, is there somewhere we could get this girl some britches—or at least something to wear that isn't white?"

"Corporal Haskins's wife may have something. I'll see what we can do."

"Thanks."

Jeff led the girl to the corral where he roped the grulla mare and put his saddle and saddlebags back on her. As he put the supplies in the saddlebags, the girl spread the blankets and deftly made a bedroll of them. Jeff tried to suppress a grin when she offered it to him. Instead, he nodded and tied it behind the saddle with his own bedroll. He motioned the girl to him and lifted her to the saddle, then took the reins and started to lead the mare.

A woman hurried across the parade ground and introduced herself. "Mister Riley, I'm Mary Haskins. The first sergeant said you wanted something for the girl to wear. Will this do?" She held up a butternut dyed shift that had been patched and repaired more than a few times. "It was my girls' until they both got too big for it."

"Ma'am, this is just about perfect. Thank you."

"You're quite welcome. This is a fine thing you're doing for her."

"We'll see. Thanks, again." He led the mare toward the gate.

A quarter hour later, they approached the crossing of the San Pedro. Jeff unsaddled and picketed the mare. Looking around, he took out his knife to dig up a yucca then chopped off the root and began peeling it with his knife. When he was done, he placed it on a rock and beat it with a stone until it was pulp. Sitting on another rock, he pulled his boots off and stripped to his long johns. Scooping up a handful of the pulp, he waded into the river and began to wash with the soapy root. A smile spread on his face when he heard a splash behind him. He continued to busy himself with getting the grime off until he heard the girl call from the bank.

"Cómo te llamas?"

"Mi nombre es Jefferson, *pero mis amigos me llaman* Jeff." He turned around.

The girl was wearing the butternut shift and drying her hair with the white one. Her once grimy skin was spotlessly clean, and she had a healthy glow about her. She smiled at him and did a pirouette for his approval.

"Muy bueno."

Jeff climbed out of the river, then started building a fire ring with stones. The girl began gathering dry firewood without a word. Soon, he had a small fire going and put a pot of water to boil with a handful of coffee in it. Suddenly, the girl put her hand out toward him with the palm facing him and put a finger to her lips. She slowly reached down and picked up a palm-sized stone. She hurled it past him, and he heard a soft thunk. Turning, he saw a cottontail thrashing in the grass with blood under its ear. Nascha raced past him and grabbed the rabbit by the ears. She brought it back and pointed to his knife holding out her hand.

Jeff chuckled silently to himself as he handed her the blade. She walked down to the river and very quickly skinned and gutted the animal, then chopped some green sticks and returned. She handed him the knife and skewered the rabbit, propping it over the fire to roast. While Jeff brewed the coffee, she walked along the riverbank picking wild onions and a few other things. When she returned, she deftly tied them in a bundle and stuffed them inside the rabbit.

Jeff poured them each a cup of the hot brew then took a small bag of sugar and the stiff brush from his saddlebags. He put a handful of sugar in her cup, stirred it with his knife, and handed it to her. She smelled it and smiled but put it down to cool. Jeff handed her the brush. She turned it over and around in her hands and looked questioningly at him. He made a motion like he was combing his hair. Hesitantly, she tried it out. A big smile blossomed on her face, and she began vigorously pulling the tangles from her hair.

Soon, the rabbit was done, and they sat down to eat. Although the meat was tasty, Jeff made sure that Nascha got all she could eat before he finished off the last bit. Nascha walked down to the river and washed the grease off, then brought the bedrolls and dropped them on opposite sides of the fire.

"A feller could get spoiled with you around," Jeff said.

"*Qué?*" she asked.

"Oh, *nada,*" he replied smiling.

Jeff wiped his greasy hands on his buckskins, then rolled a quirly and settled back with a second cup of coffee. It was barely dark when Nascha spread her bedroll and nearly instantly went to sleep. Seemed like a good idea, so Jeff unrolled his bedroll, propped his head on his saddle, and drifted off himself.

WHEN HE AWOKE, it was still dark. He rolled out and began pack-
ing his things. When he turned back to the fire, Nascha had her bed
rolled and was filling the canteens with fresh river water.

By dawn, they were back at Captain Whitside's quarters where a
private stood holding the reins to a pair of army mounts, a bay gelding, and a sorrel mare. Both looked like they could do the job. Jeff
transferred his gear to the other horses and handed the mare off to
the private.

"Take good care of her, son. I'll be back for her." After tightening
the cinches, he boosted Nascha up on the sorrel and adjusted her stirrups to fit. He mounted the bay.

Captain Whitside stepped out onto the porch. Looking them
over, he said, "Looks like you're making progress with her."

"Yes, sir. She cleans up pretty good, and she's a hand around a
campfire. We'll camp somewhere just north of Lewis Spring tonight
and should make Tombstone before nightfall tomorrow. You might
send a wire to Virgil Earp, he's the marshal over there. See if he can
find Jim Withers for us."

"I'll do that. Be safe, you hear?"

"That is certainly my intention, Captain."

Jeff tossed off a friendly mock salute and turned his horse to the
gate. Nascha trotted the sorrel up beside him and smiled. They rode
in companionable silence, staying vigilant for trouble. Every time Jeff
looked, she was a few paces to his right and behind him. Each time,
she smiled at him and didn't seem to be overly tired or uncomfortable.

About two hours out of Camp Huachuca, Nascha suddenly trotted
up close and whispered, *"Ten cuidado. Apache."* She turned in front
of him into an arroyo and stopped around the first bend. When he
caught up, he could barely see over the rim of the arroyo through a
screen of brush. A chill ran up his spine. Six warriors rode south sin-

gle file. Had they kept going, they would have ridden right into them. He looked back to Nascha, but she had dismounted and was stroking the noses of both horses to keep them quiet. It was a good half hour before the Apache rode completely out of sight, and they waited another half hour to be sure none turned back.

When he judged it safe, they remounted and continued east. Late afternoon, they skirted Lewis Spring and turned north. He judged they had enough water left, and it was best not to go near known waterholes where they had a much better chance of being spotted or tracked. They made a dry camp a little over a mile north of the spring in a rock formation which would hide them and the horses. There was no forage for the horses, so he gave them each a nosebag with some grain and a hatful of water before picketing them for the night.

———————✦———————

THE NEXT DAY passed without incident, and they arrived in Tombstone about an hour before sunset. He led the way straight down Fremont Street to the courthouse and the marshal's office. Jeff told Nascha to wait for him, and he dismounted and went inside.

"Howdy, Virgil."

"Howdy yourself, Jefferson. I see you made it."

"I guess Sam Whitside let you know I was coming."

"Yes, he did. I've got some bad news for you, though."

"What? You couldn't find her father?"

"Oh, James Livingston Withers wasn't at all hard to find. That's him in the cell there. Around here he's known as Whiskey Jim. He's the town drunk or the closest we've got to one."

"Kee-rist. After all this girl's been through, I'm supposed to turn her over to a whiskey-soaked sod of a father?"

"If'n you've got a better idea, I'm all ears."

"Is there someplace safe I can leave the girl while I try to sober him up?"

"Sure. Follow me."

Leading the horses, Jeff followed Earp around the corner, down Fourth Street, then left on Allen to Big Nose Kate's.

"Now, Virgil, this don't look like the kinda place for a young lady."

"It isn't, but Kate's got a heart o' gold, and she's tougher'n whang leather. No one will bother the girl here. If'n they try, well... we got plenty o' room on Boot Hill."

"It's your town, and you likely know best."

Jeff helped Nascha dismount, and they went inside. A loud friendly woman greeted them.

"Well, what have we here? Virgil, you damn well know I don't take 'em that young."

"Howdy, Kate," said Virgil. "This here is Miss Abigail Withers recently returned from captivity by the Apache. Her pa is Whiskey Jim. We need a place for her to stay while we sober him up."

"Ah, the poor little thing." Kate sat on a velvet covered footstool and held her arms open wide. "Come here, darlin'. Kate will take good care of you."

Nascha looked from the loud woman to Jeff and back again. "Adelante, Nascha. Está bien," said Jeff. Then to Kate, he said, "She was with them for four years and doesn't know any English, but she speaks pretty good Mexican."

"I speak good Mex myself," Kate replied, "but why do you call her Nascha?"

"It's her Apache name. It means owl. I haven't tried to get her to adopt her old name."

"Okay. Nascha it is until she's ready for a change." Jeff led Nascha to

Kate and gave her her hand. *"Te quedas con* Kate. *Volveré."* Even though he'd promised to return, Nascha seemed hesitant until Kate whispered to her in Spanish. Her eyes grew large, and she nodded and smiled.

"Looks like you've got a way with her, Kate," said Virgil. "I owe you one."

"You owe me more than one, Virgil, but we'll discuss that later."

"Thank you, ma'am," said Jeff. He and Virgil left and went back to the courthouse, Virgil riding Nascha's mare.

Jim Withers sat up in his cell holding his head in both hands and moaning. "Thank God you're back, Marshal. I need a drink real bad."

"You need a bath," replied Virgil. "You stink like a Missouri pig farm on a hot day." He left the office and returned a few minutes later with a bucket of water. He set it down in front of the cell. "If you want out, come over here," he said to Withers.

"Oh, yes, sir," said Withers stumbling to the cell door.

In one swift move, Virgil stooped, grabbed the bucket, and flung the contents in Withers's face thoroughly soaking him.

Withers sputtered and fumed. "Now what'd you go an' do that for?" he asked in a whine.

"Like I said, you stink. Now listen close. This here is Jefferson Riley. If you ever want to get out of here, you'll do exactly as he tells you. No hesitation. No complaints. Exactly what he tells you or I'll forget I ever had a key to this cell. You understand?"

"Y-yes, sir. Exactly what Mister Riley says."

"You got any coffee, Virgil?"

"There's a pot over on the stove. Been there all day, but we can make more."

"That'll do for now. The stronger, the better." Jeff went to the stove and poured a cup of coffee that could float a horseshoe. He carried it to the cell and passed it through the bars.

"Drink this. All of it, and don't spill it." He handed it to Withers. As an afterthought, he said, "Be careful. It's hot."

"I can't drink this. I need whiskey."

"I said, 'No complaints,'" said Virgil. "Now do as the man says."

Withers choked and sputtered, but he managed to swallow the whole cup. Jeff poured him another.

"Why are you doing this to me?" he asked with a whine.

"Shut up and drink it," said Earp. He went to the stove and refilled the pot from a water pitcher then added a double handful of ground coffee before putting it back on the stove. A retching sound came from the cell. Withers was puking in the slop bucket. He'd spilled half his coffee getting there. When he was finished, Jeff took the cup and refilled it.

By the time the prisoner was on his fifth cup, Jeff judged he was sober enough to hear what he had to say.

"I can't drink no more," Withers said.

"You can, and you will," said Jeff. "Now you listen to me. I brought your daughter."

"I don't have no daughter. I don't have nobody."

"You do have a daughter. Her name is Abigail. She was taken by the Apache four years ago. The Army got her back, and they sent me to bring her to you."

"Ab-Abigail? No, it can't be. She's dead."

"She's not dead. She's right here in town waiting for you."

"It can't be. Abigail? What am I gonna do with a little girl? You keep her."

"Now listen to me, you sot. That sweet little girl needs her daddy, and by God you're gonna sober up and meet her if I have to beat the booze outta you."

"Abigail? Wall, I'll be. How is she?"

"She's alone. Her Apache family was killed. She has no one but you in the whole world."

"She's here?"

"Yeah, she's here in Tombstone."

Withers was silent for a moment. Then he looked down at the rags he wore. "I can't see her like this. Look at me."

"Finish your coffee. I'll take you to get some decent clothes. It's the least I can do for her."

Withers drained the cup, and Virgil opened the cell. "Now you behave yourself, Withers. Do what Jeff says, and take care of that girl."

"Yes, sir."

Jeff took Withers on Nascha's horse to the general store. When they entered, the bell over the door called the storekeeper, a short bespectacled bald man.

"Howdy, mister. Can I help you?" he asked Jeff.

"Yes. Mister Withers here needs some new clothes. He'll want trousers, shirt, suspenders, hat, long johns, socks, and boots. I'll pay for it."

"Yes, sir, indeed. Please come with me." The storekeeper took a long look at Withers, then began pulling items from the shelves. He had a complete outfit agreed upon in no time. Jeff added a bar of lye soap and paid him the six dollars and thirty-five cents he asked without haggling. The storekeeper wrapped the purchases in brown paper and tied them with a hemp string.

"Nice doing business with you, gentlemen. Please come again."

Jeff nodded, picked up the package, and turned and pointed Withers out the door.

"Where can I change?" asked Withers.

"I reckon Virgil will let you change when we get there," replied Jeff as they mounted.

They rode back to the courthouse and climbed the stairs.

"That didn't take long," said Virgil.

"Nope. Now we need to get him out of those rags and into his new outfit," said Jeff.

"Be my guest," replied Virgil indicating the open cell.

Withers went in, and Jeff handed him the package. Withers looked uncomfortable. He looked even more uncomfortable when Jeff filled a large bucket from the pump out front.

"Get out of those rags and give yourself a bath before you put the new ones on," said Jeff.

"Hang on a minute," said Virgil, walking over to his desk. He returned with a scrub brush and a scrap of towel.

"Sir, I can't take no bath with you folks right there. A man needs a little privacy."

Virgil chuckled and motioned to the door with a head bob. He and Jeff stepped out into the hallway to await the transformation.

Several minutes went by, and then a shotgun blasted from the jail. They rushed back in. Withers, or what was left of him, lay sprawled in a pool of blood on the floor.

"Kee-rist," said Jeff.

"Looks like he just didn't have the sand to sober up," said Earp. "Hey, you better see this." He pointed to the still wrapped package which now sat on his desk. Withers had scrawled a note on it.

Tell Abby Im sory.

"Kee-rist," Jeff said.

"What are you going to do now?" asked Virgil.

Jeff thought for a minute. He picked up a blank sheet of paper from Virgil's desk and dipped a pen in the inkwell.

Sell my mare and apply my pay to the horses you lent me. If that don't cover it, write me care of GD/Cheyenne, Wyo Terr.

Riley

"Will you see that Captain Whitside gets this?"

Virgil looked at the note. "Why shore. What's in Cheyenne?"

"There's a girl up there who's been after me to marry her and settle down on a horse ranch. Guess I'll have to talk her into a package deal."

"Ride easy, my friend. Married life will suit you."

———— ✦ ————

—Born and raised in Southern California, Dennis Doty has been a carny, U.S. Marine, rodeo cowboy, Personnel Manager, and Retail General Manager before retiring and finding his true calling as an author, editor, and publisher. Since 2002, he has made his home on the edge of the Daniel Boone National Forest in Southeastern Kentucky.

Mexikanischer Cowboy by William Herbert Dunton

ACTION AT
SKELETON CANYON

ANDREW SALMON

IT HAD THREATENED rain all morning, but not a drop had fallen. By midday, the sky was pure azure, and a punishing sun beat down on Skeleton Canyon. Sergeant Pete Lovell wished to hell it had rained as he put spurs to his roan. Near-empty canteens hanging from the saddle clacked dully as the horse sprang forward. Corporal Ben Hodgson's mount matched Lovell's stride for stride as both roared up from the spring a half mile from the heliograph station.

Gunfire had interrupted their work filling the canteens for the station's detachment. Distant at first, the crack of rifles and pistols had swelled in volume before receding. They knew the guard contingent was giving some Apache what for, and when the noise faded in their ears, they surmised that the chase was on.

Thing was, the Skeleton Canyon Station was new and not outfitted with a full complement of guards. It had been set up by the 2nd Cavalry to monitor the movement of Army beef out of Texas, which had crossed New Mexico into Arizona. Once across the Skeleton Creek arroyo, the herd would break into three separate groups—

one bound for Douglas, the second to Fort Huachuca, and the last, the smallest, a mere dozen head, and, consequently, thinly manned, was bound for White's Ranch. Cochise County would eat well in the coming weeks if the Apache didn't get the beeves. It had been a hard winter and a dry, scorching spring so far, and food was scarce. Although there hadn't been any large-scale activities since Geronimo had surrendered, the herd would be irresistible to the Apache. The heliograph station was to look for the drive, and they'd spotted the cattle early that morning with field glasses as it crossed the arroyo, their mouths watering at the sight of all that good beef after two weeks of jerky. The station was supplied with thirty days of rations, but this was hardly gourmet fare. They had flashed their message to the ranch, giving the estimate as to the number of head they'd seen as well as an "all clear" report regarding the presence of hostile Indians.

Lovell and Hodgson hated to think what was going on if a large group of Apache were hitting the position. All the more reason to get up the ridge fast in case they were needed for its defense.

There was a thick stand of aspen and cottonwood rising up the slope ahead. The trees would slow their progress but provide vital cover if Apache were near. A rifle shot whizzed by Lovell's right ear removing all speculation. They'd been spotted. The shot was followed by another, and Hodgson's horse stumbled. Lovell had instinctively hauled his horse out of the line of fire while maintaining the angle to the trees on the upslope. He spied Hodgson out of the corner of his eye as the corporal slowed a hair to check his horse, and that proved fatal as an arrow took him high in the chest. Hodgson gasped before tumbling backward out of the saddle.

Lovell dug the spurs in desperately and reached the trees as an arrow buried its head in the thick bark of a trunk inches from his shoulder. He had the horse start up the incline. He could not take the path the engineers had cut when the station was set up as it was open ground. Instead, he blundered through the growth. Thick tree cover cut the sunlight, and he felt as if time had slipped forward to twilight. It was cooler as well, and the trees pre-empted more firing. Bullets were in short supply, and the Apache had none to waste in wild shots. He caught his breath in the relatively safe position.

He could not rest, however. The Apache were hot on his heels. His horse, rifle, pistol, cartridges, and water were what they coveted more than his scalp. He dared not turn around to look for his pursuers.

For the moment, he had to shake those who had targeted him, and there was only one possible way he might do that.

There was an almost sheer drop off to the left. The trees growing close to it would provide him the cover he needed. There would be a cost, however. But there was no alternative, so Lovell urged his horse forward as fast as the animal could manage. His goal was a low cave on the hillside. They'd found it while exploring the mountain and used it while off-duty as it caught only the morning sun and was cool during the hottest part of the day. It was invisible from up top. The perfect refuge while he gathered his wits.

Excited shouts behind Lovell revealed to him that he'd been spotted. He was almost at the cliff edge. Heart in his throat, he raced up and leapt off the horse as a shot whizzed over the saddle he'd vacated. His boots hit the rocky slope at an angle, and he fell heavily, his knees bashed and cut by the jagged rocks. He fought to counter his momentum before he pitched down the forty-foot drop.

As he struck the rocks, he was surprised to see tow-headed Private Tim Carver leap to his feet on the slope. The youth spent a lot of time at the cave looking for fossils.

"Pete! Is it Indians?" the boy hissed.

His head jutting above the cliff edge, one of the closing Apache put a bullet through Carver's forehead, and his lifeless body tumbled down the slope. Lovell stared in shock for an instant, but the warriors were approaching to be sure of their target. He grabbed Carver's bayonet. The boy had been using it to sift through the rocks. If the braves saw the blade, they'd climb down to retrieve it. Backing frantically, he backed into the cave as far as his body would fit. He pressed his back against the cold, damp stone, his Colt tight in his fist.

The braves were speaking. He saw dust and pebbles tumble down the slope as they shifted their feet. They were standing directly above him. He had no understanding of the various dialects spoken by the Apache but could guess from their tone and relaxed movements that they thought it was he sprawled at the base of the slope. Seeing him drop and poor Carver pop up in surprise at his sudden appearance, the mistake was understandable, and it most likely saved his life. Lovell heard his horse snort as one of them must have taken the reins. He was sorry to lose the roan, but there was nothing for it. Another shower of small stones indicated they were satisfied they'd got him, and the horse would do for the moment. Carver had his pistol, of course, and they'd want to work their way down to take that off the body as well.

This didn't leave him much time. The lure of a captured weapon and cartridges was enticing, and once down there with Carver's body, one glance up the slope would reveal his hiding place.

Lovell took this moment of relative safety to see how things stood.

The heliograph station was one of fourteen stations covering an area two hundred miles wide and three hundred miles long. This vital network provided communications for the region, but with the quick spread of the telegraph and railroad west, it would soon be unnecessary. Skeleton Canyon was the farthest east of the stations, close to the New Mexico border, in an isolated stretch of desolate terrain. Knowing the Army was up here, the Apache would most likely know why and would want to destroy the heliograph or at least take the mirrors for their own use since they had used reflected sunlight to signal one another for ages. Had the band cut the telegraph wires as well? If so, the heliograph was the only option left to warn the ranch twenty-five miles away, and he was the only one left, as far as he knew, who could use it. He had to reach to get up there and signal the ranch so they could bolster the cattle drive manpower and protect the much-needed beef. Only the hill was full of Apache. They had his horse, rifle, and water. Luckily, he carried extra cartridges for both weapons in bandoliers across his body. If they dropped him, they'd have all this as well.

Shots rang out. It was difficult to pinpoint from where the noise came as they echoed up and down the slope. But he guessed from up above. The Apache were attacking the camp. His mind raced. Who was up there? The two operators, MacDonald and Mondou, Private Patterson at most, and none of them were seasoned soldiers. No, Hodgson, Carver, and he were supposed to protect these operators and had failed miserably. The shots ceased as quickly as they started. He assumed the men were dead. Damn it to hell!

Lovell focused his thoughts and began to grasp the situation. There had to have been a good-sized group of Apache to draw the guards away. That Texas beef was too tempting a target, and whoever was leading this group had left nothing to chance. He had split his forces, using one to lure the guards off on horseback while the other crept uphill on foot to destroy the heliograph station to prevent a warning being flashed. This group would also collect what weapons and horses they could from the station before striking for the herd across the Skeleton Creek wash and before the drovers reached White's Ranch.

With standing orders to run to ground any band of attacking In-

dians, Captain Miller must have wrongly guessed that the group hitting the station contained all the Apache in the area and lit out after
them, leaving the heliograph relatively unprotected. The shooting had
ceased abruptly. Was anyone besides Lovell left? That was a sobering
thought. He wasn't even sure he could operate the heliograph. He'd
apprenticed with the telegrapher, Mondou, brought in from Mississippi for the finesse needed to work the shutter quickly and efficiently
as long and short flashes of light were used to send words the same
way messages were sent over a telegraph wire. Mondou had been at
the shutter that morning, and Lovell had chided the man, lazy in his
habits, for leaving the station telescope by the heliograph after sighting
the herd instead of returning it to the makeshift storage shed erected at
the camp. The man hated using the telescope. Lovell wondered if this
oversight might be one reason the Apache were able to draw so close
before being discovered as watch was supposed to be continuous. The
heliograph tripod was not at the camp itself. It had been determined
when setting up the network that the mirror flash was better detected
against a dark background—say, a shadowed peak—rather than a clear
blue sky. Thus the heliograph had been best positioned on the northwest side of the uppermost peak's base, while the camp was around to
the eastern side of the same peak where the ground was level and there
were trees for shade and wood for cooking fires.

Lovell had tried his hand occasionally at signaling as part of his
training, but a quick sure touch would be needed now. If he could
even get up there.

He pawed the dripping sweat out of his gray eyes and mopped
his square, lined face with the blue sleeve of his Army coat. Mid-af-
ternoon heat scorched the land, and the coolness of the cave could
no longer combat it. His throat burned with thirst. Shaving was not
mandatory at the station but recommended against the heat. Lovell

had shaved that morning and in his current state would have gladly drunk the soapy, stubble-spotted water.

The wool coat had to go. He stripped it off, leaving it deep in the shadow far back in the cave behind him lest it be spotted. His undershirt had gone the color of old bone from so much wear and even sweat-stained was of a similar shade to the earth and rocks beneath his feet. The bleeding knees weren't so bad now—he did not want to leave a convenient trail for the Apache to follow. The cuts stung, but his knees appeared otherwise undamaged.

Lovell emerged gingerly from the cave. The afternoon sun hit him like a hammer blow. He could feel the heat working on his nut-brown skin. His eyes were mere slits against the intense light reflecting off the hot stones. He cocked his head, listening. Only wind, gaining in intensity, moved through the dense branches of the trees.

He stepped back into the tree cover, and the relative coolness was welcome. The closely-packed trunks obscured all, meaning the Apache would waste neither precious bullets, nor arrows, if he was spotted, as they could not be sure of their target. At least, he hoped this was the case. The Apache were not wasteful. He was one. They were many. How many, he couldn't guess. A knife blade would do for him, once they were aware of his presence.

He started through the trees, careful of his steps over the earth littered with dry, dead branches. If there were Apache around, he wouldn't hear them approach and relied on his vision to stay alive. The station rested atop a seven thousand foot high peak, and he had a third of that distance to cover before he reached the heliograph. Necessity forced him to move more quickly than was prudent. Every crack of a branch under his boots sounded like rifle shots in the quiet gloom. The breeze had gained strength, and his skin cooled, while anxiety and desperation kept the sweat flowing down his body. Thirst was a rabid animal in his throat. He covered ground as quickly as he could. The surroundings grew darker. A cloud must have temporarily obscured the sun. Minutes raced by.

He stepped around a fallen tree and found himself face to face with an Apache brave.

The look of surprise on the lean man's face became one of stern determination as he pulled his knife and sprang at Lovell, who dodged, but slid in a pile of dry leaves and lost his balance, falling painfully to his lacerated knees.

His first thought was for his pistol. He could not use it. The shot would draw the attention of every warrior in the vicinity, and he would not survive long should they converge on his position. He would use it at the moment his life was imperiled. Until such time, he would fight hand to hand.

He seized a stone the size of a hen's egg and launched it with all his desperate strength at the brave who had no choice but to shy away to one side. This permitted Lovell to take up a stout branch in one hand while pulling Carver's bayonet with the other as he climbed painfully to his feet.

Lovell's blade ran eighteen inches to the brave's six, and his opponent kept his distance as he sought an avenue of attack. Lovell swung the branch in great arcs to make sure the brave couldn't close. It was a standoff that would have to give at some point. The brave, young and eager, darted forward at last.

The impact made Lovell drop the branch as he put his hand back to break his fall. The sweaty, bare-chested Apache snatched at Lovell's gun hand. He held tight, refusing to surrender the weapon to the warrior. They rolled down the slope. The length of the bayonet worked against him at close quarters as he could not turn the point to stab into the brave's back, but he could pummel and dig at the man's back with the hard steel socket end. He saw the man's teeth draw back from his lips at this abuse, and he had to push away from Lovell, slashing as he retreated. Lovell cried out as the blade caught his left forearm with a superficial cut.

The Apache stood, one hand pressed against his bleeding back. He shot Lovell a look of pure hate for the pain he had inflicted. Lovell had a firm grip on the bayonet, his eyes locked on the brave's. Lovell saw his opponent's gaze flick to his knees, bleeding profusely.

Lovell lunged at the man and staggered as his forward leg appeared to buckle. Thinking the white man's knees were failing, the warrior leapt forward. Lovell, not incapacitated at all, met the Apache's charge by driving the bayonet into the man's abdomen upward under the ribs into the heart. The man opened his mouth in a silent scream, convulsed, then collapsed against Lovell, who hastily pulled the bayonet and backed away. He sank to one knee.

Adrenaline had given his knees more stiffness than he could have hoped for during the battle. Now they stung and throbbed with the dirt and grit that had been ground into the lacerated skin by the roll down the hill. He got painfully to his feet and limped on, having to regain the ground he'd lost, cursing at the precious minutes this would take.

Gasping for breath, his mouth and throat turned to dust, he saw the last stretch of the ascent. The tree line gave way up ahead to lose rocks and scrub brush. He would be exposed between his position and the heliograph. If there were Apache about, he'd be an easy target. Still there was a chance. Straining his ears against the hiss of the wind, he caught no other sound.

He steeled himself for a mad dash to the top. Suddenly, he heard the scuff of moccasined feet and hurried voices. They'd spotted him and were closing in. He threw his gaze this way and that, expecting attack from every quarter in the dark expanse of the woods. A thought lanced through his brain. The Apache moved like ghosts over any terrain. So why were they dashing so noisily now?

Something hit his back.

He ignored it as he spotted a group of warriors sprinting down the path from the camp not twenty yards from his position. He crouched low behind a tree trunk. If they saw him, they gave no sign as they continued on by. Was their work completed up top? Had they found the heliograph and destroyed it?

He threw caution to the wind and ran as fast as he could manage toward the clearing in a last race to the top.

He was struck again on the shoulders and the top of his head repeatedly. In the heat of the moment, he paid the strikes no heed. The wind was so strong it must have dislodged twigs overhead.

Mind racing, he'd instinctively determined that the false twilight in the trees was due to the pervading gloom beneath the canopy of branches swaying in the wind, which was increasing in intensity by the second. Skinning his eyes for armed warriors one last time, he darted sharp glances in every direction but up. He stepped from the tree line and was peppered with raindrops the size of silver dollars.

A massive storm had rolled in while he snaked through the dense trees, and the heavens had unleashed their slashing fury. He was drenched to the skin in a minute, and his boots squelched as the torrential rain turned the earth beneath his feet to a quagmire. The raging wind whipped rainwater into his face as he blindly strove to reach the heliograph over the open ground. He did not stop even as some part of his exhausted mind reminded him that the signaling device was useless without sunlight. He stumbled on regardless, and a laugh at his folly filled his throat to mingle with the cold rain he swallowed.

All for nothing! His mind raged.

And the Apache? They had desperately sprinted down the path

to their horses spooked by the thunder which boomed like cannon fire all around. He had been the least of their concerns. Steel rods of rain lanced down unceasingly. Visibility was reduced to scant feet. The wind howled. Late afternoon had turned to darkest night. His clothes were heavy, sodden as he reached the heliograph. The mirrors dotted with raindrops also ran with tiny rivulets down their smooth surfaces. It hadn't been destroyed, at least. Lovell laughed out loud. Useless now!

He found himself standing in a stream drawn by the inexorable pull of gravity over his boot tops. He felt as if he'd been dropped into a hurricane, not a spring storm. Already drenched, he did not seek cover from the onslaught of water hitting him from all sides in the gale. He'd swallowed enough of it to be half-drowned. The cold water chilled his hot skin. He stood there beside the heliograph and thought of the long descent the Apache were making down to the horses. How they would have to calm the animals before the long ride to catch the herd outside the ranch. The rain had bought the drovers some precious minutes as a running gun battle on horse-back in pouring rain over muddy terrain was not a wise course of action for anyone. However, if they were hungry enough, desperate enough, the Apache might attempt an attack. Many lives on both sides would be lost.

Unless....

Could it be? Was there a chance?

Sloshing through the mud, he hunted for the telescope.

There it was! In its sheath. Not ten feet from the heliograph. Right where Mondou had left it, the lazy fool. The wind had kicked it down the slope a might is all.

Hands numb with the cold drenching rain, he fumbled at the cover, got the cap loose, and yanked the instrument free like drawing a saber. Dropping to his agonized knees before a good sized boulder, he balanced the telescope against it, aiming down at the valley below.

Everything was a gray blur. Heavy rain kept streaking the lens as he made frantic, though subtle, adjustments to the telescope's position which looked like wide swings of miles to his eye pressed to the viewer.

There! He had it! Barely visible through the tempest.

Skeleton Creek.

An arroyo that morning, now a raging, brown, undulating river of flash flood speed and power. Tree branches and entire younger trees were being swept along, their tips raking the air above the turgid miasma.

Lovell roared his triumph.

The Apache could never cross the creek at its current level. No horse with any sense could be forced to make the attempt. The flooded creek cut the Apache off from the herd as if a wall had sprung up to block their way. They could not intercept the herd before it reached the ranch.

Pete Lovell lay down on his back, let the water pummel his face and bruised body like grapeshot, and almost drowned as he bellowed his joy and relief against the storm.

—Andrew Salmon has won several awards for his Sherlock Holmes stories as well as the inaugural Mustang Award from Saddlebag Dispatches *magazine. He has been nominated for the Ellis, Pulp Ark, Pulp Factory, and New Pulp Awards. He lives and writes in Vancouver, BC. His novels include* Ace of Devils, The Fight Card Sherlock Holmes Trilogy: Work Capitol, Blood to the Bone and A Congression of Pallbearers (*collected in the* Fight Card Sherlock Holmes Omnibus), The Dark Land, The Light Of

Men, *and* Ghost Squad: Rise of the Black Legion *(with Ron Fortier) and his first children's book,* Wandering Webber. *His work has also appeared in numerous anthologies covering multiple genres, including a tale in* Bass Reeves Frontier Marshal, Vol. 1.

HAT CREEK

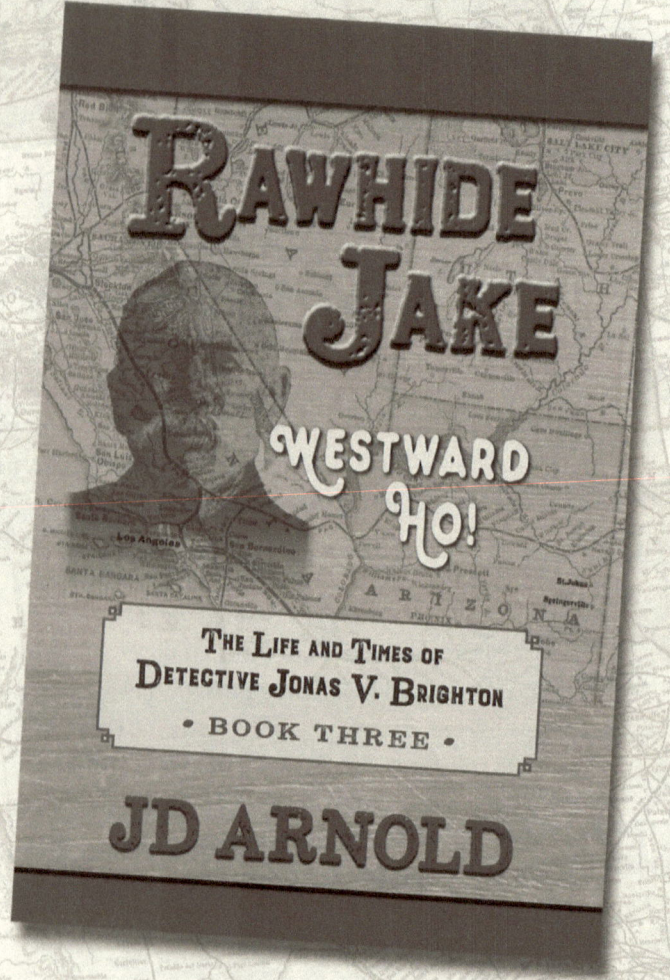

AN EPIC JOURNEY
OF RESILIENCE, HONOR,
AND THE RELENTLESS
PURSUIT OF JUSTICE.

As the trusted lieutenant of the infamous Geronimo, Chato's days are painted in the hues of raid and revolt until personal tragedy strikes when his family are taken into slavery in Mexico. Hoping to secure their release, Chato strikes a deal to aid the U.S. Army in maintaining peace with his people. But when Geronimo denounces him as a traitor and departs, all hope for Chato's family flees with him. Forsaken by his former brothers-in-arms, Chato vows to hunt down the renegades himself, becoming a beacon of the Chiricahua peace faction clinging to reservation life in the process.

"... Few who attempt to tell the tale of another culture achieve Farmer's depth of insight."

—Bestselling Western author Paul Colt

HAT CREEK

Don't Miss W. Michael Farmer's other award-winning novels from Hat Creek, including The Odyssey of Geronimo: Twenty-Three Years a Prisoner of War *and* The Iliad of Geronimo: A Song of Blood and Fire. *Available at your favorite local bookseller*

www.ingramcontent.com/pod-product-compliance
Lightning Source LLC
Chambersburg PA
CBHW051249180626
46816CB00004BA/1404